jade

jade

a novel

rebecca davis

For Charlie & Lily

Prologue

Isn't it strange how we sometimes remember the smallest details of a dream, but not the entire thing? Some pieces slip away easily, like stray feathers on a windy day, while others remain embedded in our minds forever.

This is what I remember: bits and pieces of a face that I've never seen in my waking life. Short, straight hair that's parted on the right; sometimes dull russet, but sometimes lit with sunlight, creating fiery red highlights. An ever-so-slightly crooked nose, striking in its imperfection. Strong, neat brows firmly set on an unlined forehead, and straight white teeth behind plump pink lips.

And finally, most of all, I remember dazzlingly beautiful eyes—eyes the color of the lightest jade, that look directly into my soul and seem to glow from within.

That is all.

Chapter One

Awake. I shake off my latest dream. Perhaps "latest" is the wrong term; the dream is the same as always. His face—I don't know whose and I never have. His face is all I can remember each time I dream of him. The dreams come more often now. Almost every night he's there, staring into me with those fascinating pale green eyes.

But it doesn't matter. I won't let that distract me today.

I roll from beneath luxurious cotton sheets, glaring at my alarm clock. It's 3:00 AM, an ungodly hour in anyone's book. But I have to be there an hour before sunrise, so here I am, now, awake.

The first place I go after my usual morning bathroom stop is the kitchen. Thank goodness the coffee maker has a timer on it, because I need the caffeine immediately. It races through my veins, a perceptible tingle that will help me get through this early morning.

After coffee, I head back to my room to get dressed. As I pass, I take a quick look in the mirror above my dresser. I feel different today, and it's not just the exhaustion. I feel...older, perhaps? It's almost as if I've somehow changed overnight. It is my eighteenth birthday, after all. And I guess I feel as though I should look different today, as if my body should reflect the change in my age, the change I feel in my mind and soul.

It doesn't, though. Long, wavy, dark brown hair, tangled from a rough night's sleep, flows down my back, stopping at my elbows. Big hazel eyes, so like my mother's, gaze sleepily back at me.

I stretch from head to toe, trying to wake myself up. I may need another coffee. My muscles pull taut and I feel each one extending as I reach. Suddenly glancing behind me at my reflection, I frown at my hips. Slightly wider than I'd like, as always.

I turn back around to study my face once again, leaning my elbows onto the dresser to get a closer look. I brush away a dab of coffee at the corner of my lip, then quickly wash my face because almost anything used to give me a pimple and I haven't broken the habit. My skin is creamy and clear—now—a big improvement from the years of puberty when my cheeks were always red and inflamed with acne. A few small scars still mar the otherwise smooth skin. My teeth now sit precision-straight in my mouth, thanks to years of braces and retainers. It's a pretty face, I think. Perhaps nothing extraordinary, but it's definitely pretty.

But still, I am unsatisfied by its sameness. It's my birthday. I finally finished high school only a few days ago. I stand here on the brink of adulthood, and yet I look exactly the same as I did yesterday. Just like every other year.

I sigh and turn away from the mirror, then change quickly into a pair of shorts and a T-shirt. When I finish, I head back to the kitchen and its alluring scent of coffee. This time, though,

I slow down beside the door just down and across from my own. I slowly put my hand on the ornate brass handle and turn. I push the solid oak door open to reveal my dad's study.

I walk in, my bare feet slapping the hardwood floor until I reach the soft area rug. The light automatically flips on, motion-activated. I think about how Dad would completely forget to turn it off, otherwise, always too distracted with bigger things. I look around the familiar room. It's large, with a desk on one side and a pair of cushy leather chairs against the opposite wall. The cherry-wood desk is big and covered in clutter, just like the one in his office at work. I push aside some papers to uncover the photo that my brother, Alex, and I gave him for Christmas. It's a great shot. I don't remember what Alex had said to me, but we're both smiling genuinely. The photographer had also taken one just a moment earlier, each of us doubled over in laughter. I think he may have been making fun of our coordinating colors: he in a black suit with a red shirt and white tie, me in a black polka-dotted white dress with a red sash. I touch his face through the glass frame. I will miss him.

I go around behind the desk, tug open the bottom drawer, and pull out another photo that had been tucked all the way in the back under yet more papers. This one is in an ornately carved wooden frame. The photo is older, the hair and clothing out of style, the colors fading. My mother's big eyes look back at me. My dad loves this photo of her. She looks so young in it, younger than I ever saw her. Nineteen maybe? Twenty? I think it was one of their engagement photos; the hand supporting her delicate chin is wearing a stunning sapphire engagement ring. Her dark, wavy hair is shorter than mine, but the exact same deep brown. I can plainly see the features in her face that cause my dad so much pain when he sees them in mine. The photo could easily be mistaken for one of me if not for its age. I hug it to my chest, kiss my mother on her cheek, and then place everything back as I found it.

I leave the room as quietly as I had entered. Making my way farther down the hallway, I stop again to softly touch my hand to the next door. The wood is cold to the touch. Alex is sleeping peacefully inside, the central air conditioning in the room surely blasting on high, as usual.

I jump about a foot in the air when the door suddenly bangs open. Alex, completely disheveled, stands in front of me, very obviously not sleeping after all.

At almost fifteen, my "little" brother has shot up like a weed in the past year. He's been taller than me for a while, though that's not much of a challenge. I've never been much to go up against. I stopped growing at five foot one, while he's going on five eleven. He has our dad's sandy hair and lanky build, but he's got Mom's hazel eyes, like me. A light dusting of freckles covers his cheekbones, along with a smattering of the same acne I used to deal with.

I grimace guiltily at him. He is clearly not awake yet. "I'm sorry, Alex," I say. "Did I wake you?"

"Of course not," he mutters grumpily. "I couldn't let you go without a proper goodbye, could I?"

I grin at this. "You didn't have to get up. We said goodbye last night!" But I am glad he got up for me. We're close, Alex and I. I'll miss him the most out of everyone here.

He walks with me into the kitchen and we sit down, each

grabbing a cup of coffee. He adds enough milk and sugar to his to turn it, more or less, into a warm coffee milkshake. I drink mine black this time, just to be his opposite. I grimace at the bitter taste, and he laughs at me, knowing exactly what I'm doing. In the dim lighting, I notice a dark shadow emerging over his upper lip, darker than the peach fuzz that's always been there. "What's this?" I tease, swiping at it with my finger.

"Liz!" he admonishes, bobbing his head back, away from my reach.

"What?" I ask innocently. "You've got dirt on your face."

He rolls his eyes at me and sticks out his tongue. Then he leans into the leather back of the stool, gathering his dignity. "That's my mustache," he says, smoothing it down. "Anyway, don't you have to go?" he asks pointedly.

"Nah. I figure I can hang out with my baby brother for a few minutes before I go away for a whole year." I reach over and pinch his cheek.

This time, he swats my hand away and raises his eyebrows. "Baby?"

"Always." I smile at him and he laughs. This is how we are, always teasing. But we are also a team. Us against the world. He has his friends and I have mine, but, at home, it has always been the two of us. Dad would try to spend time with us after Mom died, but he usually ended up at work instead. He got called in all the time, at all hours.

He never once told them no.

Wise beyond his years, Alex once told me he thinks that it hurts Dad to be with us because we bring back so many memories of Mom. Especially me, since I look just like her. So instead of dealing with that, Dad buries himself in his projects and leaves Alex and me to take care of each other.

His face becomes serious again. "So, you're really sure about this, Liz? I mean, think about it. No TV. No air conditioning. No light bulbs, smartphone, electricity, plumbing?" He looks down at his hands, still cradling the warm mug. "No pain-in-the-ass little brother," he adds quietly.

"Oh, Alex!" I jump up and hug him. Sitting on the high-backed stool, his face is almost even with mine for once. I look into his eyes. "You know that I'm going to miss you! Even if you are a pain in the ass." He grins. "You know that's the hardest part for me, right? Leaving you behind."

He nods and sighs. "What about the rest of it? How will you survive without your computer? Your blow-dryer? All that other electronic crap you use every day?"

"I'll live. Our ancestors did, after all."

"Yeah, but they never had to lose something they were used to having." He pauses. "Why are you really doing this, anyway? You've never really explained it to me." He stares straight into my eyes, looking hard.

I sigh. "You were almost five when Mom died, but you remember her, right?"

"Of course," he replies indignantly. "Well, some things about her, anyway," he amends. His brow crinkles and he closes his eyes. "I remember the way she looked when she smiled at me. The way she smelled, always like vanilla and lavender. The way her voice sounded when she would read stories to me. She always did the best voices, remember?"

I nod and smile, recalling these memories with him.

"I remember how she would dance with me, so very slowly, to get me ready to sleep… What was that lullaby she used to sing for us? Oh, right." He smiles wistfully and sings softly, "*When you wake, you shall have, all the pretty little horses…*"

His voice is clear and sweet, almost right on key. Mom used to sing it every night at bedtime. She had many talents, our mother, but singing was not one of them. She never sounded as good as Alex does now. And yet, what we wouldn't give to have her sing it to us again, just once.

Alex continues, "And I will always remember the look on her face when she would tell me she loved me." He pauses, sighs. "But not too much more than that. So much has faded away." He looks back at me sadly. I hug him again.

"Well, I remember much more than that," I tell him. "I still miss her every day."

"You know I do, too."

"I know. But this is just…my way of coping, alright? It has been since the beginning. I started working on our family tree right after she died. Before the funeral, even. I had to try somehow to keep her alive in my mind. And now with this missing piece…" I think for a moment. "I just…I feel like it's the only way I can keep her with me."

"Fine, Liz, I'll give you that," he says resignedly. "But you do know you're obsessed, right? Because this is seriously kind of crazy. No, you know what? Not even kind of. It's just plain crazy. Just to find this one woman who knew absolutely nothing about our mother? Finding this old lady won't bring Mom back, so let it go already. I don't even know why Dad's allowing this."

"You know why, Alex?" I say, getting angry. "Because, in case you missed it, he's even more obsessed than I am. Where do you think he's been disappearing to every year, like clockwork? You really think he was telling the truth when he said he had to go away for an overnight conference *every* March for the past four years? You think it's just a coincidence that this 'conference' falls on his birthday each year, even though there's never been one before? Think. He was the first test subject and he's been going back ever since. What else would have motivated him to create the device in the first place?"

He looks at me, dumbfounded. For once, I've noticed something he didn't. Sometimes I guess it just takes one to know one, and, yes, we *are* both obsessed. He startles as a loud snort rings through the room, otherwise quiet now that the echoes of my rant have died away. Our dog, Penny, has shifted in her sleep. He lowers his voice. "He's visiting her?"

"Of course he's visiting her," I answer, matching his tone. "We both know he hasn't been the same since she died. No matter how much he loves us, we can never make him happy like we could have if she were still here." I pause, not sure if I should tell him more. I decide that he's old enough to know if he didn't already.

"I overheard Edna and some of the lab guys talking one day. Did you know that before he started work on the device, they all thought he'd kill himself? He was depressed for months and talked of nothing but death. They tried everything they could think of to bring him out of it, but nothing worked. They tried and tried to get him to see a therapist, but of course he wouldn't go.

"Then one day he just snapped out of it. He went into the

lab to work on this amazing new idea. They all thought he was crazy, but he wouldn't stop working on it until it was a reality. Almost six years later, it was.

"So that's why he's letting you go?" Alex concludes.

"So that's why he's letting me go," I echo. "Because he understands what it's like. I need to do this."

Alex nods and hugs me one last time. I hold him tightly. Then I turn around. On the way out, I give Penny one last pat. She opens her eyes and wags her bushy tail, then settles back to sleep. I wave at my brother, who is watching me go. Then I walk out the door.

Chapter Two

Away from the emotional pull of my brother, I start to feel excited. The door leads down to our garage. I turn on the light and see shelves of unused tools, scraps of lumber, unopened paint cans. All is neatly stored and showing no signs of use. Dad spends too much time at work to do any projects at home, despite his best intentions. Thank goodness for the housekeeper, the weekly visits by the landscapers, and the contractors who are called in when something breaks. We'd be living in a rundown shack without them, because Dad would never get to any of it.

My phone beeps. I check the screen to see that my friend Donna has woken up early to send me a goodbye text. "See u next yr," it reads. "I'll miss u so much!" I bite my lip and take a deep breath. I'll miss her too. I pause to send her a quick reply before continuing on my way.

My car is parked between the shelves, a small black BMW convertible. I climb in, press the button to open the garage door, and slowly guide the car down the drive. As I go, I look back at the house I grew up in. It's too dark to see much. Sunrise is still nearly two hours away, and our house sits back in the woods, away from glaring streetlights. Only the security light is on, illuminating the garage door as it closes.

If it were lighter out, I would be able to see our pretty home one more time before I leave. Our house is not white or tan like many of the houses in the area, but painted a pale lavender above a faux stone foundation. It's also much smaller than the huge homes—mansions even—of our neighbors. That's the way my mother wanted it. She and my father had this house built just after I was born. The small second-floor balcony leans out on stone pillars, white trim frames the windows and door, and the two-bay garage opens from the one wall of the basement that's not entirely underground.

My favorite room in the house, the sunroom, is visible only by the bright white security light reflecting on the glass. I love it because it's so warm in there; I often say that I'm always cold. The sunroom is decorated with plush, pale-blue furniture, a light wood table, and is brimming with blooming hibiscus trees in shades of pink and yellow. I can spend hours reading in that room with the sunlight warming me through, or enjoy late nights there, just gazing out at the moon and stars. The sunroom is the place where I did most of my research when I wasn't at the library. I would sit with my feet up on a hassock and my laptop humming, delving through anything I could dig up.

The research I did was in tracking my family tree. Well, my maternal family tree, anyway. I've mostly only researched my mother's side. Hers is more important to me, as it's all I have left of her. She died of cancer when I was eight.

My mom came from a wealthy family. The Woods have been so wealthy for so long that they consider themselves to be "old money." And we aren't bad off even without them. My dad is the head engineer at his own science and engineering firm. But none of that could save her. No matter how much money anybody threw at the doctors, near and far, the cancer was relentless.

So that's when I started my research into her family. I have seen the Woods, generations of them, in my mind's eye as I read about their names, their occupations, their lives. I have tracked her family into the past, well into the 17th century. And I have tracked it through my own generation, as well. I know about all of my distant cousins whom I've never met. I have written them letters, and I even spoke to a few on the phone. But I have been frustrated for a long time while looking for a single missing limb on her family tree, my great-great-great-great-grandmother, Elizabeth Wood. She is the one I aim to find now.

I suppose I can't honestly say why finding her is so important to me. Maybe it's because she shares my name, Elizabeth. Because of that, I sort of feel a special link with her. Or maybe it's just simple curiosity, along with the frustration of defeat. She is nowhere. She is a ghost. For the rest of the family, there are records everywhere, going far deeper into the past than Elizabeth's time, which was in the Victorian era, specifically the 1870s. There are newspaper articles, birth and death certificates, obituaries, marriage records, and more for all the others, and yet there is almost nothing about her. It's almost as if she never existed. The mystery is intriguing.

I think another part of it is also a desire to clear her name, our shared name, of a supposed crime. The sole record of Elizabeth Wood that I've been able to find shows that almost exactly 140 years ago, June 20, 1878, she was hanged for murder.

I know it could be true. But it just feels wrong.

But I can find Elizabeth Wood nowhere else in the historical records. Birth certificate? None. Maiden name? Nope. With only that one record of her death, but nothing about her birth, I don't even know how old she was when she died. She married a very prominent young man, William Wood, and yet there is no record of their wedding, not even a mention in the local paper. There is no way that a Wood wedding would have gone unannounced. But Elizabeth's name isn't even on the birth certificate of her son. There is just a clear, washed out spot like someone deliberately erased it instead.

The only mention of her anywhere is this very small death notice tucked into the back corner of the local newspaper:

On this day, 20 June, 1878, Mrs. Elizabeth Wood, wife of Mr. William Wood, is to be hanged for the brutal Murder of Mr. Damien Gracen of Thorne Hill, Connecticut. May God have mercy on her soul.

Nothing more. Those four lines are all I've ever found about her.

These same thoughts run through my head as I drive through the wooded back streets to an old farming area a few miles north of what used to be downtown. I pull in about a half hour before I need to, at a quarter to four, but I find two vans are already here. They are big white vans with the logo "Franklyn Engineering" in small black letters on the sides. Both have their headlights pointing at the trees and spotlighting an old stone wall running away from us a few meters in.

The door to one van opens and my dad steps out. He is tall

and lanky, like Alex. He towers over me. He wears a white lab coat that hangs loosely around his thin frame. His light brown hair, which has been slowly graying and receding for as long as I can remember, is slightly disheveled. This is nothing new for him, day or night. He rarely considers his appearance. I step out of my car and come around to him. As I get nearer, I can see his handsome brown eyes, which have little flecks of gold in them. They look tired. And why not? He wasn't at home, so he either left before I woke up, or he spent the night in the lab again.

When we reach one another, he gives me a quick hug and a smile. It may just be how tired he is, but his smiles never seem to show in his eyes anymore. I don't think it is the exhaustion, though. I haven't seen him truly happy—the way he used to be—since Mom died. I still remember the way his smiles looked back then, with full flashes of teeth and his bright eyes sparkling. He never looks that way anymore.

All the same, I know he's happy to see me.

"Lizzy!" he says. "I've missed you. Are you ready? How are you feeling?"

"I'm fine, dad," I answer. "I've missed you, too." I hug him again, then look up at his face. "I'm ready."

Chapter Three

Last week, Dad tried to keep me here by telling me that he needs me to take care of Alex. That may have been true once, but Alex can take care of himself now. He's never needed me to cook or clean for him, even when he was little; our housekeeper takes care of all that and always has.

Because despite my reasons—valid ones, I think—my dad doesn't actually want me to go through with this. He doesn't like that I'll be gone so long. At least a year, by the very nature of the device. Twelve months from today will be the soonest I'll be able to come home. I don't know why, or how, but I do know that it will only work on the date of one's birth. So, I guess I could come back within twenty-four hours, technically, as he has done before. But we all know it's highly unlikely that I will accomplish my goal in that length of time, and I am okay with that, even if he isn't comfortable with it.

But today he says nothing. He knows of my determination. The time for convincing me is past.

He simply nods. "They'll be setting up in a minute."

It's actually almost five minutes before the setup begins.

There's really not too much to set up anyway, which is good, because there is only a team of six people to do it, including my dad. I help, too. Seven people.

A floodlight on a stand is placed in the center of the area. A lightweight frame and curtains are assembled to form a changing room. Two large garment bags are hung up on a stand just inside the curtain. A mirror goes in beside the stand. A brown leather travel bag is propped up against the frame. A tall chair and a basket of hairbrushes and accessories are set out on a small table.

My dad, never a man of many words, raises his eyebrows at me and motions with his head towards the chair. I sit. Edna, one of my dad's employees, comes up behind me. She is an engineer, too, but she has always had an interest in cosmetology, so she likes to help. Paul, however, is in charge of my makeover, being the firm's outside consultant on all things beauty-related.

In their hands, I am transformed in very little time. Using only antique-style hairpins, my long hair is swiftly pulled into a chignon. Paul pulls out a few short tendrils and eases them into soft curls that float gently down the nape of my neck. Then he takes out a hat and begins pinning it to my hair. It has a similar shape to a man's top hat, but it's smaller and has a brim that's curled slightly upwards along the sides.

While he deals with my hair, Edna applies my makeup. It's easy, because it's very minimalistic: powder, to make my complexion ever so fashionably pale; very light rouge for just that hint of a blush on my cheeks; balm to add a touch of shine to my lips. The natural look is very "in" where I'm going.

Next I move on to the changing room. Edna follows me with

another woman, Sara, a costuming consultant. As with my hair, we've practiced this ritual so many times that dressing doesn't take long either. Chemise. Pantalettes. Petticoat. Bustle. Corset. Underskirt. Overskirt. Bodice. Gloves. Lace-up boots. I am handed a parasol and turned around so I can see the mirror.

The effect is magical. Earlier this morning, I had wanted to look different. Now, I most certainly do.

My figure is largely unchanged. Thank goodness for the genes that allow me to wear this corset without cutting off my air supply in order to achieve ridiculous historical beauty ideals. But still, I look so different. Stately. Elegant. Poised.

The dress is deep blue with cream trim. It hugs my body throughout the length of the high-necked, double-breasted jacket bodice, down the laced back, and then it flares at the hip. The skirt front falls straight down from there. The back, however, is lifted by the bustle. It's just a small one. By the mid-1870s, large bustles had fallen out of fashion. The over-skirt is tugged and gathered in under the bustle by pulling the underlying layers of fabric in to create an almost mermaid-like silhouette. The ruffled and pleated underskirt below completely covers my feet, which are clad in modern reproductions of late Victorian boots, and drags behind me in an almost imperceptible train.

My gloves, parasol, and hat are all blue, matching the shade in the Victorian traveling dress perfectly. The hat sits forward on my head, catching the top of my upswept hair in the back and shading the top of my forehead under the brim in front. It is fully adorned with feathers and blue and cream-colored ribbons.

I look exactly as though I have stepped out of history. Which is perfect, considering what I'm about to step into.

When I come back out, Dad is waiting. He looks at me intently. "Do you have any questions?"

I shake my head. "I've been through everything about a hundred times."

"Well, I'll tell you again anyway."

I sigh, defeated, rolling my eyes in teenage exasperation.

"*Do not* lose track of time. You can't exactly forget your window date, but you can easily forget what day it is and let it pass you by. You will have twenty-four hours, starting at midnight. Don't miss it unless you absolutely have to."

I nod.

"We'll have a team waiting for you here when you're ready to return. So don't forget where your departure point is. If, for some unforeseen reason, you cannot make it, we will wait for you at the next window."

"Got it, Dad," I say, not too impatiently. Of course I've been through all of this dozens of times, but I know he wants to make sure I'll be safe, so I try to stay calm and let him continue. Instead, he surprises me.

"Then you're ready?"

"Yes," I say, taken aback that these are all of the instructions he plans to give. "Yes I am."

He smiles. "Then let's go."

The departure point is a bit farther into the woods, at the intersection of the stone wall we'd seen earlier in the headlights and another just like it. We walk in the light of an ever-brightening sky. The wall is very old. As we pass, I see decades worth of ivy, moss, and lichen blanketing the stones. The wall has collapsed in places, and we make our way around and through the woods slowly. Edna loops my train around a button in back even as I lift the front hem. The walk isn't easy in this outfit.

When we make it to the intersection of the walls, they help me climb up onto the stones. Sara hands me the leather travel bag, which I sling over my shoulder.

Then my father finally pulls out the actual machine. I look skeptically at the small device in his hand. I've seen and used the models before, but somehow, I still expected something much grander in reality. Its black color and small rectangular screen are reminiscent of my cell phone.

"Dad, seriously. Is your time machine just an iPhone app?"

Everyone laughs, even my dad. "You've used the model, so I'm not sure what you were expecting, Lizzy. Something out of the movies? Big and flashy with all sorts of whirligigs and bright lights? Or maybe a DeLorean, hmm? A big blue police box? We're quite a bit more sophisticated in real life. It is 2018 after all."

Still the overprotective parent, he shows me once more how to use it. I'm eager to go, but he rightfully tests me to make sure that I am absolutely clear on what to do. I dutifully answer his questions. It would be really bad if I were to screw this up now. When everything is finally done, I say my goodbyes all around and thank everyone for their extensive help. I thank my father last, not sure that just a few words can encompass everything I am feeling.

"You're welcome," he says, smiling even though I see the beginnings of tears in his eyes. He hugs me goodbye and plants a kiss on my cheek, his scruffy chin tickling my face.

"Good luck, Lizzy. Have fun, be safe, and come home to us. I love you."

I know that he does, but he doesn't express it very often. It gives me a warm feeling inside to hear him say the words. I smile down at him just as the first rays of the sun peek up over the horizon. "I love you, too, Dad."

I make sure to hold my case tightly, and take one more look around at the surrounding forest.

Then I tap the button.

Chapter Four

Wow. What a feeling. The sensation is strange and disorienting and yet absolutely amazing at the same time. I can't even describe the enormity of what just happened to me, except to say that I know it's quite possible that I will never be the same again.

A few short moments ago, I was standing on a stone wall in the forest, surrounded by my dad and my team of helpers. An instant later, I'm here. I'm on the very same stone wall...and yet it's not the same. I'm all alone now, standing on a much newer wall. The plants that had overgrown it are gone, and it is whole, squared off, and sturdy. Birds are flitting over the meadow. Yes, a meadow. The trees that were around me are not even sprouts. I'm surrounded instead by fields bursting with clover and wildflowers. There are small birds and rodents and insects all chirping and bustling about. The trees that had been there seem to have jumped back much farther afield, hazy in the distance.

Before me is the dawn of a new day. When I woke up early this morning, it was June 21, 2018. A mere two hours later, I am watching the sun rise on June 21, 1875.

Oddly enough, one of my first thoughts is that I've spent my suburban life very sheltered. Sure, our house is set back in the trees, but did I ever go out for a walk among them? Not really. Most of my exploration took place at the shopping mall. Did I ever walk barefoot through a field of wildflowers? Never. I saw someone do it in a movie once, but I've never really paid much attention to a field of anything. I vow to change that now. And I'm suddenly glad that I'll be able to experience nature along with everything else I'll be doing here.

I shift the heavy bag on my shoulder and remember its contents, all painstakingly collected for this trip: Spare underthings, toiletries, and accessories perfectly replicated from antique versions…and, most importantly, gold and silver coins and paper money—all correct for the time period, of course. I place as much as I can carry into my purse, my pockets, even my undergarments. The rest—and there is still a lot left—I leave in a sack that I hide beneath a pile of small stones in the wall that I can come back for, as needed. The economy is very different here than it is back home; a few hundred dollars will get me a long way. The thousands I brought will get me much further, but not if they end up stolen.

I begin the long walk south towards the town. Thank goodness that my shoes are actually fairly comfortable.

With nothing to distract me from the day, I start to truly take in the world around me as never before. I notice mist rising up off a nearby pond and the sun rising over the distant hills to my left. It's turning the clouds around it into the most beautiful mural of bright pink and orange. I am awestruck at this simple beauty. Perhaps I should have woken up earlier all these years. It seems a shame that I've missed eighteen years of sunrises.

My breathing picks up. It's a very warm morning, even for the end of June, and very humid. It's definitely not an easy walk in an ankle-length traveling dress and leather-soled shoes. I put up my parasol for shade, but it barely helps. The dark color of my dress catches the heat and, though everything is linen, I still have many layers underneath. There is no breeze to waft through my skirts and cool me down.

Inside my gloves, my palms are wet and sticky. It's no more than half an hour before I'm sweating like crazy. No, I almost forgot; ladies don't sweat in this day and age; they perspire. Or is it glow? My grandmother, my Mom's mother, once told me that horses sweat, gentlemen perspire, and ladies glow. Whatever it is, I am doing it profusely, because no distinction in name changes the feel of these salty drops that continue to form all over me and glide unendingly downwards.

I'm resting for a moment when I notice a change in the fields ahead of me. Instead of wild grasses and flowers, there are neat rows of crops and recently tilled soil. Small figures in the distance work the land. It looks like I've made it to a local farm.

I still have to get to town, but I need a drink first. I am desperately thirsty, and I wonder if the farmer will be hospitable. Besides, I suppose it's as good a place as any to begin my search. I doubt I'll find much news of my rich ancestor here, but, who knows? No stone unturned and all that, right? I angle my trajectory towards the sunrise in the direction of the distant farmhouse.

As I come closer to the main buildings of the farm, I see

the silhouette of a single man heading towards what I think might be a chicken coop. I aim for that building. While I walk, I pull out my handkerchief and attempt to mop my face into some semblance of serenity. I have a feeling that my efforts are futile, but I try all the same. I am almost 100 yards away when the man walks out of the building holding a basket. He heads to the house, not seeing me. I smile to myself as he does a double take, catching sight of me out of the corner of his eye. He walks my way.

As the man approaches, I begin to see more of him. He is still backlit against the rising sun, so at first, all I can make out is his build. He's muscular, presumably from tending to these fields by hand. He has broad shoulders and he looks to be close to six feet tall. He is a bit taller than my brother, at any rate, but not as tall as my dad—though there is no lankiness in evidence here.

More details become clear as he gets closer still. Brown hair glints with red and gold highlights in the morning sun. I know girls who would pay hundreds of dollars for hair like that. His walk and build suggest a young man, I think. He's wearing a dingy old button-down shirt rolled up at the sleeves, and a pair of brown pants made of what looks to be very itchy fabric. The tops of his boots are clean and polished, but the sides are covered with what I hope is nothing more offensive than mud. I can just make out a small smile forming on his face.

"May I help you, Miss…?" His voice is deep, strong, and vibrant.

"Elizabeth Franklyn," I answer demurely. In my head, I tell myself that I respond in such a tone simply because it's how a proper lady should, but the reality is that his voice has a power over me that I can't understand.

That's when he turns into the sunlight and I see it. I see exactly the reason why his voice resonates in my mind. This man is as familiar to me as if I'd seen him every day of my life. Which, in a way, is almost true. I'd recognize that face anywhere.

The man before me has full pink lips under a slightly crooked nose. I've never seen him smile before, but he does now, and small dimples peek out around his mouth. He has strong, neat brows, and his eyes are surrounded by a halo of enviously long, dark lashes. And what eyes—indeed, the eyes of my dreams. His eyes are pale jade, bringing to mind early spring leaves and stones of peridot. Somehow, the sun glinting off of them makes them seem to glow, such a familiar sight and yet one I've never truly seen before in my life.

"Miss Franklyn, I must own to being surprised to have a visitor so early in the day. Especially a young lady such as yourself. What can I do for you?" His voice has a musical quality to it and I never want to stop listening.

"I…um… I…" I'm completely speechless. Not an unusual circumstance, to be sure, but this…this is different. The man standing no more than two feet away from me is the owner of the face that I've been dreaming of for as long as I can remember. How am I supposed to make polite chitchat with him?

"Are you quite well? Please, come in, and I'll make you a cup of tea." He frowns with concern for me. My heart sinks. Already I am loath to see anything but a smile on his lips. I feel terrible about putting a frown on his face because of my strange behavior.

But still, every muscle in my body is completely tense. I cannot act normally because this cannot be real. Somehow I can effortlessly believe that I've traveled back in time by nearly a hundred and fifty years. That's easy. No problem. Why not? But to see *this* man standing before me? Speaking to me in cold, hard reality? My mind cannot wrap around it.

I'm using all of my strength just to keep myself from reaching out to touch his face. How else can I make sure this is real, that it truly is him? I've dreamt of this exact face for so long that I'm sure it can't possibly be genuine.

I finally manage to croak out, "Yes, please." It's polite, but slightly sickly. "Some tea sounds lovely."

In a move I've only ever seen in movies, he easily offers to carry my travel bag for me, then presents his arm to help me to the house. It seems that even a farmer of this century can handle the ins and outs of being a gentleman far better than anyone I've ever met back home. My prom date didn't even bother to hold the door open for me. I was right behind him, but he let it slam in my face. And yet he still expected a goodnight kiss. Along with a grope, as a matter of fact. What a loser he was.

As this man assists me, the bare skin of his arm touches mine. Only the tiniest strip of flesh is exposed at my wrist, but still, I feel goose bumps immediately arise. I notice that the fuzz of reddish-brown hair on his arm is standing up at my touch as well. I smile wonderingly. Can he possibly feel it, too?

He turns to me suddenly as we walk and gives an apologetic look. "Forgive me, Miss Franklyn. I almost forgot to introduce myself. My name is James." *James.* His name resonates in my head. So this is the name that goes with the mysterious face. It fits, I think, but for some reason it seems just the slightest bit off. "James Percival," he finishes with a warm smile.

If I were a true 19th-century lady, I suppose I might simply swoon. His smile, the sound of his voice, and the touch of his hand on mine might be too much. That's what you always hear about anyway, the frail and delicate flowers who faint away at the drop of a hat. But no smelling salts are necessary for me. The 21st-century girl in me feels confused and conflicted, but also excited. I'm way too keyed up to faint. All I want to do is stay right here at his side and bask in the glow of his presence.

But wait. Time out. What the *hell* am I thinking? I need to put these thoughts out of my mind. In twelve months, I'll be back home and he'll be long dead. Dreams or no dreams, I have a life to go back to and he has one to get on with here. But, oh, how I wish it were otherwise.

I need to focus. I take a deep breath and concentrate on speaking.

"It's a pleasure to meet you, Mr. Percival," I manage to say, forcing my lips into a smile. It's really far too stiff to pass for anything but a grimace, but either he doesn't notice or he's simply too courteous to mention it. He opens the door to the weathered old farmhouse and motions for me to walk through.

"May I ask where you're from, Miss Franklyn?"

"Please, it's Elizabeth." His eyebrows raise a miniscule amount in what I take to be an expression of amused surprise. I pause, wondering if I've already messed up. I did pay attention in the Victorian etiquette classes I took, honestly, but things seem to be slipping from my mind like water through a sieve. I probably shouldn't have asked a complete stranger to call me by my given name just yet. I move on to more rehearsed answers. "I'm from Watch Hill, Rhode Island." This is a white lie, of course. But I can't very well tell him the truth, that I'm actually from the future Thorne Hill, Connecticut, now can I?

"Really?" he asks. His green eyes twinkle mischievously. "That is quite a walk. I'm impressed."

I laugh awkwardly, unable to meet those magnificent eyes. He's teasing me, isn't he? Oh, my. I feel like I'm about to hyperventilate.

I breathe deeply and slowly while I wrack my dismally slow brain for the rest of my cover story. Parts of it seem to have gone missing. "I… I only just got here," I stammer stupidly. "I sent the carriage ahead, er, with most of my luggage—so I could walk into town?" I say it almost as a question. I am failing so miserably right now. The sweat is building up on my forehead again, but I push on valiantly. "It's so beautiful out here. Too nice to spend any more time in a stuffy carriage, isn't it?" Finally finished with the lie, I manage a quick glance up at his face. It's enough to make me blush and I look back down at my hands again.

I've always been the world's most terrible liar, but somehow he buys my story anyway. Or he seems to, at least. I feel ashamed, dirty even, for lying to him, but I'll do it again if I have to. It's the price I have to pay.

"I very much agree. I love the fresh air and the feel of the woods." He pauses to gaze out the window for a moment. "So what brings you here? Why did you leave Rhode Island?" He begins making the tea, so different a process from the one I'm used to. Gone is the microwave to warm up a mug full of water, or even the ceramic stovetop and stainless-steel teapot that Linda, our housekeeper favors. Instead, he places a cast-iron kettle onto a hook attached to the mantle. He rotates the hook out and over the flames and stokes the fire below. Instead of neat little tea bags, he scoops loose leaves into each cup that will settle in the bottom and have to be strained as we drink.

My mouth feels dry as I prepare yet more lies, but they come out a little more easily this time, a little more naturally. "My father wants me to get out and meet people." I grimace. "'People,' meaning wealthy young men, I think. It seems there are far too few eligible bachelors at home." I roll my eyes. "You know how parents are."

He nods knowingly. "Yes. Yes, I do. Mine would be only too happy for me to find a wife."

I make the mistake of making eye contact again, only to become lost in his eyes, the soft green irises pulling me in. I begin to babble nonsensically and soon enough, without meaning to, I'm talking about the true reason I'm here. "Though actually, I'm also looking for someone. Do you know the Wood family?" I ask, flustered that I can't control myself around him.

His face shows recognition and I go on. It's too late to turn back now. "They are, um, family friends. Well…actually I'm mostly interested in their son, William. Do you know of him by any chance? Have you heard if he's married yet?" I blurt out.

I pull my gaze away from his almost violently and focus on the floor. It's bare wood; simple but neat. I scarcely notice. All I can think is that this is getting worse and worse. *Why* can't I think clearly? No one has ever had this effect on me before.

From the edge of my field of vision, I can see his expression, which looked only a moment ago as if it might never be anything but a smile. But now it has faltered. "No," he answers shortly. "I don't think he is married yet." His warm tone has disappeared along with his smile. "I am not generally well versed with the comings and goings of the gentry these days, but as far as I have heard, Mr. Wood is out of town on business right now."

I mentally berate myself for being so stupid. I should have just kept my mouth shut. Why couldn't I have just shut up? I need to come up with a reply that won't make me sound even more dim-witted.

"Oh?" I say. *Good one,* I think sarcastically. At least I somehow manage to say it almost nonchalantly. But he looks upset. *Oh, crap, why is he upset?* I wonder.

I mean, if I had put any thought into it at all, I wouldn't really have expected him to know much about William, never mind his potentially having a problem with him. After all, this man is just a farmer, right? He wouldn't exactly be best pals with one of the richest men in town. Though I suppose he might have a dispute with him, or the family. What if he does? But still, I can't stop now. He might know more. I hate to ask the question, but I do, cautiously. "So, I guess you don't know when he will be back then?"

He chuckles darkly. "I'm sorry, Miss Franklyn. No one seems to know, and believe me, the entire town wishes they did. It's all I overhear people discussing any time I'm in town, though I'll admit I'm not there often." He makes a disgusted sound. "Honestly though, the only reason anyone cares at all is because he's wealthy. They cannot wait to marry one of their daughters off to him," he states matter-of-factly. His voice, which had been so warm and welcoming earlier, is tinged with bitterness.

I cringe away slightly from the coldness in his demeanor, upset at myself for not thinking before I spoke. *I just had to go ahead and blurt it all out*, I think again. *Stupid, stupid, stupid.* I feel certain that he regrets inviting me in now that he thinks I'm a gold-digger.

I stop myself yet again and sigh. It is of no importance. A gold-digger or worse, who cares? I keep forgetting that it doesn't matter in the slightest what this James thinks of me. We can have no future together. Literally.

After that exchange we sit in absolute silence while we sip our tea. Not, of course, the companionable silence of old friends, but that awkward, uncomfortable silence of two people with absolutely no clue what to say to one another. I've finally met the man of my dreams, and the first thing I did was screw it all up. Surely he hates me already.

And the worst part is that I'm not even supposed to care.

I can't stand it. I need to get out of here, away from his silence.

Our words may have faltered, but his politeness has not. He stands with me as I rise quickly with a quiet, "Thank you." His pale eyes lock on mine once more and my heart speeds up. A hummingbird would have trouble keeping up with its fluttering beat. After what feels like an eternity, he smiles again, gently. So gently. And yet he manages to light up the entire room with the brilliance of that smile.

"Will you allow me to walk you to town, Miss Elizabeth? A lady should never have to walk unattended, and it's still a few miles away." With just those few simple words, my heart is soaring once more. He's surely just being polite again, and yet I suddenly feel more peaceful. His smile has erased any thoughts of my escaping. Now all I want to do is stay with him as long as possible.

We leave the house and begin walking, James carrying my bag and taking my arm again while I keep my parasol up against the still climbing sun. We make our way in silence, my heart still beating wildly, reacting to the renewed contact of his skin against mine. I may have purposely tugged the trim of my sleeve out of the way as much as possible.

And the feeling is almost unbearable.

Just as I start to think that we'll walk all the way to town without a word, he turns to me suddenly, as if coming to a decision. "Miss Elizabeth, forgive me if I'm being forward, but... may I ask you something?"

I nod, glancing his way for just a moment before turning back to the path.

"I'm curious," he continues. "I've never met anyone who would send her carriage ahead so that she could walk miles on her own through dusty fields—and with her traveling bag, no less. Please don't take offense," he adds quickly. "But you must agree that it could be seen as a bit...odd."

What can I say to him? I don't want to tell him another lie. I know I'll have to lie again soon, but for now I want to give him something real. I think hard, racking my brain for some small bit of truth to tell him.

"Perhaps I *am* a bit odd," I laugh, stalling for time. "But that's not a question."

He smiles. "I just meant, well, who are you? If you know

what I mean..." He trails off with an exhaled chuckle, looking at the ground.

"I really am just a normal girl," I tell him. "I play the piano, sing, and dance, just like most ladies my age." It's all true. I took years of lessons of every classical skill imaginable so I would be able to blend in here. "I like to walk and to ride, which is why I wanted to finish this trip on foot, out in the fresh air. My bag," I say, motioning to it, "contains things I'd rather not leave alone with anyone, even my father's coachman. So I brought it with me."

He nods. "Understandable, at least to me," he says. "But then, I love walking through the outdoors myself."

"It is beautiful here," I agree. "I've never seen a sunrise so lovely." *Or at all*, I remind myself, but he doesn't need to know that.

"And what of your family?" he asks.

"Well, my father is...a doctor." This is not technically a lie; he does have a doctorate. "Dr. Jonathan Franklyn. I have a younger brother, Alexander. He'll be fifteen in a few months. They're both back home." I feel almost proud, managing a whole sentence of truths about myself.

"Your family didn't come with you?"

"No. My father has too much work to take care of."

"Well, I suppose it must be bad for a town's health if the doctor were to up and leave."

"Yes!" I nod a bit too enthusiastically. "Right. Yes, of course."

I truly am such a horrible liar. I don't know how James doesn't see right through me. Though once again the thought occurs to me that maybe he does, but he's just too nice to call me out on it. I continue regardless. "He can ill afford to take an extended break from work without a replacement. And my brother is too young to come with me yet; I'd have to look after him instead of making a life here for myself."

"And how old are *you*, if I may ask?"

"Why, sir!" I exclaim, feigning shock. "Asking a lady her age?!" He blushes.

I laugh at the sight and then answer his question. "I'm eighteen. Just today, actually," I tell him almost proudly. "It's my birthday."

"Well then, happy birthday, Miss Franklyn." He pauses, just realizing something. "You've mentioned your father and your brother, but what of your mother? Is she not able to join you?"

I look at the ground and take a deep breath. "My mother died ten years ago."

"I am so sorry." He truly sounds grieved. "Please forgive me, Miss Franklyn."

"It's not your fault." I try to lighten things up. "And I do believe I asked you to call me Elizabeth."

He becomes flustered. "Of course, Elizabeth. I'm sorry."

"Don't be," I tell him. "I still miss her terribly, but it was a long time ago now. It doesn't hurt so much to talk about it anymore." Regardless, I change the subject before either of us gets too uncomfortable. No one really knows how to react when I tell them about my mom.

"What about you, Mr. Percival? Won't you tell me about yourself?"

He smiles at me. "Well, first of all, if I must call you Elizabeth, then you ought to call me James."

I try, unsuccessfully, not to appear too pleased with this

unexpected development. Instead, I end up pathetically breathing his name to myself. *"James…"*

I snap myself out of it quickly. I need to keep cool.

Thankfully, I don't think he heard me.

I manage to continue lamely, "Of course. James. You were going to tell me about yourself…?"

"There's really not much to tell, I'm afraid. I own a farm, work the land along with a few hired hands, and I don't have time for much else, especially during planting and harvest. It's a busy life."

"Well, what about your family?"

"My family. Yes." He frowns. "Well, my parents, of course. My father is in business. My mother keeps the house. I have an older sister; she's been married for about five years now. We don't talk much. And I have a younger sister, little Mary, whom I just adore. Blonde curls and great big hazel eyes, like yours. I guess I've always doted on her, being the baby. She's fifteen. You know, she plays the piano so beautifully, you would swear you were listening to Mozart himself. You said you play?"

I laugh at that. My piano skills were notoriously bad when I took lessons as a child, and while they've improved a lot since then, I have a way to go before I reach Mozart's level. "A little bit. I don't make time to practice as I should. She's probably been playing her entire life, and surely she has natural talent that I lack. I can never get my fingers to move fast enough; they're just too short." I hold up my hand and wiggle my small fingers to show him. The dainty gloves make them look even shorter than they are.

He holds his hand up to match mine, and I stop moving my fingers to press my hand firmly up against his. His long, elegant fingers extend more than an inch beyond each of mine. They look far better suited for the piano than my own do. He looks at our hands side by side for a moment before his gaze slowly meets mine. "I think they're lovely," he says softly.

I take a shaky breath. "Perhaps I just need more practice then." I match his gentle tone.

He seems to catch himself and pulls his hand from mine. He looks down to the forest floor, no longer willing to meet my eyes. "Forgive me, Miss Elizabeth. I've overstepped my bounds."

Before I can reply he expertly changes the subject. "What were we discussing again? Oh, yes, my sister."

With the moment passed, he somehow seems to become completely comfortable again even while I am left reeling.

"She has indeed been playing ever since she was a toddler; surely that's why she is so wonderful at it. Sadly, I don't get to hear her play very often anymore, since my parents are...not really on speaking terms with me right now."

Despite the state he's left me in, I'm intrigued. I wonder what could have happened. "I'm sorry to hear it. That's so sad. Why not?"

"My father disapproves of the way I've chosen to live my life." He says it very matter-of-factly, turning to stare off into the distant woods.

I frown. "That's awful. Is there something so terribly wrong with farming?"

He shakes his head. "Not exactly. It's just that they had hoped that I would take over for my father and run the family business. You know, actually make some money, and do something with my life. I'm the only son, so they expect me to uphold the family name.

"What they can't understand is that I want to make my own way. I don't want to ride my father's coattails all through my life; I want to be my own man. So I saved enough money to buy this small farm and hire a few hands. We're actually doing quite well. It turns out that I have my father's eye for business, if not his love for it. Though I suppose it doesn't hurt that I also kept in touch with a few of his old contacts." He smiles before continuing.

"But the best part is that I'm actually happy here. I am quite sure I never would have been content as a businessman. I love working the land with my own two hands. It makes me feel alive. It's the most amazing feeling to watch fields of seeds you've sown grow up into acres of plants ready for the harvest. And there is nothing sweeter than living off of food you've grown yourself. It's very satisfying."

His passion for what he does shines through with every word. I'm impressed. It takes a lot of character for someone to go his own way against the wishes of his family. That's especially so if he gave up a stable middle-class life for the unsure existence of a farmer.

"You really are something, James," I tell him.

"What do you mean by that?" He looks genuinely perplexed.

"Just that I've never met anyone with the conviction you have about what you do. No one I know would ever take a chance like you did. You gave up a safe, solid life for one of hard work and uncertainty. You put your blood, sweat, and tears into a harvest, and yet the entire crop still depends on the whims of nature. On top of that, you went up against the pressures of your family to do what makes you happy. I think it takes a very brave person to do that, and I truly admire you for it."

He doesn't get a chance to respond because suddenly the forest opens up in front of us to reveal a bustling town about half a mile away.

Businessmen in jackets and top hats make their way towards work on Main Street. It's a very different place today than what I remember. Vendors with carts and shop owners open up and hock their wares. Horses and carriages move up and down the cobbled road. No asphalt, no cars, and not one person is staring into a smart phone.

So here we are. We've made it into town proper. Funny that a short while ago I wanted to get away from James, but somehow we've gotten here way too soon.

"Where are you staying?"

I give him the name of the inn we had chosen for me. "The Maples."

He gives me a curiously thoughtful smile. "This way." He leads me off the wagon path and onto a deer trail just at the edge of the woods. I hesitate. "A shortcut," he explains. And I know I'm supposed to be more cautious, that I should think before leaving the established road with a strange man. But I cannot make myself distrust him. In my mind, it's as though I've known him forever. Besides, we've come this far.

My trust pays off. We walk quietly around the outskirts of town, coming out to an open meadow. A tree-lined gravel drive runs down the center and at the end stands a massive three-story building. It's built in the Grecian style. The building is white, with wide columns along the front and sides. The roof angles up in the center of the building to form a peak, while the sides are flat-topped. This building doesn't exist in my time. We found out about the inn itself through lots of research, but there are no traces of it in 2018. In fact, I think there's a diner in this spot now. But I've seen plenty of buildings like it. Even so, I absolutely adore it: the location, the look, everything. It's perfect.

At the front steps, James turns to me, his dazzling eyes shining. "You know, that was one of the nicest things anyone has ever said to me." I'm confused. It must show on my face, because he clarifies. "Back there, in the woods…that you admire my decision. To go my own way."

Oh. I pause, debating how to answer him. I should have kept my mouth shut. This is an emotional subject, and I can't afford an emotional attachment here. Though if I'm honest with myself, I know that it's already far too late for that.

I decide to tease him, trying to keep the tone light. "Really? *That's* the nicest thing anyone's said to you? I take it you don't get many compliments."

But my witty banter is lost when he answers me very seriously. "No. Not really. And the ones I have gotten, well, they weren't from anyone whose opinions really mattered to me."

And my opinions matter? The question burns in my throat. I want so badly to ask it, but instead I just motion toward the elaborately carved door, nervous all over again. How quickly I've forgotten that I'm not going to get emotionally attached.

"I…I'd better go," I stutter. "Thank you for the walk."

"It was my pleasure."

He brings my hand to his mouth and kisses it, all the while

looking into my eyes from under his long lashes. How I wish I didn't have this stupid glove on, this barrier between us!

He holds my gaze and again I am lost; I feel I could stand here just like this for a hundred years or more, basking in his incredible eyes until the future world I left is completely built up around me. He finally releases me and hands my travel bag to the bellman who has just opened the door, though I hadn't even noticed. I'm gasping raggedly as though I've been holding my breath. *Have I been holding my breath?*

James smiles one last time, flashing his dimples at me, then turns and walks away from me into the meadow we came from. I go inside and watch his retreating form through the window. He turns around just once to look back at the inn, but he's too far away; I can't see his face. All too soon, he disappears, completely blending in with the trees. I let out a sigh as the bellman leads me through to the front desk.

This can't be happening. *How could I have let this happen?* It's insane. Less than two hours alone with this man and already I'm beginning to fall in love with him.

Chapter Five

As I walk through the inn, my thoughts are still taken up by James. I barely notice the foyer or the richly furnished sitting rooms. I try to pay attention while I speak to the man behind the desk. He's not sure about me at first, all dusty and sweaty, but soon enough the bellman is leading me to a third-floor suite. I'm pretty sure that between the elegant clothing I am wearing under all of this grime and the money I brought forth, the hotel clerk could surely tell I'd be worth his time. I vaguely hear someone mention something about a small restaurant downstairs, but my concentration quickly disintegrates.

When I get to my room, I lie down on the bed, still fully dressed, the small bustle making an odd bump in my lower back. I roll quickly onto my side. I close my eyes and, unbidden, James's face is the first thing to appear in my mind's eye. I reach out inside my daydream to touch him as I cannot do in reality. My previous dreams of him had always ended with a certain longing, but never this painful ache that I feel now.

I allow myself ten minutes to wallow before I pull myself together. It's time to get moving. I do my best to push James from my mind as I stand, but he lingers.

Still, I think I'll be able to function now. I sit up, take a deep breath, and look around my rooms, willing myself to take everything in.

It's hard to believe I missed all this when I came in just a few minutes ago. The place is stunning. Deep red and gold draperies hang over the windowpanes, dark hardwood covers the floors, and the golden sunlight glints on the burnt orange and deep plum bedclothes, making the whole thing reminiscent of an autumn day. The gleaming floors are partially covered by plush white rugs, while the pure white velvet upholstered furniture looks too fancy even to touch. *Is there any way I'll be able to sit in one of those chairs without fear of ruining it?*

I force myself to move around, though there's not really much for me to do, as I have almost no luggage. I pull a snack out of my bag, a handful of strawberries from back home—they're in season, so as not to raise suspicion—and eat the sweet fruit quickly. I find a safe in which I store my cash so that I don't need to carry so much on me. The rest I keep in my purse so that I can remedy my luggage problem immediately. If I'm going to meet people in the circles I need to be in, I'll have to be seen in more than just one traveling outfit.

Which reminds me...almost as important as the clothing, I'll need to hire myself a lady's maid. I'll never get anywhere in this town if they think I can't even afford the most important of servants for a young woman such as myself.

I'm not sure where to start looking for a maid, so after I clean myself up, I ask the concierge and he directs me to an agency back in town. I am provided with a carriage for my use, and the coachman brings me on my way.

A half hour after walking into the agency, I leave with the promise that an experienced live-in lady's maid, Miss Lanie Smith, will be at my room this afternoon, promptly at four.

With that out of the way, I go shopping. I am able to buy my way through the few high-end dress shops in Thorne Hill. I'll have to wait for most of the items I purchase, but I am able to pay extra to have a few pieces fitted and completed for me to wear today. I leave one dress shop a few hours after entering, wearing a stylish cornflower-blue-and-white-striped walking dress with a matching hat, gloves, and parasol. After my full morning of shopping, my original travel dress, a plain morning dress, a much fancier dinner dress, and a very extravagant evening gown, along with accompanying underclothing, will all be delivered to my rooms at the inn much later this afternoon. Oddly enough, all of that clothing is for one day alone! Victorian ladies are changing constantly, though thankfully it's usually only the top layer that needs to be switched. Even still, it's a wonder that they ever get anything accomplished.

And even with all the gowns I purchased today, still more such dresses will be arriving over the course of the next week or two, because, of course, should I manage to break into society, I should never be seen in the same dress two days in a row.

Like my traveling dress, these are all gorgeous and frilly, if a bit uncomfortable to wear. It's not so bad, though, because I refuse to tighten the corsets too tightly. And there is a fun, "let's play dress up" quality to them, like when I was a kid, trying on my mom's fancy gowns. So far it is more enjoyable than not.

Mostly though, this whole thing just doesn't feel real to me yet. It's so hard to believe that just a few weeks ago I was buying low-rise jeans and bikinis at the mall and driving home in my cute little Beamer. Now, dress-shop clerks are delivering custom-made Victorian gowns to my rooms by horse-drawn carriage. I shake my head in wonderment.

By the time I get back to the Maples in the coach, it's well past noon and I'm exhausted and starving. I remember vaguely being told about food, so I inquire and am led straight to the cozy restaurant on the first floor. Even though I am completely exhausted from my early rise and so much excitement today, I know I won't be able to nap without some food in my stomach.

The restaurant is located in what they call the northern wing of the inn. It's small and very elegant, and apparently is a popular lunch spot not only for guests, but for the wealthier townspeople, as well.

White silk tablecloths cover the small round tables, each adorned with a golden vase containing fresh flowers. The china is a beautiful rustic plum that contrasts perfectly with the white backdrop. The glasses are of intricately cut crystal, perfectly faceted so that the light shining through them creates miniature rainbows throughout the room.

Large windows let in the early afternoon sunlight and are propped open along with the side doors to let in a refreshing breeze on this hot summer day. This is a necessity since, as Alex mentioned, air conditioning hasn't even been invented yet.

The view from this room is stunning. The inn sits in a meadow that extends for another few hundred feet or so. At the edge, only a few feet away from the tree line, a small brook twists merrily around, burbling excitedly through a rocky bed. Up until the brook, the meadow is well manicured, with trees and flowers strategically placed for the best look. Beyond it, just before the trees take over, wildflowers of all colors seem to dance delicately in the gentle wind. A single rabbit lopes through the flower beds, bending often to nibble at a blossom. I think I like the far side of the brook much better.

Back inside, the waiters are attentive and cater quickly to my every need; soon I have a plate full of bread and butter to start, and I dig right in. I people-watch as I eat to keep myself from impolitely wolfing down my food.

The couple at the nearest table to me catches my attention first. The man is old; at least sixty. He is clearly wealthy—anyone eating here has to be—and wearing a very finely tailored suit over his robust figure. His black top hat sits on the table beside him while he conspicuously enjoys a hefty lunch. His companion is a young woman who can't be more than twenty-five. Judging by the huge rock on her finger, she seems to be the older man's wife. She is fairly pretty, but the ever-present scowl on her face takes away from her youthful glow. While the man is obviously enjoying his meal immensely, the woman has yet to eat a bite, sending back everything that has come to her, including her place settings, with one complaint or another. She loudly berates her husband to speak to the manager on her behalf, but he keeps his head down and his mouth full of food.

At another table, I spy a little girl dressed in her finest, no more than eight. She sits quietly with two older women. If one of them speaks to her, she merely nods or shakes her head, impassive. On one occasion she smiles, but it's a polite expression that doesn't reach her huge dark eyes. I've never seen anything like it. I've heard the old saying that children should be seen and not heard, but this is my first time observing it in action. The little girl seems less like a child and more like a miniature of the women next to her. She lacks the energy and life so evident in the children I have babysat for back home. It's so sad to me to see a child so…empty that I have to turn away.

Fortunately, at that moment, my meal arrives and I can concentrate instead on the delicious flavors going through my mouth. Of course, it doesn't take long before the ache in my hungry belly goes down and my mind wanders again, the urgency to eat having been depleted. I try to use the time wisely, beginning to consider my strategy for finding Elizabeth Wood. If William Wood is out of town as I was told, then it's going to be more difficult to track him down than I had thought. Nothing I'd read had indicated that he was gone. I was counting on William to lead me to her. After all, there are plenty of records about him. It's strange that in my research I didn't uncover anything about him traveling on business. There should have been gossip in the newspapers about it at least. I must have missed something.

I realize this could become really difficult without having William to follow. After all, I can't just go up to people and ask questions like I did with James, which was a foolish thing for me to do, anyway.

Of course, it will not even be possible to make a stupid mistake like that—never mind undertake a real investigation—with the upper-class set unless I make some connections. I'll need to somehow become part of his social circle if I want to speak with anyone who might have knowledge of his relationship with

Elizabeth, hence the new dresses, the fancy inn, the new maid; I'll never get to talk to anyone if I look like a pauper. Now the only problem is going to be getting introduced.

I'm about halfway through my lunch, slowly chewing and thinking and watching, when a young man walks through the door of the restaurant. His confident gait catches my eye right away, taking my mind off of my problems for a moment. He is tall, thin, and rakishly good-looking with sun-streaked blonde hair and sparkling brown eyes. His top hat sits at a jaunty angle atop his head. I'm not a fan of facial hair, so in my opinion he'd look better without the thin, light mustache atop his upper lip, but even so, he's an attractive man. Not as attractive as James, but handsome nonetheless.

I pause to shake that stray thought from my head.

This young man glances slowly around the room until his eyes alight on me. He walks my way without taking his eyes off of me, smiling as if we're old friends.

"My dear lady, there cannot be any reason in the world that a girl with beauty such as yours should be dining alone!" His boisterous voice carries throughout the restaurant, but my neighbors politely pretend not to notice. His English is lightly accented, and not merely with the posh upper-crust New England accent that's so common around here. He probably grew up on some fancy estate not far from London or something. "My dear, may I have the exquisite honor of joining you?"

I laugh inwardly. It's almost too bad I can't answer his smarmy line with one of my own. But these days, something to the effect of "How do you even manage to breathe with all of that bull crap spilling out of your mouth?" probably wouldn't go over very well.

But if my expression seems amused instead of delighted at the honor of his presence, he doesn't notice. I look closely at the fine suit he's wearing. It's every bit as nice as the one the old man is wearing. Maybe even nicer, and perfectly tailored, to boot. By the look of him, Mr. Bull Crap here could be my ticket into the world I need to enter. I take the chance and let him join me.

"I would be delighted to have some company, sir. Please, sit down."

"Wine!" he calls out exuberantly to a waiter while removing his suit jacket. "We must have wine here!" He turns back to me; his teeth are ever so slightly crooked, but they are white and glossy and they gleam as he smiles. "Now, lovely lady, allow me to introduce myself. Damien Gracen." He bows with a flourish before removing his hat and taking a seat, though I barely notice. My blood began running cold the moment he spoke his name.

Oh, this man can get me into the proper circles, alright. He even has a close connection to Elizabeth. Way too close of a connection, in fact. After all, in almost exactly three years' time, she'll hang for his murder. I think back to the newspaper blurb. *"Elizabeth Wood…to be hanged for the brutal Murder of Mr. Damien Gracen."* The handsome man sitting across from me is a dead man walking. It's only a matter of time.

"Is everything quite alright, my dear?" He gives me a concerned look. This is the second time today I've worried a new companion with my strange behavior. I seem to be making a habit of it.

But his voice jolts me slightly out of my reverie. "What? Oh, yes. I'm terribly sorry… It's just that I've had a very busy day already and I'm actually quite exhausted. It's kind of just come upon me all at once." There is still food on my plate, but suddenly my appetite is completely gone.

"Say no more, my dear lady! We must get you home immediately! You'll need to be well-rested for this evening, when you allow me to take you out for dinner and dancing." He flashes me a roguish grin. "Where to?"

Despite myself, I laugh weakly at his audacity. I'm well aware that no matter what his fate, I still need his help. So I agree to the date, though it goes against my better judgment. After all, I have no guarantees that anyone else will help me. I need to take all the opportunities I can get. Things are already starting to get complicated.

"It's no trouble getting me home, Mr. Gracen. I'm staying right here at the inn."

"How convenient, then! Tell me: Are you a visitor or a new arrival to our quaint little town?"

"I suppose I'm a new arrival, but—"

"Say no more, my dear, this is perfect. We need all the lovely young ladies we can get around here, my darling. You go and get some rest now, and I'll pick you up at eight." He gives me a charming smile, and then looks toward our server. "Waiter? The check, please!"

Though it goes against all my notions of feminine equality, especially since he didn't even get to eat with me, I allow him to pay the bill and walk me to the stairs when he insists. I suppose it is nice to have someone look after me. Besides, it would look extremely odd if I didn't accept. High-society women don't pay when they dine with men, period. I turn to go but he stops me.

"Miss, wait! I don't even know your name, you splendid little creature!"

I can't help it—I giggle and blush as his choice of pet names finally tips the scales from silly to ridiculous. "Oh, right, of course. My name is Elizabeth. Elizabeth Franklyn."

"Enchanted." Like James, he kisses my hand in farewell. But unlike my earlier experience of longing, what I feel with Damien is mostly sadness and anger. Sadness for his destiny, for the future that I know he'll never get. My anger is at fate, at time, and especially at the person who is responsible for his untimely death.

I just hope it's not her.

I need to find Elizabeth Wood as soon as possible. I don't think I can stand to be here when Damien dies, now that I've met him. *How long will it be?* I can't remember the date off the top of my head. One year? Two maybe? *And what if she really is the killer? What have I gotten myself into?*

Chapter Six

"Oh!" I wake with a cry to the ringing of the alarm clock. I had thankfully managed to set it before I passed out to wake me at 3:45 in the afternoon, just before my new maid is due to arrive.

I'm disoriented. I don't remember much, but I definitely had a nightmare and the feeling of terror lingers. I shudder. I think Damien Gracen was in it. He was dead. Dead and bloody, and yet staring at me with wide, frightened eyes. I pat my clothes, feeling wetness. I look down, almost expecting to find myself covered in gore, but it's just more sweat. I take a deep breath and shake my head, clearing the dream. And then I laugh because Alex was right; I truly miss air conditioning.

Despite the heat, I make some tea. It soothes my mind as much as the laughter did. I also forget about my aversion to the fancy white chairs. My brain is a little too fried to care anymore. I'm already sitting in one before I think of it.

By the time the knock on the door comes, I feel much better. The tea has helped immensely. I've washed my face and fixed my hair, and I feel almost human again.

I answer the door to the bellman escorting a pretty girl who seems close to my age. She wears a shabby brown dress that falls just above her ankles, showing the tiniest peek of thin brown stockings and tattered, worn-down shoes under the dusty hem of a petticoat. She has gray-brown hair and eyes, high cheekbones that are dotted with brown freckles, a long nose, and small but full lips. Her face is smudged with dirt, but still she has an eager smile and a curtsy when she greets me.

"How do you do, Miss Franklyn?"

"I'm quite well, thank you, Lanie." I tip the bellman and bring the girl inside. "And how are you?"

She looks surprised, like she's never had someone ask her that before. I suppose it could be true; I've noticed in my own time that many of the wealthy employers don't bother to think of their servants as people. "I'm quite fine, Miss Franklyn. I'm very pleased to meet you," she adds brightly.

I smile back at her; her happy demeanor is contagious. "You as well," I tell her honestly. She looks around the room. "Please, sit down." I motion to a chair and, to her utter astonishment, I pour the girl a cup of tea. She takes one look at the immaculate white chair and flatly refuses to go anywhere near it in her dusty dress, but accepts the tea and leans against the wall instead.

So we drink tea and discuss her employment, including her on-duty hours, her responsibilities, and her pay. I wasn't really sure about having a live-in maid, but it turns out that Lanie doesn't really have anywhere else to go. Like me, her mother died many years ago. Unlike me, her father is an abusive drunk who threw her out of the house for the simple fact that she's not the son he'd always wanted. She tells me this only after much prodding on my part, and a vow of secrecy. Since I don't want to send her out to live on the street, I set her up here instead, in the rather plush servant's quarters off of the main suite.

Lanie is a very sweet and happy-go-lucky person, which I find amazing, considering her background. We get along so well that it's easy to forget that we are technically employer and employee. We spend almost two hours talking before she looks at the clock and jumps into action.

"Miss Elizabeth, didn't you say you were going out tonight? It's nearly six!"

Getting ready to go out during the Victorian era takes a lot of work. Lanie heats up the water for my bath and, while I soak, she fixes up my hair, which has become disheveled throughout the day. No hat this time, just elaborate bows. I get out and we do lotions, powders, and makeup—slightly more than I wore this morning—and then strap me into the dinner dress I purchased earlier.

Thankfully, with Lanie's help, I'm ready to go with a few minutes to spare. I look at my reflection in the mirror in awe, once again hardly believing that I can still be the same person I was this morning.

I'm decked out in a gorgeous silk gown of my favorite color, peacock blue. The gown has elbow-length sleeves with swooping white lace cuffs. The bodice has a much lower neckline than my earlier dresses, with a wide opening at the neck that is almost off the shoulder. It is boned and fits me like a glove—a really, really tight glove. More lace, plus beads and bows and flounces, accent the gathers that tuck in the skirt beneath the bustle. It sounds like a lot for one dress, and it is, but, somehow, it all works. However, I am sure that this is all the pretty one outfit can handle. The train on this dress is even longer than that of my traveling dress, though not nearly as long as the evening gown that's being made for me. It's beautiful, but I have to practice not tripping over it each time I turn around.

At precisely 8:00, a different bellman knocks on my door to let me know that Mr. Gracen is waiting in the lobby. I tell Lanie to order dinner for herself and not to wait up for me, and then I head downstairs to meet Damien.

As I round the last turn of the spiraling staircase, I gently remind myself to smile.

And actually, it's not so hard. Damien Gracen is a naturally upbeat person. He's charming and confident, and his demeanor puts me right at ease.

"I hope you don't mind, my dear Elizabeth, but I've been invited to a dinner party and I would love to take you along. After all, we never did get to dine together earlier, did we? After dinner, I promise to take you out to dance the night away. Will you come?"

A dinner party? *That should be perfect. Getting into society is turning out to be much easier than I'd thought.* "Of course, Mr. Gracen. Do remember that I am new in town; surely you must know that I'm in need of all the new acquaintances I can get."

"How could I forget, my divine friend? I'd certainly remember you if I'd seen you around here before! Such loveliness simply could *not* be forgotten!" I laugh at this new audacity as he raises his eyebrows cheekily. "Now, let us be off!"

Chapter Seven

Damien tells me all about our hosts as we ride in his personal carriage to the dinner party at the residence of Mr. and Mrs. Albert Hanson. I listen intently, and my ears perk up when he mentions their daughter, who is close to my age and might just know the gossip about William and Elizabeth.

Her name is Glory. Luckily, it seems that we'll be spending some time with her and her friends this evening, so I'll probably even get a chance to find out what they know. I hope I'm able to be friends with these ladies myself. It would certainly make life a lot easier.

What could make that difficult is that even though Damien doesn't mention it, I sort of get the feeling that he is dating this girl. Or even several of her friends as well. As charming as I've already known him to be, I don't doubt that he could do it. He definitely has a player vibe.

We get to the Hanson residence and I gasp. It's not that I haven't been around fancy houses before; I grew up in a town of wealthy businessmen with their colossal homes. My grandparents own the biggest mansion in town. But this particular house has been condemned in my time, just another old Victorian home that is ready to be demolished so that something new and grand can be put up in its place.

But here, in 1875, the house is brand-new and in its glory. Windows gleam, unbroken, and the paint on the round-shingled siding is no longer faded, cracked, and peeling. It looks freshly painted, a deep evergreen, and it picks up hints of color from the setting sun.

Even cloaked in the growing shadows, I can see that the grounds surrounding the house are well-maintained now, not like the overgrown scrub that has taken over in my day. It is classically landscaped and looks very beautiful. I imagine that the gardener must put in a lot of hours here.

The front walk is already lit with torches, and elegant guests walk from their carriages to the house. Men in black tie and women in beautiful dinner gowns with frilly trains like mine go up the stairs onto the inviting wraparound porch. Some of the men mingle and smoke pipes or cigars outside while the majority of people make their way into the house.

We follow the other guests indoors and find that the inside is every bit as lovely as the outside. The grand staircase is our first sight as we walk in. The banisters are ornately shaped and stand taller than me. The staircase is carpeted in a beautiful Oriental design, full of greens and blues. It is one of those stairwells that opens up as it descends, the bottom stairs wider and rounded out towards us, almost welcoming guests up those waiting steps and into the most private rooms of the house. The rooms, of course, that no dinner guest may enter.

We move through the entranceway to a sitting room.

Hand-carved pieces of furniture adorned with luxurious and colorful velvet cushions stand on clawed feet around the perimeter of the room. A grandfather clock, its dark wooden base carved with intricate swirling designs, rests by a marble mantelpiece, loudly ticking away with a long golden pendulum. Rich tapestries, gilded sconces, and lavish frames filled with fine paintings hang on walls. Thick, soft rugs cover most of the hardwood floors, while gold-and-crystal chandeliers give off warm, flickering light from the ceilings.

And, oh, what ceilings! I glance up to take in the sparkling light only to find that the ceilings have been painted with floral murals, geometrically laid out from a wreath of peach-and-cream-colored daylilies around each chandelier.

The glittering light from above joins the lingering daylight coming through the windows and bounces off of the mingling guests to bring out the colors of the ladies' gowns. These ladies, decked out in all different hues and covered as they are in ruffles and flounces, remind me of more flowers, blooming in the fading glow of sunset.

This stylish group gathers in a large room off of the dining area that literally serves no other purpose than to entertain guests before dinner. Servants move stealthily about the edges of the room to allow the guests plenty of space to enjoy themselves, while still being close by in case something is required.

Maybe two dozen of the richest and most influential people in town, young and old, mix and mingle with their peers, friends, and acquaintances. Damien is already proving to be much more helpful than he knows.

He leads me easily through the crowd to the three people

who seem to be hosting this gathering. As we approach, an older man speaks first, in a gruff but jovial tone. "Gracen, good to see you, my boy! So glad you could come to our little party! You remember my wife, I'm sure, and of course, my little Glory." He gestures to his two female companions.

"The pleasure is mine, Mr. Hanson." He glances at the wife. "Ah, Mrs. Hanson, you look enchanting as usual." The older woman blushes as Damien takes her hand and bestows a small kiss upon it. "As do you, Miss Hanson," he says, raising one eyebrow. He kisses her hand, as well, but receives only a cold stare in return.

"And who is this delightful young lady?" Mr. Hanson continues, ignoring his daughter's icy glare.

"Ahh," Damien says. "This lovely creature is my newest acquaintance, Miss Elizabeth Franklyn. She is new to our fair town, so please, my dear friends, help me show her all the delights we have to offer here." He smiles good-naturedly and, much like her father, ignores Glory's wrathful look.

"I do hope we can show her a good time!" Mr. Hanson booms. "My dear Miss Franklyn, I am very pleased to meet you. This beautiful lady is my wife, Mrs. Dorothy Hanson, and our lovely daughter, Miss Glory Hanson." He motions at each woman respectively.

"It is a pleasure, ladies," I answer with all the politeness I can muster. "Please, sir, I have been quite delighted already just by entering your beautiful home." I smile demurely while he glows at the compliment. His wife, too, seems pleased, but Glory is wholly indifferent to the praise of her house, still staring daggers at my companion. I'm not sure yet whom I should feel bad for in this situation, Glory or Damien.

Glory's expression may be one of doom, but she is still possibly the most striking girl I've ever met. And while it may simply be the pure, raw hatred on her face, she seems to me like the kind of person that just has to be horrible. She just has to be, if only because if she's actually a lovely person on top of being so beautiful, I might just die from the injustice of it all. No, it's not fair, and yes, one should never judge a book by its cover, thank you very much. Nor is it that I don't think I'm attractive; I do. It's just that next to Glory Hanson, I feel a bit like a poorly dressed pre-teen boy standing beside a *Victoria's Secret* model.

Glory is, in a word, glorious. She has a mane of fiery red hair, currently bound in an elaborate updo. Tiny tendrils frame her face, which is pale like porcelain and stands in stark contrast to her deep crimson lips. My own face is rounded, but Glory has a perfect heart-shaped jawline and cheekbones that I couldn't hope to replicate even with a dozen YouTube contour tutorials. Her emerald eyes are lovely; though they are definitely no match for James's, even with the subtle eye makeup she wears to complement them. Her lashes, however, which seem to stretch beyond any normal reach, make up for that. Somehow they're longer even than his. She is also a good six inches taller than me and her luscious figure leaves me feeling inadequate in comparison.

However, her beauty is inconsequential at the moment when compared to the emotions running across her face. Her stares are no longer merely cold. Her expressions run from longing to loathing, and everything in between.

And then she shifts her gaze to me.

Those dark green eyes look upon me with the vengeful fire of all the demons in hell. I imagine that if looks could kill, poor Damien and I would both be dead many times over. I can almost see the ruffles of her emerald gown quivering with her righteous fury.

It's clear to me that I've arrived on the arm of a man she's tried to claim as her own territory. This is definitely *not* the good first impression I was hoping for.

Fortunately for Damien and me, Glory has been raised as a lady and would never embarrass her parents by being openly rude to a guest in their home, even guests as repugnant to her as we are now.

"Mr. Gracen, so wonderful to see you," she says politely, though for all her courtesy, her voice is cold enough to induce frostbite. "Please, allow me to steal away your guest. Being new in town, I'm sure she'd love to be introduced to my friends." She smiles coldly at me as I freeze. "She needs to meet some young ladies; what would people think if she were to spend all her time with you, and with no one to look out for her? I'm sure she will fit right in."

Her icy tone clearly suggests that I will *not* fit right in. I feel very much like a gazelle would, if being led to meet a pride of lions in their den.

Her parents, of course, think that this is a fabulous idea and happily wave me off to the lion's den without a thought. And dear Damien is only too happy to let me go with her as long as he needn't follow.

As I'm pulled away from his side, I manage to whisper just

one small sentence in his ear.

"I will get you for this." I add my own daggers to the ones Glory is still staring after him.

He just laughs. *Bastard.*

◊

For the most part, Glory and her friends are just as frightening as I had feared. While this fact does alleviate some of my guilt for wanting to hate her on sight, merely because of her good looks, it doesn't make the next half hour before dinner any more tolerable.

By far, the nicest girl of the group is Angelica Prince. Angelica is older than her friends—who all seem to be close to my age—and practically an old maid in this time period, still unmarried at a shocking twenty-five years old.

Honestly though, I'm not sure why. She seems to be a sweet girl who has a good opinion about nearly everyone. I suppose that some people might consider her a bit plump in a time when the long and lithe look has just come into fashion, but I can't see how that would keep her single. She seems nice, she seems smart enough, and she's very pretty, with sweet blonde curls and big brown eyes.

Except... I wonder: Is her dress just a bit plainer than the others around her? Are her shoes slightly worn down at the heels? That might explain it then; perhaps she's not as rich as they are. It makes me wonder why she's a part of this group in the first place. After all, they hardly seem the charitable type.

As the evening goes on, I watch the group dynamic and it

occurs to me that Angelica is desperate to fit in. She laughs when they laugh and sneers when they sneer, not so much because she agrees but because it makes her one of them. No wonder they let her in their group; I bet she'll do almost anything they ask of her. They would want someone to walk all over, wouldn't they?

The group goes downhill from there. Emily Grenier is apparently seventeen, and much more annoying than I remember being a year ago. She is tiny in every way—and I know tiny, considering my own stature. She stands a good three inches shorter than me, but that's just the start. Her pale pink bodice cannot accentuate what she doesn't have, so her boyish figure shows through with the exception of the bulging bustle behind her. Even her face looks pinched with her small features: thin lips, a tiny beak-like nose, and closely set eyes the color of a mud puddle. Her mousy brown hair is lanky and flat.

Her appearance, however, is not a factor in my judgment of her. I could easily like her if she wasn't, well, herself, for her character is so much less attractive than her person. I only spend a limited amount of time with her, but, from what I can tell, she loves nothing more than talking badly about people behind their backs. Or to their faces. So I guess she just enjoys putting people down in general, really. Her only other occupation seems to be fawning and simpering over every word that is spoken by Glory...or even worse, Libby.

Miss Libby Hunt is undisputedly the alpha dog of this little clique. She's not as drop-dead gorgeous as Glory, with her weak chin and a long, pointy nose, but her blonde hair is glossy and her china-blue eyes are clear and deep. She is only slightly taller than me, and her petite figure fills out an expensive lavender dress in all the right places, though it is diminished next to Glory's impressive curves. Everything about Libby's dress and demeanor just oozes money, while everything about her expression just oozes disdain.

It's easy to see from the beginning that even Glory can't beat Libby in that area. She is a master. In about a quarter of an hour I watch her send no less than three girls away crying. All the while, not a single cross word leaves her lips. No, her talons are hidden behind sugary sweet words and smug but very real smiles. Only when the other young ladies turn their backs do Libby's claws come out.

"Aurelia, have you lost weight? Only fifty more pounds to go, and you'll look divine!" she says to a lovely girl with no more "extra weight" than Libby's own friend Angelica. She smiles in her saccharine way as if her compliment was merely that. Aurelia's face crumbles as she turns away, and Libby sneers behind the girl's retreating back. "God, what a cow." Her voice changes instantly from syrupy sweet to haughty bitch, not caring for second if Aurelia hears her.

Not one to be left out of spiteful comments, Emily chimes in, "My God, what did she eat for breakfast, a whole leg of lamb?"

The four of them laugh, though Angelica's is stunted and she looks strained. She murmurs, "I think she looks quite nice actually…"

Libby gives her a flinty look. "You would."

Angelica quickly shuts her mouth and looks at the ground. It might be sick, but I can almost see her reasoning for what she does. She is used and abused by these girls. But still she must feel that she's in a better position than one of the girls who just went away crying. *At least she's part of the winning team?*

That may be fine for her, but I'd rather be prey than join these harpies in their sport. However, unlike the other girls, I have every intention of fighting back. They won't send me away crying.

For the most part, they ignore my presence in their circle in favor of vicious gossip, tearing the other girls apart behind their backs when they're unable to do so to their faces. I decide to try and sneak away once I'm sure I can't listen to one more cruel barb.

With eerie timing, they change the subject right as I'm about to make my move. The conversation turns to the men about town and I'm pulled back in like a black hole dragging an innocent planet away from the safety of its orbit and into the lightless void.

"Of course, Damien is to die for, but you know that, don't you, Elizabeth?"

I give Libby a tight smile. "Indeed. He is quite fun to be around, and such a charmer." I don't mention that I'd much rather spend my time with a certain farmer than that swaggering smooth-talker, any day.

"Oh, yes," adds Glory. "But he's quite a cad, you know. Nothing pleases him more than trying to make one girl jealous by walking in with another." She sounds confident now, like she would never fall for such a thing—as though it wasn't she who was green with envy when Damien walked in with me.

I raise my eyebrows. "Trust me, ladies, I'm not interested. He's been very sweet, and nice enough to bring me here to introduce me to all of you…" I pause so I can finish with a straight face. "Wonderful people. And as I said, he certainly knows how to have a good time." I smile sweetly.

"Well, even if you did like him, you would have quite a bit of competition!" Emily looks knowingly from Glory to Libby while Angelica giggles. *Both of them?* How unsurprising.

A look from Libby silences them both. "Forget Damien. Glory can have him. I'm still waiting for dear William to come back to us," she says.

My ears perk up. Maybe this torture session will be worthwhile after all.

"I can't stand that he's gone and left us for so long." She frowns prettily, pouts, and then goes on. "We all used to have such fun. Do you remember that time he and Damien took us all to the city? God, what a lark! The two of them drank so much wine that they waltzed together in the street while singing us a duet—"

"An awful duet," Glory interjects. "Those two imbeciles are completely tone-deaf," she says, smiling fondly.

"Ha, yes! It was terrible! Though the subject matter wasn't bad…a song of our never-ending beauty, as I recall. The stupid fools danced and sang in the middle of Fifth Avenue, at three in the morning, no less!" The girls are giggling like mad. Even I manage to crack a smile at the thought of Damien and my great-great-great-great-grandfather (who, in my mind, looks like the old photos of my mom's father) singing in the middle of the night, drunkenly entertaining these girls. I can see the two of them in my head, drunken idiots hand in hand, waltzing up and down the city streets. I can almost hear their terrible singing, discordant and out of time. Some upbeat song, I imagine, extolling the virtues of beauty and youth in a woman.

Then Libby opens her mouth again and my daydream disappears, popping away like a soap bubble in the hands of a child.

"And all that money he's got!" she continues greedily. "How sad that he should leave us to travel the country, even if it is to bring home more! How many ladies do you think he's meeting in Manhattan, Boston, Chicago, and wherever else he's gone off to? I would never forgive him if he were to go and marry one of those girls instead of me!" She sighs dramatically before turning to me rather smugly.

"You know, our parents agreed some time ago that we'd be a perfect match. We belong together. He was practically begging me to marry him before he left. If he hadn't had to go away, I just know he would have proposed by last Christmas." She turns back to the others and whines, "So when is he going to come back and marry me?"

Well now. William Wood and Libby Hunt are an item? And, if Libby is to be believed, they're practically engaged.

But she can't be my ancestor, can she? My great-great-great-great-grandmother's name is Elizabeth. But wait… Libby Hunt. Libby. Of course! How could I have forgotten? Libby is one of many ways to shorten my name. *Her name.* My nana used to call me Libby when I was a little girl and I'd hated it.

How did I forget that?

No. That's not right. It can't be. I must be mistaken, that's all there is to it. Libby cannot be the one I'm looking for. If it were her, wouldn't she have been in the historical records that I combed through so carefully? There would be no reason to hide anything if Libby and William were to get married. There would be a paper trail. It's not as if she's some random woman off the streets. She's from a wealthy family. Any wedding of that size would have been in the society papers, if nowhere else. All the highborn ladies would have had to know about her huge ring, what her dress looked like, and how many bridesmaids she would have.

I'm right, aren't I? Or am I just rationalizing to try and convince myself against the obvious?

No, it can't be. I refocus my eyes and glance her way.

"Deborah!" The sugary voice is back. "You look so pretty this evening! One can barely even notice the acne! Tell me what trick you've used to cover up your nasty little problem!"

Oh, man, I hope not....

Chapter Eight

The rest of the night gives me even more insight into this world and the people I'm looking for.

Dinner is soon served, a full seven-course affair that surprises me by offering wine even to the youngest of guests. I've never tried it before, so I sip sparingly of the deep-red beverage and then stick to water after that. Honestly, I don't care how much they paid for it, the stuff tastes vile.

I reunite with Damien and sit beside him at dinner. We sit in chairs even fancier than the ones in my suite and eat off of gold-rimmed white china dishes with real sterling silver utensils. And the food, well, the food is delicious.

There is bread, warm and steaming, with fresh creamy butter and golden honey. Light, frothy soup bursts with flavor. The fish is white and flaky, and so fresh that it was probably caught earlier today. Lamb chops, tender and savory, are smothered with the most delectable gravy I've ever tasted.

Damien goes in and out of conversations with his neighbors, but mostly he talks to me. Earlier, I gave him a huge dressing down about his abandoning me, but he has this way about him and I can't seem to stay mad.

When I'm curious about my tablemates, I ask and he tells me their names and anything else of interest that he can think of. We make a game of it. I randomly motion to strangers, challenging him to come up with something, anything, to tell me about them. He rises to the challenge every time, never skipping a beat, though I refuse to count the older British couple that he knows everything about. Of course he knows his own parents.

Over dessert, I listen intently to Damien's description of Libby's parents, just in case the worst is confirmed and they are related to me. Judge and Mrs. Hunt live in a huge mansion on top of a hill on the outskirts of town. Libby is not their only child, but she is their youngest and the only one still living with them. They also have two sons, Alfred and Jeremiah, both in their thirties and married, living with their wives and young children in the city. The judge is a very prominent man in Thorne Hill and holds a lot of sway over everything that goes on in this town.

As the evening wanes, I say a silent prayer of thanks to the powers that be for sending Damien to find me today. I couldn't have asked for a better guide to lead me into society. He is so popular; he knows everyone worth knowing—and more.

With his help, I'm sure I'll soon find the thread that will lead me to Elizabeth Wood. I add a quick amendment to my prayer of thanks—a request that the thread leads me far away from the Hunts.

The one thing bringing me down is that I hate knowing that my friend will soon be gone. I feel helpless because there's not a thing I can do about it but try to learn the truth about what happened.

And strangely, Damien *is* my friend. I listen to his softly accented voice, so smooth and full of life, and I realize something: Regardless of it all—his obviously eventful dating life, his outrageous charms, or even the horrible knowledge that his future will end abruptly—there is no way that I can do anything but like this man.

Back in the present, I find Damien waiting for my words to start the next round. My move is obvious, but still he holds off. Using the spoonful of decadent strawberry shortcake still in my hand, I motion toward the only people left. "Only one more couple to go, my dear sir. What about them?"

These last two make a very handsome pair. The gentleman looks older than his wife, though both are probably in their forties. He has brownish-gold hair streaked with gray at his temples and tired-looking green eyes. He is fairly fit, but, like many wealthy older gentlemen of this era, he sports a small gut that rests just behind the buttons on his waistcoat. His wife is tall and slender and very elegant. Her eyes are clear and gray, and her hair very dark, almost black, a beautiful contrast to her alabaster skin. Both faces bear tiny wrinkles, crow's feet, and laugh lines, and yet both have stood up well to the test of time.

"Ah, yes, the Woods."

I nearly choke on a strawberry. The Woods are here? How have I gone this whole evening without knowing that? Damien has got my undivided attention. I want to know as much as possible about William's parents. My ancestors.

"Two daughters: the eldest, Mrs. Lucy Payne, is married and at home awaiting her first child. It won't be long now. The youngest, Miss Maribelle, is only just too young to be joining us this very evening. She's a lovely girl. *Very* lovely. I really can't wait for her to come out into society." He winks and I roll my eyes while silently urging him on. "I quite regret, however, that her elder brother, William, surely won't let me anywhere near her. He knows me far too well, I fear, being my best friend and all.

"But lucky me—I don't have to worry about Wood until the bugger makes his way home. He's been traveling around the country taking care of his father's business or some such nonsense for far too long now. Not to mention…" he looks thoughtfully at the ladies around the table, "I doubt that he'll have much time to stop me when he comes home. Each and every one of these girls is waiting to trap him the moment he arrives."

He sighs theatrically. "I always have to remember that they'd all drop me in an instant to have a chance with Will—or his inheritance, at least." He feigns a look of heroic stoicism. "He's a fantastic fellow but let's be frank: He's filthy rich. His is the only inheritance in town that is larger than my own. That is why, despite my superior looks and many charms, I will always come in second."

He winks at me again and smiles brightly, no trace of bitterness or jealousy on his face. He completely understands that around here, the most important love is the love of money.

Even if I'm disappointed by his lack of faith in humanity, I'm encouraged by Damien's knowledge of the town—and especially of William. I have stumbled upon much more than I could have ever hoped for. In coming here, I thought it would take weeks to even make my first acquaintance in high society, never mind the chance to get to know close friends of my grandfather. Yet somehow on my first day, I meet his best friend, who is also (or will be) closely connected with Elizabeth.

Of course, I still have questions. So many questions. *Does Elizabeth come from town, or will my grandfather come riding home with her in tow? If she's from here, have I already met her?* As much as I don't want Libby Hunt to be my mysterious relative, my research will become a lot more complex if he brings the future Mrs. Elizabeth Wood home from his far-off travels.

Then again, a scenario like that might explain why I couldn't locate her in the municipal records. I can picture it now: He meets Elizabeth. Perhaps she's the daughter of one of his business contacts—no! A simple barmaid he meets while trying to unwind after a long day. They fall in love, but she's poor; she'll never be accepted by his family if he brings her home unwed. So they elope, furtively exchanging their vows in the dark of night. The family is appalled when he arrives home, hand in hand with this slattern he calls his wife—complete with a child in her arms. They refuse to acknowledge the marriage and hide the union from the world until something happens...the murder. She stands accused, then convicted—but even then the media is left out in the cold, printing only a tiny snippet and shielding her lowly background from an unforgiving society. *Hmm...It has potential.*

I look at poor Damien. As much as I hate to think of it, when the murder occurs, all of the pieces will start coming together. But that's a long time from now. Surely I'll have things figured out long before then. I don't want to be here when it happens.

In fact, I would give almost anything not to be here when Damien dies. But how else will I find out if it truly was my ancestor who committed the crime? I can't clear her name without knowing more. My head, so full of hope a minute ago, now burns with dread.

But Damien has no idea that my thoughts have darkened, a meadow suddenly blocked from the sun by a massive thundercloud. No, the sun is still shining over his mind.

"Now, my dear, the night is young and it's time to dance!" I look down at my plate, surprised to find it has been cleared away. *When did I finish eating? Did I finish eating?*

"Let us say our goodbyes and follow the young and beautiful crowd to a magnificent ballroom where we will dance the night away!" I just nod, decisively draining the wineglass that still sits in front of me, hoping the alcohol will deaden these dark thoughts. I grimace at the flavor.

He grins widely; he's been downing drinks all night. "That's the spirit!"

We head to yet another mansion, smaller this time, but in a beautiful neighborhood made up of only such grand homes. The streets are lined with elegant torch-lit streetlamps and I count three parks as we drive by, all empty, save for a lone man in one park walking towards a bench. It's dark over there, out of reach of the lamplight, and I can't make out his clothing. I wonder if he is just out for a walk on a beautiful night or if this bench is his only place to come home to.

The mansion belongs to a young newlywed couple. They're holding a ball to christen their new home. Most of the younger ladies and gentlemen from the dinner party joined the migration to the ball when we did, and they arrive within minutes of us. Then there are the people who were already here, creating a group of about three dozen of the most affluent young people in town.

It's almost funny how excessively rich this gala is. Only a few weeks ago, I attended my senior prom with four hundred of my classmates. We pranced around in expensive gowns and tuxes, with fancy hairdos and sparkling costume jewelry, yet this is so different, it's laughable.

Obviously, I notice the music—here, there are no Ed Sheeran or Taylor Swift songs blasting way too loudly through giant speakers. Instead, music is provided by a string quartet in the corner of the old-fashioned ballroom. This is music suited to a much different style of dancing than what I saw at prom. There is no inappropriate grinding going on here, or groups of girls dancing barefoot in a circle with their uncomfortable high-heeled shoes left sloppily under a table somewhere. Here, ladies and gentlemen dance gracefully in pairs, barely touching one another, and all shoes remain firmly ensconced on their feet.

But truly the biggest difference is the pure extravagance. I had thought then that we were a bunch of spoiled rich kids, but prom cannot hold a candle to this. Interestingly, I had always pictured the past as I had seen it in black-and-white pictures: dull, faded, and lifeless. But it's so much more vibrant than I had imagined.

This room has color everywhere. The walls are covered in deep-brown wood paneling on the bottom, while the top is painted a delicate pale yellow, the exact color of a daffodil right before it blooms. On those walls are original artworks in some of the most elaborate frames I've ever seen. Portraits of the owners, landscapes, and still lifes are all brought to life in a rainbow of hues. The ceiling is painted like the one in the Hanson family's mansion, though not with flowers this time, but clouds and cherubs in full color that almost seem to float above us. Once more, the furniture around me is exquisitely hand-carved and upholstered in vibrant silks and velvets.

The extravagance does not just extend to the room itself, but also its inhabitants. Each lightly bustled gown is more elegant than the next. Even the designer prom dresses of the wealthiest girls in school can't compare to these works of art, each hand-made with yards of the richest and most decadent silks and brocades. And not even those designer girls were sent to prom wearing their parents' prized heirloom diamonds, but here, the young ladies drip with jewels meant to draw male attention to their most endearing features: their money.

The young men move about in tailcoats and black-tie accoutrements, behaving like true gentlemen in ways they probably don't when alone. They bow to their partners and dance with complete confidence in a way that I've never seen in real life. Most of the boys at school thought that dancing meant bobbing awkwardly to the beat of whatever cheesy pop song was playing. Maybe a few jerky hand movements if I were to get really lucky. If I was unlucky, it meant feeling them attempt to grind their crotch against my backside. There was definitely no bowing involved.

No, the closest modern comparison I can come up with is a party I once attended at my grandparents' mansion—descendants of the handsome couple I saw earlier this evening. It may even have been in the same house that couple currently lives in.

It was supposed to be my sixteenth birthday party, but I barely knew anyone but the two of them. My mother's parents always wanted me to experience their definition of real life, which, to them, meant being forced to pander to a bunch of people you don't like or that you've never met before. The party was in their huge entertaining hall, and the guests were all the *best* people they knew. In reality, those people were the *richest* people they knew, but the words were interchangeable to them. They still are, in fact. Or, rather, will be when I get back. Whatever.

As I stand here in this mansion and see all the glitz and glamour around me, I'm reminded of that night. Except for one thing: Even though it was my birthday party and I was the guest of honor, no one paid much attention to me. The Woods' youngest granddaughter was not what had drawn all of my grandparents' friends and acquaintances to their home. I spent the evening sitting alone on an antique sofa, bored out of my mind as I watched them mingle.

But I am not alone now.

I walk around on Damien's arm for a while, and he introduces me to friends with whom he stops to chat. They try to include me, and I do my best to be charming, smiling modestly at their compliments and laughing at their jokes. Most seem nice enough. But Damien doesn't talk long; he's not here for the conversation. Soon enough, he pulls me out onto the dance floor.

I took dance lessons—lots of them—in preparation for my trip to the 1870s. However, more than a century's time can change the way a dance is performed, so my style and timing are a bit off. Luckily for me, Damien is a great dancer and, by following his lead, I'm soon comfortable on the dance floor. We dance until we're breathing heavily, and then stop to take a break lest one of us—*gasp!*—should start perspiring.

"So, what do you think, Elizabeth?" Damien asks as he hands me a glass of wine, which I quietly exchange for one of water. "How are you enjoying Thorne Hill society? Are you completely bored of this town yet?"

I laugh shortly. "Not quite. Look," I gesture around me. "There are still people I haven't even met yet."

He's about to respond when a young man comes up to me and bows. "My dear lady, I couldn't help but overhearing. Let me help you remedy that." He offers his hand. "My name is Amos Fishbourne."

"Elizabeth Franklyn." I smile politely while his lips lightly brush my hand.

"I'm delighted to meet you, Miss Franklyn. Would you do me the honor of dancing with me?"

I look first at Amos, who has prematurely graying hair that curls cutely around his ears and eyes of mossy brown, and then look to Damien for direction. I have no objection, myself, but I am technically his date. He shrugs and sweeps his hand, motioning for me to proceed.

"Have fun, and I'll see you later, my lovely Elizabeth," he says with a smile.

So off I go with Amos. He's not as good a dancer as Damien. However, after watching the other couples around me, I don't think that anyone here is.

Something must have clicked in the room when Amos asked

me to dance because suddenly gentlemen seem to be crawling out of the woodwork requesting the same. My dance card is soon full. Throughout the night, I meet more than a dozen young men, each eager for a turn or two about the room with the new blood. I dance with them all, and Damien again as well, beaming all the while and having the time of my life.

After dancing with the other men, it turns out that my conjecture was right. Damien is the best dancer here, no contest. He moves without faltering, gracefully and confidently. He can lead even the most inexperienced girl and have her moving like a princess. He is the one man every girl wants to dance with. And, being the way he is, he asks them all, including Glory, Libby, Emily, and Angelica.

They each take their turn, even Glory, but these four have other entertainments for the evening as well. Not ones to waste time, when they're not dancing, they quickly revert to gossip and mockery.

Oh, yes, it looks like we'll be great friends alright. I roll my eyes at them.

At one point, I pass behind them unnoticed, moving towards the refreshments, and I hear Libby mention someone who can only be me.

"...new girl is utterly ridiculous! Can you even believe how awfully she dances? I swear she looks like a monkey on a street corner doing a jig!" They laugh.

Really? I don't think I looked that *bad.*

"Where did Damien pick her up from anyway?" adds Glory. "Out of the trash? Did you see her hair? I've never seen straw so dull and lanky."

I sneak a peek at one of my dark, silky tendrils. I know for a fact that my hair looks gorgeous; there's no way they can be talking about me now. My voluminous waves are anything but dull and lanky. Libby picks up again, "And honestly, where are her parents? They just let her travel unchaperoned wherever she wants?"

"I know!" chimes in Emily. "I cannot believe she came all the way here alone from…er…wait. Where *is* she from, anyway?" Her pinched brow wrinkles as she glances between the faces of her friends.

"Who knows?" Libby sniffs with disdain. "But do you know what I think? *I'll* bet she was poor before she came here. Daddy probably made a little money and now she wants to play rich. She's trying to make a new name for herself in a town where people don't know about *that* little tidbit." She gives an exaggerated sigh. "Ugh, I'm so thirsty! Angelica, be a dear and fetch someone to bring me some wine."

"Of course, Libby! I'll be right back."

So they are *talking about me.* Or, rather, they're talking about the girl they wish I was, so that I won't seem to be competition. Rolling my eyes yet again, I move in. I shouldn't, but I can't help it. I have to play around with them just a little bit.

I catch Angelica before she gets too far. "Oh, Angelica, could you have them bring some water for me as well? Thank you so much!"

She beams at me and walks away while the other three eye me warily. I play dumb.

"Good evening, ladies! I've been so busy dancing, I haven't even had time to say hello. How are you?" I throw in all the sweetness and sincerity that I can muster. I can play this game, too.

Libby answers first. "We are doing just grandly, aren't we, ladies?"

Oh, she's good. A moment ago her tone was full of venom; now it's sugary and light.

They nod, stiff like bobble-head dolls. Glory, eyes narrowed, attempts to speak politely, but she doesn't have the talent Libby has. "How is your evening, Elizabeth?" she asks through clenched teeth. I guess she's still slightly bitter that Damien brought me instead of her.

Again, I shouldn't rub it in...but I do.

"It's wonderful! I'm having such an amazing time meeting so many new people! And I've been dancing all night; I've hardly had a chance to sit down. Every time I try to take a break, Damien grabs me for another dance!" I laugh. "He's so entertaining, too. Every time we move past someone, he spills all their dirty little secrets!" Libby and Emily feign laughter, and Glory attempts to join in.

"Well, I hope he didn't say anything about us..." Glory begins primly.

I laugh gaily. "Of course not! Well, nothing too bad anyway." I pause. "I think."

Coming to her friend's rescue, Libby speaks up sweetly. "I'm so glad you're having fun, Elizabeth. What a pleasure it must be to be the new girl in town!" She puts on a look of concern. "Though I'm sure your feet will be very sore tomorrow. But, don't you worry, these gentlemen will surely leave you alone from now on. They are always *so* interested in new ladies, but they lose interest quickly once a lady is no longer..." Here, she pauses for effect. "Fresh. It will be much easier on your poor feet very soon, I'm sure."

How does she do it? She sounds so innocent and sincere, yet, from behind that veneer, her insults lash out like switchblades.

Happily for me, Damien catches my eye from across the room and motions for me to join him. I ignore her barb and flash back a charming grin. "Thanks for the tip. But if you'll please excuse me, ladies, Damien wants my company."

I walk away confidently and I feel as though I have just won a major victory. I even make it halfway to my date before I berate myself for what I just did. I really should have resisted the urge to start anything, but it just gets on my nerves that they think they're so superior. If they knew the truth, they'd probably be sucking up to me. While I may or may not be descended from Libby, my bloodline through the Woods is clearer than even hers. In the end, that's all that seems to matter to them.

Well, that, and the fact my family has more money than these girls could even dream about. Even allowing for inflation, my grandparents make the Hunts look like paupers. Six generations of smart investing will do that. They have no idea who they're dealing with.

But my biggest problem with the whole thing is why any of that should even matter to them. It really is entirely beyond me. Of course I'm aware of class distinctions and bloodlines; I wasn't raised under a rock. It's just not possible in the community I grew up in. But I did grow up fairly sheltered from the luxuries and responsibilities of that life.

My parents didn't want to raise us that way, so they bought a beautiful but modest home instead of a massive mansion filled with things we didn't even use. No, we went to my grandparents' house for that; my parents were never interested in that kind of life.

Because of their influence, I grew up with friends from both sides of the tracks. I liked and respected each of them for who they were, not for how much money their parents brought home or who they were connected to. So when I see this kind of discrimination, it disgusts me.

I put them out of my mind when Damien grabs my hands and leads me back to the dance floor. He's been drinking a lot since we got here, and he is even more exuberant than ever, though still fully a gentleman. There is plenty of daylight between our bodies.

Hours later, Damien and almost everyone else are completely drunk, and people are finally starting to trickle out the door, though perhaps stumble is a better word. I stopped drinking after that one glass at dinner, so any buzz I felt is long gone.

We ride in Damien's carriage back to the inn, with him occasionally slouching into my shoulder with a snore, even as he tries to keep up his end of our conversation. He's so drunk, I begin to worry that he might get overly affectionate with me, the way I saw him get with a few of the other girls at the ball. But he only kisses my hand in farewell as he leaves me in the care of the concierge.

"Goo'night, divine Elish-beth! Shleep well, my dear!!" he calls as he staggers back to the carriage.

I'm so exhausted, I can barely laugh, but he is absolutely

ridiculous like this. I correct him gently, "Good morning, Damien; it's nearly three AM. Get home safely."

I head upstairs and change into nightclothes with some difficulty. Lanie is fast asleep, slumped in a corner on the floor waiting for me. I wake her gently and send her off to bed before she can protest.

I tiredly climb into bed and blow out the bedside candle, the gas-lamps long extinguished. The soft mattress is like heaven against my weary body. I lay my head onto the fluffy down pillow only to find something loud and crinkly occupying that space.

I groan. *What now?* I want to leave it until morning, but something makes me reach for the matches instead. Somehow I manage to clumsily relight the candle and the dim, flickering light reveals an envelope reading simply, "Miss Elizabeth Franklyn," in loopy, swirling script.

I tear into the envelope, curiosity beating out exhaustion. Too tired to bother with trifles, I skip straight to the last line to find out who sent it.

"Yours, James Percival."

Wait, what? James Percival?

Suddenly I feel wide awake, adrenaline coursing through my veins in an instant. I quickly run my eyes back to the top.

Dear Miss Elizabeth Franklyn,
I apologize dearly for being presumptuous, but I truly enjoyed our time together this morning and it seemed to me that you may have as well. It would give me great pleasure if you would be willing to repeat the experience. I

shall be waiting at the edge of the forest path near the inn at 7:00 am if you would like to meet me for breakfast. I know that this is most unconventional, as early morning is an unusual time for calling hours, but my days are quite filled to the brim. I shall wait for you until 8:00. I would be much obliged if you would send a message along should you be unwilling or unable to come, though I must say that I very much hope to see you tomorrow.

Yours,

James Percival

My eyes are round as saucers as shock takes over, and it quickly turns into elation. All thoughts of sleep are banished and I begin dancing wildly around the room. "He wants to see me!!" I squeal. I repeat it again and again, turning it into a chant, "He wants to seeee me; he wants to seeee me!" Laughing with glee, I run over to the writing ledger in the other room.

I hear a noise from Lanie's room and guiltily shut my mouth, although I'm unable to stop grinning like a fool. I glance quickly at her door, hoping I didn't wake her and that she didn't see me.

The door is closed and the suite is still and silent once again. If Lanie heard, she's not investigating.

The thought of a witness to my giddy display sobers me quite a bit. Enough, at least, to let a strong dose of reality seep into my sleepy brain.

And the reality is that I must be crazy. I want to go spend time with James. Very much. I want to be with him so much that even the thought of not going to him creates a physical ache in my chest.

But *that* is exactly the reason why I shouldn't go. I don't need anything holding me here when it's time to go back. And I have to go back.

True, romantic interaction was never expressly forbidden. I couldn't, for example, somehow prevent James from meeting his future wife, so that his ancestors cease to exist. My father explained to me that time is not as linear as we think it to be. It is, actually, more of a loop. And that means that anything I do now can't change the future: Anything that happens here, in the past, has already happened in my own time. The consequences for the future, if any, have already been set through the actions I *will* take here in the past.

Which makes this decision all the more difficult. *Technically*, there's no way I could harm anything by going to see James. If I might somehow change fate by seeing him again, then I simply won't be able to do so. And yet...I can't afford to get attached. Everyone is waiting for me back home. Alex. Dad. My friends, and all the others, who think I'm away on a tech-free tour of Europe for a year. And then I think of James, and of saying goodbye to him in a year, after spending time with him throughout that span. And I can't bear the thought.

I sit at the desk and start to compose my own note. I will stay strong and stay away. It's for the best.

Dear James,
Thank you so much for your kind invitation. I regret that I will be unable to join you this morning. Please do accept my sincere apologies. I was ever so grateful for your assistance yesterday, and I do hope to someday repay the favor. Feel

free to call on me again should you ever ~~want to see me~~
need anything.
Thank you again.
~~Love,~~
~~XOXO,~~
Sincerely,
~~Liz~~ Elizabeth Franklyn

I crumple up my pathetic attempt at a letter and toss it into the wastebasket. The least I can do would be to go and let him down in person. It would be much more polite, and I'm too tired to write a proper letter just now, obviously.

Besides, he most likely just wants to be my friend anyway. I'm probably projecting my own feelings onto him.

With that resolved, the exhaustion takes hold once more. I lay down again and, this time, I drift straight into the peaceful oblivion of sleep.

Chapter Nine

I wake up late. Understandable, considering how late I got to bed, but I berate myself for not thinking to set the alarm. I rush into Lanie's room as soon as I'm up so she can put me together. She helps me climb back into my walking dress from yesterday. Even with her help, I arrive at the edge of the forest more than fifteen minutes after eight.

I look around, breathing heavily, but see no sign of him. I'm too late. I know it shouldn't, but disappointment hits me hard anyway. I sigh and turn around to go back to the inn.

"I didn't think you were coming."

He speaks very quietly, in that hushed tone reserved for mornings and libraries, but still I startle at the sound of his voice. He smiles at me softly as he comes out from where he had been partially hidden behind a tree.

"I didn't think I'd made it in time," I say, copying his soft tone. I open my mouth to tell him what I came to say—thank you for the invitation, but I can't go with you, so sorry to keep you waiting—but I make the mistake of looking into his eyes as he walks towards me. My heart leaps into my throat. He moves in close to me and a lock of hair falls into his face. I resist the urge to sweep it aside.

Holding my hands firmly at my sides, I try again. My rehearsed apology becomes a mumbled excuse for being late. "I went to bed very late last night. Or rather, very early this morning," I say meekly. "I'm still very tired…"

"Do you want to go back in then? You need your rest." His eyes are wide with concern. "You could have sent a note. I would have understood."

"No!" I say, forgetting myself entirely. "I'm fine, really. It was only dinner and dancing. I mean, it went on until quite late, but I'm fine." *What are you doing?* I berate myself internally. *That was your chance to decline!*

He raises an eyebrow, not at my inner turmoil, but at my statement. "Enjoying the delights of the Season on your first day?" he says archly. "Well now. Do you have friends in town?"

"I didn't," I say, giving in and going with it for now. "But I met quite a few people yesterday." I list some of my new acquaintances. "I was introduced through my new friend Mr. Damien Gracen. He came into the Maples restaurant for lunch and found me eating alone." I give him a wry smile. "He seemed to decide it was a shame to let that happen, and then he made it a point to introduce me to everyone he knows, so that it won't happen again." I laugh.

"Gracen?" He tries to match my smile, but it looks off. "And how did you find him?" he asks, in a manner much stiffer than just a moment ago.

I'm taken aback by this reaction. *What could be the cause?* Then I remember that he had a similar reaction to William's name yesterday and then we didn't talk for twenty minutes, so I continue cautiously. "He's a very pleasant sort of fellow, isn't he? I think he'll be a good friend. Do you know of him?"

"Some. He tends not to spend too much time at farms, you know. I doubt I'd be in his class." Perhaps, like me, he has a deep disdain for the astounding arrogance of the elite. He wouldn't know that Damien seems to have very few concerns about class, though I suppose it's highly unlikely he'd befriend a farmer, in any case.

"You *will* be careful with him, won't you, Elizabeth? I don't trust him. What I do know for certain is that he is the kind of man who is out with a different girl each night of the week."

This makes me smile, even though I know I shouldn't. *He's worried about me.* "I never said that I trusted him, only that he was fun to spend time with," I tease. "I have no interest in becoming one of his conquests." James seems to relax a little at that. Or it may just be my overeager imagination....

And then he suddenly changes the subject. "Do you want breakfast?" he blurts. "I can't take you out," he adds, seemingly embarrassed, "but I have freshly baked bread and plenty of eggs and bacon back at the farm." He looks at me so hopefully that I couldn't bear to say no even if I wanted to. I *should* tell him no. But perhaps we can just be friends, he and I. That's probably all he wants from me anyway. It surely won't hurt anything to be friends.

I tell him yes.

He smiles at once, and I can't help but feel elated that it was me who put that expression there. He grabs my hand, which is bare because I scandalously—and accidentally, of course—left my gloves at the inn while rushing to head out. It's a simple gesture from him, meant only to lead and guide me, but my skin tingles at his touch.

I hesitate and a shiver runs up my spine. James looks back, eager to be off.

"Come on," he encourages gently. "Let's go!"

◊

We don't walk as far as we did yesterday; we round the last bend of the deer path to find a pretty chestnut horse tethered just out of sight of the main wagon trail, her long tail whipping flies off her flank while she waits patiently for her master.

James boosts me up, apologizing profusely for not having a sidesaddle for me. Because of my skirts, I sit awkwardly in sidesaddle position anyway. He makes to walk beside the horse but I threaten to jump down if he doesn't mount up with me. Partly because I am truly likely to fall off if I don't have someone to lean on...but even more so because I want to be near him. *In a friendly way, of course*, I tell myself.

He quickly gives in and expertly mounts up behind me, steadying my clumsy stance with his body. I lean into him and allow him to reach around me to hold the reins, completely comfortable now that I'm encircled in his arms.

Time begins its crazy dance once more, beginning to pass much too quickly when I am with him. I concentrate on burning this moment into my memory. I never want to forget the feeling of his strong arms around me.

We talk as we ride, and I fill him in on the details of my

first day in town. James is a good listener; he doesn't butt in with his own anecdotes, but merely laughs or frowns in all the right places.

He chuckles at my over-the-top impression of Libby and her friends making fun of the other girls. "They really said that?" he asks incredulously.

"They really did."

"But that's horrible."

He seems particularly taken aback when I tell him what the girls said about me.

"How dare they!" he exclaims. His voice softens as we continue along the dirt path. "I can only imagine how lovely you must have looked last night. Even now, you're simply the most beautiful woman I've ever seen." The blood rushes to my cheeks and an automatic smile comes to my lips.

I try to hide it by dropping my face toward the ground and biting my lower lip. But from the corner of my eye, I see him flick his startling gaze quickly in my direction, and I know that he knows my reaction as surely as if I'd spoken it.

To cover my embarrassed delight, I mumble, "Well, they were probably right about my dancing anyway..."

"I doubt that. Someone as graceful as you cannot possibly be a bad dancer." His grin fades and he sighs. "You know, I find women like that truly abhorrent. They think the world revolves only around them and all they care about in others is money and status—so that they might raise themselves up by the connection. There is more to people than that. Believe me, I know!" He shakes his head.

"I do believe you. Why is it that they are unable to accept

people for who they are?"

"Do you know what I think? Honestly, I think it's because they cannot accept themselves. Each of them has been raised in the same environment—one in which even *they* truly cannot tell if someone likes them for who they are or for what they have. And, as I said, it's mostly about what they have. It's sad, really."

We keep talking as we ride, and we soon arrive at his farm in a little over half the time it took to walk yesterday. We bring the horse to the stable and head for the small farmhouse.

I pause. "James, perhaps this is a stupid question, but, why didn't we take one of the horses to town yesterday? Wouldn't that have been faster?" I can barely admit it to myself, but I'm actually very glad it didn't go faster. Still, I'm curious.

"Probably." He smiles and then continues matter-of-factly, "But then I'd have had less time to talk to you."

My face brightens to crimson once again and I look down at my skirts. I can't help myself.

He just grins and gently offers me his arm to lead me to the house.

He asks me if I want a tour before breakfast. I accept, and together we wander the first floor of the farmhouse. Apparently the upstairs area is only spare bedrooms and storage space.

I wasn't paying enough attention yesterday to notice, but unlike me, James keeps everything in his home neat and clutter-free. In his kitchen, cast-iron pots and pans hang from large hooks on the walls. A freshly scrubbed wood stove for cooking and a neatly swept-out fireplace reside in one tidy corner. A tan canvas tablecloth, free of crumbs and debris, covers a large wooden table with pitted legs. Threadbare curtains of brown and yellow drape across spotless windows, while similar rugs adorn clean, but rudimentary, wood floors.

The living area is similar, with unsophisticated and eclectic wood furniture placed neatly about the room, so unlike the elegant pieces I saw yesterday at dinner and the ball. I feel more at home here, though. A large cast-iron wood stove sits in the middle of this room as well, ready to ward off the chill of the cold Connecticut winters.

The walls are mostly bare of ornamentation except for one small portrait of three children dressed in what must be their Sunday best, each staring unsmiling at the camera. To one side stands a girl of about thirteen, clad in a bustled gown like a miniature adult, her dark hair braided over her shoulder, a bow holding the long ends together. Her skirts, unlike in today's sleek style, are full and they cover much of the backdrop, which looks like an elaborate playroom. Sitting next to her is a young boy of about ten, looking handsome in a dark suit and tie, his hair combed back neatly. On his lap rests a chubby toddler, two or three years old, dressed in a little white gown. The child's dark curls tumble down to her plump shoulders. I stare at the photo, fascinated. The boy's features unmistakably belong to James. Even in black and white, his pale eyes stand out.

I glance at him, but he's looking the other way, ready to move on.

There are two other small rooms down here: one that's been made into a sort of office and study, and the other is James's unadorned bedroom.

One wall of the study is taken up by a handmade bookshelf that is overflowing with books of all kinds. They all bear the unmistakable signs of being well-read, dog-eared and worn, some with broken spines.

Even though I know in the back of my mind that he wrote me the note—in better handwriting than my own—that brought me here this morning, I'm a bit taken aback at first. Many farmers in this era don't know how to read. But then I remember that he comes from the middle class, not from a farming family. He has a background in business and surely attended school, maybe even university. Of course he knows how to read. There is also a simple desk, piled high with handwritten papers and ledgers, and one chair to work from.

I only get a quick peek into his bedroom before he closes the door, but it's plain and contains little besides a small bed, a washbasin, and a shaving mirror. A very small wardrobe sits tucked away in a corner. In startling contrast to my bedroom back home, there is no evidence of his personal life within these four walls. There is much more character in the study, where the tattered books declare that the owner is a reader and a thinker. Nonetheless, I blush at his bedroom door like I've just peeked into his private sanctum.

Back in his kitchen, James is able to create a fantastic breakfast, despite the fact that it is lacking all the modern amenities. He pops a loaf of fresh brown bread into the hearthside brick oven, to be pulled out in a few minutes, warm and ready to smother with fresh honey and homemade butter. He packs me off outside to pick a basket of the best strawberries from their leafy nests while he mixes fresh whipped cream—skimmed from this morning's milk—to top them. He fries up eggs and bacon atop the wood stove in a sizzling cast-iron skillet while

I set the table, not for two, but for six.

It turns out that his farmhands have been here since the crack of dawn. James is the best cook, so he makes breakfast for the five of them each morning. It's a good thing, too, because it looks as though he's made enough food to feed a small country. I ring a large bell that's been set up outside to call the workers in.

The four men come quickly at the sound of the bell. I can tell they've already been working hard under the hot morning sun; each is damp with sweat.

The men stop in surprise as they enter the kitchen and see me. I can't tell if it's because James has a woman here for breakfast or because the light blue cotton dress I'm wearing is far fancier than anything in the room. Actually, it's probably the fanciest thing within a three-mile radius.

Four questioning looks are directed at James before he can introduce me to his employees, who also happen to be his very good friends: Thomas, Walter, Gus, and Michael.

After the initial shock wears off, the boys warm up and start talking. They're not talking around me or speaking as though I'm not here, but including me in the conversation. It's not, however, so difficult for them to do, since the biggest topic of discussion is the news.

Walter is the source of this news. A newspaper sits at his elbow, declaring today's headlines in bold print. In between bites of food, Walter picks it up and reads haltingly to the group in a deep, rich voice. Once he finishes each article, the debates start. Each man seems to have a different opinion on each story, and, as the newbie, they all look to me for corroboration.

But I hold my own. They take turns groaning or cheering

when their views gain my dissent or support, and I even manage to throw in a few clever opinions of my own.

Still, I keep quiet for much of the conversation, watching and listening. Not because I'm not included, but because I want to learn more about my companions.

Thomas is the comedian, always cracking jokes—often at his own expense. Along with his jokes, Tom has an infectious smile and loves to laugh; the smile lines that crinkle his face attest to that. He's very short—and his height is featured frequently in his self-deprecating jokes—but he's also very well built. He's only an inch or two taller than me, but I can easily see his muscles bulging through his brown muslin shirt. I think he's about thirty years old, but prematurely wrinkled from sun weathering and from years of laughing. His auburn hair is sun-streaked a sandy blonde in places, and his short, scruffy beard has been bleached into a pale fuzz.

Walter is much more serious than Tom, but his deep chuckle resounds more than once across the table after a particularly funny joke. Of these four, Walt is the only one who can read—a skill taught to him by James. He asked to be taught not long after getting his job on the farm, it seems. Apparently, it used to be James who shared the news over breakfast each morning, but ever since Walt read his first slow and stuttered word, he hasn't given up a chance to do more. His reading is still deliberate and somewhat childlike, and it does a lot to tone down his imposing countenance.

He is imposing because besides his serious demeanor and his deep voice, Walt is over six feet tall and covered in lean muscle. He wears his work shirt sleeveless, which shows off the powerful muscles etched in the flawless deep brown skin of his arms. His face, though, has a sweetness to it that belies his true character. He has a twinkle in his dark eyes and the set of his mouth gives him a pleasant smile when he shows it.

Gus is different from the others, being shy and incredibly sweet. He only thinks the best of anyone, and I can tell from his rarely stated opinions that he's a very empathetic person. However, he's so shy that at first he barely speaks in front of me at all. When he does, he talks quietly in a mild southern accent and keeps his eyes firmly fixed on the floor.

His shyness may come from the fact that he falls quite short of society's standards for attractiveness. He's maybe in his early twenties, but he is already losing his oily, straw-colored hair. His eyes and mouth are small and overshadowed by a very large, very red, and very hairy nose. He's missing one or two teeth and the rest are brown and crooked, marred by years of improper dental care. His face is deeply sunburned and half covered by a scraggly beard without a mustache. It seems a bit off-putting at first, to have his manner be so at odds with his looks, but it just goes once again to prove that old adage about books and their covers.

Michael, on the other hand, could not be more opposite than Gus when it comes to appearances. He is the epitome of tall, dark, and handsome with tousled brown locks and eyes like deep, shadowy pools. He's the youngest man here, probably only a year or so older than me. If I hadn't spent years dreaming of James, I surely would have been completely smitten with Michael. He is, however, not the sharpest tool in the shed and quite lacking in anything resembling common sense. But he is kind and sweet, and his bumbling is well-meaning.

Even after we finish eating, the talking and debates continue until the sun looms brightly over the trees through the eastern window, reminding the men that there's work to be done in the fields.

The four hands bring their dishes to the water basin and shuffle along outside, leaving James and me alone. He moves to clean up the dishes. When I come over to help, he tries to wave me away, but I insist. I end up with spots of grease and dirty water on the front of my beautiful dress, but it's worth it. Who wouldn't want to rub arms with James for ten minutes, even if it meant scrubbing pots and pans?

When we finish cleaning up from breakfast, we go back outside and, without a word, he offers me his arm. With no hesitation, I thread my own arm through, knowing only that regardless of what we might do, I want to be near him.

He smiles at me, his jade eyes soft as new growth in early spring.

"Are you ready to see my magnificent estate?"

I giggle, looking around me at the slightly run-down barn and henhouse, then drop into a flowery curtsy, my lips curled inward to conceal my enormous smile. "Of course, Mr. Percival. Please, lead on."

And so, he takes me on a tour of the farm. We make our way around everything—barns and fields, chickens and horses, pastures and ponds. He even walks me to the very edges of his land, a good half hour's walk, into a beautiful flower-filled meadow with a familiar stone wall meandering through and meeting another to form a T.

We don't pass close enough to the wall to see the spot on

the other side where my things are buried, but I can see it in my mind's eye. The time machine itself, hidden in a concealed pocket that I had constructed into my petticoat, seems to burn through and heat my skin beneath. I am uncomfortable being in this place with James, knowing what it means for us. It means that when the time comes, I'll have to leave.

We walk away, through fields planted with crops of all sizes, up and down neat rows, through fields lying fallow, through a small orchard filled with leafy green apple trees which are just waiting for the right time to produce their sweet fruits. The best part is that we don't stop talking the entire time. Not just about the farm, but about everything: family, town, religion, politics. And once we leave the stone wall, it's all too easy to forget that I'll ever need to go anywhere but here or be with anyone but him.

The sun is high in the sky when we return to the house and I am yawning uncontrollably.

"No, I'm fine," I murmur unconvincingly through a yawn. "I want to stay."

Not surprisingly, he sees right through me and insists on bringing me back to the inn. Once again we take just one horse, this time a black-and-white mare. Except for her, the stable is empty. The other two horses are out working in the fields, pulling carts that are being slowly filled with weeds and rocks, two things that both seem to grow with abundance in the area.

During the ride home, I can't keep my eyes open. James holds me tightly against him. Snug and safe in his arms and lulled by the even stride of our mount, I drift off, burrowing myself more deeply into the protection of his embrace.

It only seems like a moment later when I'm jolted awake by the lack of motion all around me. I look up, disoriented, as James gently tries to wake me, his soft whisper soothing but insistent. We are here.

Lanie is standing outside the inn to meet me, perhaps having seen us coming through the crystal-clear panes of an upstairs window. She and the groom help me down so that James can climb off as well.

"Are you alright, Miss?" She is obviously very concerned.

Eyes still full of sleep, I stretch and yawn. "Yes, Lanie, I'm fine. Just tired is all. Will you give me a moment?"

Lanie obediently backs off to the front door to wait, and the groom moves off to the side with the horse, checking her over.

"Thank you for the ride," I say quietly. "I'm sorry I fell asleep."

"It was no trouble at all. My pleasure." His contented smile is enough to set my heart pumping in my weary chest. Once again, his attention alone is enough to hold my exhaustion at bay.

This is why, when he bids me good day by chastely kissing my hand, I can barely contain myself. My heart rate is speeding along feverishly and my palms are slick with perspiration, the result of more than just the midday sun....

It doesn't bother me as much as it should to know that my plan to let him down easy has seriously backfired. If I thought I was falling for him before, it's nothing compared to what I feel now. It's like I'm walking on a cloud, lighter than air and floating free with every step. I am lost, hopelessly lost, in him.

So when he asks me if I'll meet him again tomorrow morning, I don't think. I just say yes.

Then I turn slowly to go inside, holding his mesmerizing

gaze even when the rest of my body is turned away. I don't look away until Lanie closes the door between us, blocking him from my view.

I let her lead me up to my room, once again ignoring my surroundings to better imagine the man I just left behind. I move through the suite with a spring in my step, my heart full to bursting, and my mind too occupied to remember that I'm supposed to be exhausted.

Once in my room, Lanie helps me strip to my chemise. Somehow, I manage to sleep, dreaming, this time, only of the face I now know so well.

I wake later that afternoon to find that calling cards have been left for me throughout the day. It seems that a few of my new acquaintances from last night's ball have visited. I am flattered, but still, I ignore them for today. I have too much to do to get my life going here.

First, I take Lanie shopping for her new uniforms. The few dresses she owns are threadbare and stained, so we also find something for her to wear on her off time. She tries to refuse, telling me it's too much. Most servants are expected to provide their own uniforms, never mind other clothing. But I won't have it. When I won't take no for an answer, she insists that I merely purchase patterns and fabric, rather than the more expensive finished items, so that she might make the dresses herself. Since she'll be spending so much time alone at the inn, I can only agree. If it were me, I'd need something to fill the hours as well.

Back at the inn, we eat dinner together in my rooms. At first, we eat in silence. Lanie, coming from years of servitude, knows that her conversation is not usually welcome. She still sits in awe that I've invited her to join me in my meal at all. But the stillness grates on me and after a few false starts we manage to begin a conversation.

In the beginning, she does nothing more than just answer my questions. She is still as kind and smiling as she had been in our first interview, but she is more awkward now as my official employee. Soon enough though, she warms up and begins to add little details. My questions for her become increasingly personal, and she answers these with the same simple innocence as any of the others before them.

It does, however, take her a long time to ask any questions of me, having long since learned that the life of an employer is none of her business. But finally, my kindness and her curiosity seem to get the better of her.

"Miss Elizabeth?"

Hoping we can be friends, since we'll be living in such close quarters, I tell her, "You may call me Liz or Lizzy if you want to, Lanie."

"Oh!" she exclaims, blushing. "Thank you, Miss Liz... It's just... Would you mind...if I were to ask you a personal question?"

"Of course not." I smile kindly to show her that I am happy for her interest. "If I have a problem with your question, then I just won't answer it."

She smiles shyly in return. "I was just curious..." She giggles softly. "Who was that handsome man you were with today?"

I can't help myself, I grin broadly. "His name is James. James

Percival." I sigh. "He is perfect, isn't he?"

"He seems very nice, Miss. You must like him very much."

"More than I should," I reply glumly. It's hard to remember that no matter how much I like him, we can never be together. *But surely it can't hurt to be his friend?* I can't think straight when it comes to him, so I change the subject.

"But what about you? Is there someone, somewhere, who catches your eye?"

Lanie turns bright crimson and bows her head. "Well…not right now. I used to like this boy, Josiah." She glances back up toward me with a wistful look. "His father was a butler for the last family I worked for. But he got married to another girl." She looks down at the floor. "I was at the wedding. It was quite nice, really. His wife, Judith, is my friend." She scuffs her foot. "But I never see either of them anymore. The family they work for left town. I haven't met anyone I liked since then."

I pat her on the arm. "I'm sorry."

"No, it's okay. It's not so bad. Maybe someday I'll meet someone who will sweep me off my feet." She pauses and then adds shyly, "Like this James has done to you. Tell me, what does he do?"

By bedtime, we are chatting like old friends. We get to bed early so that we can be awake tomorrow morning in time to prepare me to head to breakfast with James again.

We awaken to birds chirping noisily outside of our open windows. Their melodic voices are bright and awake, and, having gone to bed early, I actually am, too.

James is downstairs waiting for me when I get there. Though I watched the windows as thoroughly as possible in between dressing and hair and makeup, I never saw him arrive. Nevertheless, here he is, calmly waiting for me in the entryway as if he belongs here.

I take his hand and follow him, all the while knowing that if he asked me to, I'd follow him to the ends of the earth.

Chapter Ten

Days go by and visiting with James becomes routine. Each morning, Lanie and I wake to get me dressed and ready to meet him around 7:00 in the entryway of the Maples. Each day, we take a leisurely ride to the farm where I help him make breakfast, always with fresh, warm bread and some sort of plump berries straight off the vine. Each day, we share our food with my new friends: Gus, Tom, Walt, and Michael. Each morning, we laugh and talk and listen to Walt improve as he reads the day's news.

After the men go back to work, James and I talk for hours. We mostly walk through the woods, arm in arm. Once, when it rains, we sit contentedly on a long bench swing set up on the wraparound porch, watching the rain water his crops.

One day, he takes me out on a rowboat on the pond. I had found out in our first few days together that James has never read my favorite classic novel—Jane Austen's *Pride and Prejudice*—and so I begin to read it aloud to him while he fishes for dinner. He guesses that Elizabeth Bennet and Mr. Darcy will end up together right from the start.

Oddly enough, I feel like one of the best things about our

conversations is that we can joke and banter even while we effortlessly discuss anything and everything under the sun. I'm not sure why, but James's little hecklings feel every bit as sweet and intimate as his compliments do, and I love the way his laughter echoes through the forest around us.

It takes about a week of spending my mornings this way before it finally occurs to me that he's skipping hours of work each day to be with me. It also makes me suspect that our friends are probably picking up the slack. I can't let them do that for me.

This seems like the perfect, though painful, opportunity to call off my visits. I don't want to, of course, but I've known all week that I'm in way too deep. It isn't healthy for either of us to get so attached. But I just can't stop. His presence is like an addiction to me. Now that I've been with him, I don't want to be without him anymore.

Yet, I have to try.

"James… How are you finishing all of your work after spending all morning with me? You must get very behind."

He's quick to answer. "I don't mind! I just work a little faster and a little longer, that's all." He's a better liar than me, but still I know he's not telling me everything. The guys must be doing a lot to catch up. Even when it's not full-on harvest season, farm life is hard enough. There's no need to work extra hours in the dark.

"You know I can't let you do that for me. It's just not right."

He sighs. "Elizabeth, I *want* to spend this time with you. I don't care if I have to make up time later." He looks at me, his green eyes willing me to understand, all the while not knowing how well I do. I stiffen my resolve. *I can't let that stop me.*

"Well, I care," I counter. "I don't like doing that to you. And what about the guys? Do they have to stay late as well? Do they care? How do they like making up for your wasted time?"

He makes a frustrated noise. "They like it just fine, since I pay them extra to stay late—"

"Pay them extra? James, I can't have you throwing away your hard-earned money on me!" I am horrified that he may be putting even more into this than I had thought.

But he won't be deterred. "Never mind *that*. What do you mean 'wasted time'? You think I'm wasting my time when I spend it with you?" he asks. I shake my head ever so slightly. "That my money is wasted for using it as I see fit?"

I shrug helplessly.

"What are you saying, Elizabeth?" he asks, gentler now. "That you don't want to come anymore?"

I should be prepared for this question. It's what I was just leading up to, after all. But, now that it's out there, I don't know what to say. I know I *shouldn't* come anymore; I should never have come in the first place. I take my time to think about how that fact hasn't stopped me yet. I sigh. It's not going to stop me now, either, I can tell. Apparently, I have no willpower whatsoever.

So I tell him the truth, marveling at how easy it is to forget my painful idea regardless of the sense it makes to cut this off before we get deeper. "I want to visit with you. Very much." I pause to think for a moment. "Here's what we'll do. Tomorrow, you will work and I will come with you. We can still be together while you keep busy. This way, no one has to work late because of me."

"Out in the hot sun?" he asks skeptically. "You don't want to watch me work."

Slowly, but firmly, I answer him as though I'm speaking to a small child. "I'll wear a hat. I want to spend time with you, but you need to get your work done. This way I won't feel bad for causing extra hardships. A compromise, see?"

He gives a long-suffering sigh. "Fine. We'll try it."

We do try it. My brilliant plan lasts all of a day.

It turns out that one day is exactly how long I can—in good conscience—sit around and watch someone else work.

I decide early in the day that the plan isn't right for us. Afterwards, I take off during afternoon calling hours to go shopping as I've done once before, leaving friends and acquaintances to drop their cards and head off for their next destinations disappointed. Instead of the fancy dress shops that I went to before, their insides filled with rolls of decadent fabrics and their dressing rooms with full-length gilded mirrors, I stroll through the town's small general store along with the workaday throng in search of something much plainer.

So the next day when James picks me up, I'm wearing the plainest day dress I could find—one not so different from one of Lanie's uniforms. Unlike the frilly gowns meant for parties and balls, this dress has no ruffles, no flounces, no bows, no beads. It's basic and boring and brown with nothing that will impede my movement. In short, it is perfect for the morning

I have planned. My hat is large enough to shade my face and shoulders, so that I won't need the parasol I've been carrying for the past week and a half.

The bellman and the groom, though by now accustomed to seeing me come and go each day with James, look at me very strangely as I make my way out. They are not used to me being so small and drab; my ordinary outfits are more like colorful blossoms than the brown withered husk I surely resemble now.

But they do know who I am. No one tries to throw me out, thinking that I'm someone's maid. Though I suppose it helps that I tip them well on my way out each morning, and today is no exception.

James's brilliant eyes light up when he sees me, the pale green glowing in the early morning light against his sun-kissed skin. I suppose mine light up as well, but my hazel eyes, though pretty, are boring when compared to the sparkling peridot of his irises.

His look transforms into amused confusion when he notices my outfit. "What's this? Have you lost all of your pretty dresses?" he asks with a teasing lilt in his voice as he fingers the rough fabric of my sleeve.

I don't answer, so he shrugs and helps me onto the horse, then climbs on behind me as usual. We start riding and, and like every day, I revel in the sensation of his strong arms holding me tight.

But he won't leave it at that, just as I'd known he wouldn't. "Well…?" he prompts.

"Of course not," I finally answer with mock curtness. "Don't be absurd. I've simply decided that I can't sit and watch you and the others work—"

"So I won't," he interrupts quickly.

"I'm not finished," I warn. "I cannot sit and watch you work while I do nothing. I want to help you—"

"Absolutely not." I'm taken aback by his forceful tone. I've never heard him speak like that to anyone. He stops the horse and looks at me.

I narrow my eyes, my stubborn streak coming out at this unexpected opposition. "But I—"

"No. I won't have it." His tone has softened but he's insistent.

"Why?" I ask defiantly.

We start moving again and make it through the meadow and into the serenity of the forest before he stops us again. His words are slow and controlled, as if he's chosen them with great care.

"Elizabeth. You are a lady. A highborn, upper-class lady. Now look at me. I am a farmer. I am decidedly lower class, no matter how you look at it. According to society—"

I scoff, "Society!"

"Yes. According to society, you should not even *be* here with me. Every day, I feel like someone is going to knock on my door and tell me that you have been forbidden from ever visiting again. By their rules, you should be happily ensconced in a manor somewhere, far away from me. Not working on *my farm*—in servant's clothing, no less! No. I will not have it."

"James, you are being ridiculous!"

"*I* am being ridiculous? I am?! I am not the one from a highborn family who wants to spend my time flitting about, trying to be a farmer!" An odd look comes over his face and he refuses to meet my eyes for a moment. He shakes it off quickly and pulls himself together. I think he knows I have a point.

"Perhaps not," I retort. "Perhaps you're not some snotty,

hoity-toity, lazy, over-privileged jerk like so many of the 'gentlemen' I've met are. And that is exactly what I like about you! You're not afraid to work hard and get your hands dirty. But don't forget that you didn't start out as a farmer, either. You told me yourself that your father owns a business that he wanted you to take over. If I'm not mistaken, that puts you squarely into at least the merchant class, if not higher. That's hardly slumming it."

"Liz, it doesn't matter. My past is not the question here. The answer is still no. I won't let you."

That does it. I look at him incredulously. "Won't *let* me?" My voice goes up an octave. "*Won't let me?!*"

And that's when I realize that he's bluffing. There is no way he can keep me from doing just as I said I would. My stubborn scowl slowly gives way to a mischievous smile. "So," I say conversationally, "how exactly are you going to stop me?"

He stutters, not expecting this tactic. "I— Well— I— um… We'll turn around right now. I won't take you anywhere near the farm until you've given up this silly idea." He lowers the reins and plants his hands across his chest.

What can I do? I start laughing. I laugh until his face turns red, embarrassed. While he's distracted, I jump down off the horse. I'm on the ground before he can stop me.

"You won't take me? Well, I've got news for you, Mr. James Percival. I know my own way there." I start walking in the direction of the wagon trail. "And then I'll ask one of the guys to help me. They'll show me what to do." And they will, too. I've seen it before; they'll do almost anything I ask simply for a smile.

James knows this. I can tell he knows that he's been defeated.

"I don't like it," he grumbles, bumping his heels into the horse's flanks to catch up to me.

"No one ever said you had to," I say sweetly, knowing that I've won. I smile brightly up at him and pat him condescendingly on his leg, before extending my hand impatiently. "Now, help me back up and let's go!"

◊

James still doesn't agree with my new plan, but, after breakfast, he grudgingly shows me what to do anyway. He steadfastly refuses to let me do any heavy work, but considering that it's nearly August, I still manage to work up a sweat under the hot New England sun.

What he does let me do is help him take care of the animals, bringing each their morning meal. The cows are easiest; we just let them out to pasture and they mow down as much as they want. One of James's cows gave birth not long ago, having been mated with a strong bull belonging to a neighbor. The calf follows her mother closely, nervous to stray too far and always ready to find her udder should she get hungry.

The pigs, too, are easy enough to feed. A bucket of slop, what would have been our compost pile at home, makes a large part of their morning diet. Like the cow, a large sow is followed around by more than half a dozen piglets, adorable little babies that clamber all over one another to reach her swollen teats.

As the days pass, the animals come to know me and begin to trust me. The horses love me for the sugar cubes I smuggle away from my afternoon tea in town on their behalf. The calf, more trusting than her mother, lets me scratch her gently behind her fuzzy ears. Even the scruffy old tabby cat, who lives on a diet of mice in the barn, rubs contentedly against me after I begin to leave him small saucers of fresh, fatty cream every few days.

I learn how to milk the cows and collect the thick white fluid in pails and then allow the milk to sit and separate. I find out how to skim the cream off the top and churn it into thick yellow butter or whip it into fresh whipped cream.

I learn to collect the eggs from the henhouse, careful to stay far away from the isolated room where hens rest gently upon fertilized eggs, waiting for tiny chicks to hatch into a new generation. I learn how the rooster helps protect his hens, and that the hens will each be receptive to his advances in their own time.

James shows me how to groom the horses until they gleam and their long manes and tails hang glossy against their neat coats. He shows me how to check over their hooves to make sure nothing is stuck in their shoes. He shows me how to strap them in and out of their harnesses and saddles so I might help prepare them for the fields or for our rides.

He also teaches me to cook. I was never much of a chef back home; my signature dish was mac and cheese from a box. If I was feeling especially adventurous, I might even have added some ground turkey to it. I would brown the meat and drain it, all the while slopping it everywhere and making a mess. Meanwhile, my most advanced breakfast dish was instant oatmeal in the microwave, which always did come out thick and lumpy.

Yet with James as my instructor, I somehow learn the ins and outs of creating a perfect omelet, of scrambling soft and fluffy eggs, or grilling up crisp, greasy rashers of bacon. I once would have thought fresh buttermilk biscuits were beyond my feeble abilities, but, after a few tries, I manage to make a batch we can eat. They're not the light, airy biscuits that James bakes, but nor are they the rock-hard lumps of my first attempts.

He teaches me how to mix the ingredients and knead the brown dough for the dark, crusty bread we eat each morning. I often wish I could be around in the evenings to smell the freshly risen dough as it bakes into that hearty bread, its insides dotted with nuts and seeds. I know though, if I were here, I'd have to bake an extra loaf each night, a spare loaf for me to eat warm and fresh out of the oven, smothered with jam or melted butter.

James also teaches me to prepare the small amount of meat that we eat, though even with his help, I'll never be an expert. It's alright, though. Much of it we smoke and dry into jerky, a good way to keep it preserved for a long time without the aid of a fridge or freezer.

The fruits and vegetables are a lot of work as well. Most of the summer veggies are brought to the market to be sold, though we eat plenty of them ourselves, of course. But the rest need to be saved for winter, which is why I soon learn the art of canning. Most veggies we pickle in a thin, salty brine, while the fruits swim in a thick, sweet syrup. Then the jars are stored away on shelves to use during those lean winter months when the thought of fresh produce will be a far-off dream.

I also learn a lot more about my companions. Each of them has a fantastic work ethic, working harder and longer than even my dad and his crew. They wake up at the crack of dawn to be here, and occasionally stay well into the evening, especially during harvest season.

But they are also friends. The five of them spend time together in and out of work, and even while working hard, they manage to have fun together every day.

Besides their work lives, they each have lives going on at home. Gus's wife works in a textile mill outside of town six long days a week. They have seven children, and his eldest daughter takes care of her younger siblings instead of attending school. They live in a small house near the mill, and Gus is saving his money for the day—soon, he hopes—when his wife might leave her treacherous job.

Tom is the third son of a blacksmith. He spent many years beside his father at the forge, which explains his muscular build. But his older brothers took over the shop when their father died and, because of a feud, they left him out in the cold with his wife and two sons. They were begging for scraps in the streets when James hired him.

I am saddened when I learn that Walt's parents were slaves on a plantation in North Carolina. Thankfully, they escaped and ran north before the start of the Civil War, and spent months huddled inside closets and under trapdoors. When the war began, his father went back and fought to maintain his freedom. He died in battle, leaving a wife and two small children. But Walt and his mother and sister were free, and his mother raised the two on her own. His sister is now married, and Walt and his wife live with his mother, taking care of her in her old age. They have three young daughters to care for as well.

Even young Michael has someone counting on him. His aging father is ill, and he has two younger siblings to look after. His easy cheerfulness seems much more poignant when I find out that even at the age of nineteen, he is a widower. His young bride died of smallpox more than a year ago, only three months before she was supposed to give birth to their first child. But he—and all the rest of them—come in every morning with smiles lighting their faces.

I'm glad to see them happy, and it makes me even more enamored with James to hear that he's a generous employer and a great friend. He works hard by their sides and then compensates them well with both crops and money to care for their families.

He saw the potential in them. Tom tells me that when James hired him it changed his life. James gave him a means to feed his family, and with it, he gave him hope. And it's similar for the others. They're all intensely loyal to him, and love him like a brother. *How can I not love him for it as well?*

Sometimes I work alone with them. More often, James is with us, too, a group of us working together. But most of the time, James and I work by ourselves—taking care of the house, the food, the animals—while they work out in the fields.

I've tried many times to get him to let me help out there, but he won't let me near any of the heavier work. Besides, there's plenty for us to do all morning; I go home each afternoon utterly exhausted.

I think that he's still upset with himself for letting me work at all, but I've already told him that I'm not going back to just watching him.

I did enough of that in my dreams; now is the time to join him.

Chapter Eleven

While I'm busy with my morning routine, my afternoons soon fall into a pattern as well. I feel like I'm living two completely different lives, so dissimilar are the two halves of my days.

Around noon, James brings me back to the inn. After lunch, I will typically take a nap in my room, one of the luxuries I've come to adore here. I haven't had naptime since preschool, and I enjoy it much more now than I did back then.

I wake up in time to get changed and refreshed for the afternoon calling hours, now a part of my schedule, even after I rudely ignored everyone on my first few days in town. Visitors pour in each and every afternoon, though twice a week I put on one of my walking dresses and make my own rounds.

I'm glad to have this experience, too, because I use these visits to ask gently probing questions about the Wood and Hunt families. I have no shortage of people telling me the obvious, like how wealthy they are, and that William is away, but some have vaguely useful information.

The Woods, as it turns out, are involved mostly in real estate ventures throughout the country. The money is even older than that, though; Mr. Wood uses existing funds to make even more. Since he first inherited the capital twenty years ago, he's more than doubled it. Word is that he's counting on his only son to continue that tradition.

The Hunts are full of old money, as well, but Mr. Hunt settled into law instead of real estate. He started off as a lawyer, becoming well known after a few high-profile cases. Now, many years later, he is a prominent judge here in town. His only daughter Elizabeth, a.k.a. Libby, is the apple of his eye and his last hope for making a truly advantageous family connection. Both of his sons married well, but not outrageously so.

As for my search for William, well, I hear that there's a good chance that he might show up in Newport. All of the wealthiest families own property there, and they'll spend a month or so in their cliffside mansions later this summer. I'll have to try to find a way to get there, as well; there's no way I'm giving up that opportunity.

Sadly though, the one thing that no one seems to know definitively is when the prodigal son will return home to his family.

After visiting hours, Lanie helps me to change *again*, into dinner or evening wear. The Thorne Hill Season is in full swing, and each night there are parties, plays, shows, and dances to choose from. Some are open to all, while others are by invite only, but even if I'm not specifically invited, I often attend on the arm of someone who is.

For despite Libby's prediction, the young men are still interested in my company even as the weeks roll by. Each afternoon, I get an invitation to go out with one gentleman or another, sometimes more. But, I must admit, more often than not I attend on the arm of one young man in particular: Damien Gracen.

There are still nights like that first exhilarating evening where I stay out with him or another date into the wee morning hours. But I've found it's easier to make myself a general rule that I will not stay out past midnight no matter how much my new friends beg. And beg they do. But, unlike them, I am up by six each morning to be ready to meet James. Some of these fellows don't go to bed until that time. I can't afford to stay out so late.

In my first few days of waking early, I worried that someone might see me slipping out of the inn each morning with James and disapprove. He is, after all, merely a lowly farmer in the eyes of my upscale associates. It turns out that I'll never have a problem on that front. The employees at the inn are discreet and don't care enough to tell anyone if they weren't. As for Damien and his ilk? Well, most of them never wake before noon, and those that do knock back an old-fashioned hangover tonic—one that includes nearly as much alcohol as they drank to become hungover in the first place—and go straight back to bed.

My secret is safe.

Chapter Twelve

The summer rolls on and the Season with it. The men who escort me to our various outings are all gentlemen—in the sense that they're chivalrous and gallant to me and the other highborn ladies, pulling out chairs and holding doors. Some of them are sincerely nice guys: men who are sweet and gentle and kind to everyone. These are the ones I will attend with more than once, should they ask me.

Some of them are snobs, though they may seem like great guys at first. Of these, many even *are* good in some ways, but they are snooty and aloof to the many they deem to be below them. Yet they also care greatly about what others think, especially if those others are the select few that are level with or above them in status. These are the men who are happy to accept daddy's money but too good to put in a hard day's work to earn it; the men who enjoy the benefits of a servant's hard work but sneer with disdain over her stooped and downtrodden form.

A select few of the men in town are complete jerks with whom I refuse to associate. These men are of a countenance so vile that I can't bear to spend an entire evening in their company and have to plead illness. These are the men who, like Libby, compliment you one moment and tear you to shreds the moment your back is turned. They treat the servants as if they were lower than the mangiest stray dog. They are absolutely positive of the world's love for them, even as they stumble from your side during a party, don someone else's dinner jacket, and then loudly and drunkenly proclaim exactly which prostitute they'll be visiting later on.

And yes, I saw precisely that scenario play out.

The women are much the same, with Libby and her gang of harpies making up the despicable end of the spectrum. I spend more time with the nicer girls, but the problem with them is that so many of them have been raised to be two things: completely vain and utterly dependent on the male sex. So, if they're not talking about the latest fashions, they're usually discussing increasingly desperate tactics for catching a husband. The only thing I have in common with most of them is the torment that Libby rains down upon us.

And there is plenty of that. As I've become more popular, she and the others have only become more vicious. Of course, they always speak to me politely to my face, even when something nasty is spewing from their mouths. It's the way they work—it would wreak havoc on their dainty lives to be caught being impolite.

Of the group, only Angelica treats me kindly, and that is only when the rest of them aren't around. She wouldn't dare be nice to me in front of them, knowing how much they despise me. When they are present, she usually just keeps her mouth shut.

Only two people so far break the stereotype. One is Aurelia Goodwin. She is feisty and independent, the daughter of a suffragette mother. She is by far the favorite of my new female friends, reminding me much of my friend Donna from back home, whom I often miss. We talk about books and politics and women's rights…and men, and even fashion on occasion, because it's okay to discuss those, too, even if I don't want to revolve my entire life around them.

Damien, of course, continues to be the major exception to any label. He's kind and friendly to everyone, while also being an unapologetic drunk and a notorious womanizer. He doesn't care a bit about what others think of him, and it doesn't bother him in the slightest to spend an evening in a cheerful bar full of average working men. He freely hands out cash to beggars, and will hire men off the street for day work. Yet he won't lift a finger himself—not because he feels he's too good for it, but because he simply couldn't be bothered. And like most upper-class men, he doesn't have to. Many parents, like William's, it seems, feel that working builds responsibility in a young man. Perhaps Damien's parents feel that way, too, or perhaps not, but until they cut him off from their fortune, he'll surely continue his life of leisure.

Despite all his faults, though, I adore Damien. I've never met anyone like him, so confident, charismatic, funny, and effortlessly warm to everyone. Even though I sometimes think about James during the evenings, when I'm with Damien and Aurelia it's never anything more than a passing thought. Damien is always ready to make me laugh with a witty comment or a saucy remark, and they both are always up for a deep conversation.

In a way, though, I feel that my relationship with Damien is even worse for me than the one I shouldn't be having with James. After all, James will probably find someone else to love, and live a long, happy life with her after I'm gone. It breaks my heart, but at least he'll live.

Damien won't have that luxury.

Mostly, I try to just pretend that I don't know about it, blocking the thoughts from my consciousness with an ease that's almost scary. But my subconscious still remembers. My sleep is haunted by nightmares in which he's murdered repeatedly and I'm helpless to stop it.

But by day, I don't let them linger. I'd go crazy.

Instead, I try to use my time constructively. I haven't forgotten that I came here for a reason—not just to play around with people's hearts. I continue digging for clues about my ancestors. Unfortunately, the pile of discarded soil grows ever larger, the hole gets deeper and deeper, and yet I find no more than I already knew.

Most of the information I gather about William's location comes from gossip and hearsay, so I can't even be sure of its validity. Even the goldmine I'm standing on is full of relatively useless information. For of course, Damien, his best friend, is a good friend of mine. Naturally, I've pumped him for all he knows. How could I not?

I look down at the piece of paper in my hand. It's covered with my handwriting, notes about the past. *Or is it the present?* I'm never sure exactly what I should call it. I read over what I've collected so far.

- *Traveling since March 1873.*
- *Over two years now. Where is he?*
- *William's father visits him when he stops in Manhattan.*
- *When will he be back in New York? Maybe I could take the train out and follow his father there.*
- *Sent away to keep him out of trouble? What trouble??*

I stop there to ponder that last notion. As usual, I find it intriguing. I heard the rumor from a lot of people—that he wasn't just sent away to groom him to take over the business. They told me he was, like Damien, a cad and a louse. Only *his* parents decided enough was enough and sent him off to work for a living.

I flip to the next page, the one where I transcribed a full conversation I had with Damien, the one where he told me all about his past with his best friend. I came back that night and sat, exhausted, over my writing desk, wracking my brain to make sure I didn't forget a detail. Who knows what could be useful?

I read over my notes, remembering that night as I go…

We had met up for dinner—just the two of us—before we were to go dancing later that night. We had been talking about our pasts, him sincerely, and me trying my best to give him the pertinent details without obviously lying through my teeth.

He'd told me about his childhood in England, life on a huge estate, and the plump young governess who raised him until he was twelve. After that, they moved to America and left her behind, as she was unwilling to leave her family. He'd described how, once in America, he was packed off to boarding school where he met the boy who would become his best friend, Will.

"Will? William Wood?" I'd interrupted. "Oh, yes, you had mentioned you were friends."

"That's right, my dear, none other than Mr. Elusive himself. Can you imagine, the last correspondence I got from him was almost four months ago? The old boy's got me rather put out with him."

"That's a shame. I suppose even you don't know when he's coming home then, either?" I had thought I was being clever, just throwing that in there, but he'd caught on at once.

"Oh, Lizzy, not you, too!" he'd cried in mock indignation.

"Whatever do you mean?" I'd asked him, a little too innocently.

"I mean that every girl in town is biding her time so that she can be ready to impress when Wood gets home." He had paused then, and chuckled to himself. "I just thought of something incredibly droll. I would laugh and laugh if my dear friend Willy were to come back home with a lady in tow. Then all of you hens would have to go scratch somewhere else, wouldn't you?"

Of course he had no idea just how far off he was. I merely continued, playing the part.

"Oh, ha. You do think you're funny, don't you? Well I'm merely asking out of curiosity, my dear, not out of any desire to ensnare him upon his return. So if he does come home with some stunning beauty on his arm, it will be all the same to me. Now, will you satisfy my curiosity or won't you?"

"Well, when you put it that way, my love… What do you want to know?"

"Why don't you just continue as you were, from the beginning?"

"*Fine then. From, the beginning…*

"*Will was thirteen when I met him. We had all the same courses, and soon we began goofing off together, doing homework together, playing sports together. In very short order, we progressed to skipping homework and ditching class together, usually to drink or smoke in the trees behind the dormitories. Somehow, we both managed to scrape by with passing grades. After that, we tried university, and once again we were together, both of us dropping out within six months of the other.*

"*Not that we weren't having fun, mind you. We did spend all our time there drinking and gambling. And, of course, heading away from the campus to meet gorgeous young ladies such as yourself. So you see, if we hadn't dropped out, we would have failed all of our courses and been thrown out of university, and no one wanted that. So, we came back home and did much of the same thing here.*" He had grinned ruefully, not mentioning that such activities were still his daily occupation.

"*Now, you know me, Lizzy, so I won't try to lie to you. I do love women, all of you. Short, tall, thin, or fat—I love you all. I've never claimed to be anything but the cad that I am. But here, Will was always different from me; he loved women, too, he just preferred to love them one at a time. That was one of the few things we ever really quarreled about. He was constantly trying to convince me to do the same. He's always thought that it will get me into trouble one day, and I suppose he's probably right.*

"*Still, Wood was never with a girl for long. It was inevitable that he would break it off with her, usually within three months. And whenever he broke it off, he would inevitably complain that she only ever liked him in the first place because of his money. Every time, without fail. And I could never disagree with him; it was true. They do the same to me. It just doesn't bother me like it did him. Whether they were interested in my mind, my body, or my money, well, they were in my bed, either way."*

"You're terrible!" *I'd gasped, more to scold him playfully than from any real sense of shock. I had already known him well enough then that he couldn't truly surprise me with a statement like that—not to mention that I'd heard much worse back home.*

"It's true, though," *he'd responded glibly. His face had softened and he'd flashed me his toothy grin before continuing.*

"In any case, Wood was just beginning to court Libby, and he basically stopped the relationship before it had even started. He told me that his parents were furious; they had been very hopeful of that union. When he broke it off, they told him that they had finally had enough of his carousing and that it was time to take things seriously."

"And that was it? He just left and never came back?"

"And that was it. His father was getting tired with all the traveling he was doing, trying to expand the business. He decided to send Will instead, and he hasn't returned home in more than two years. I didn't see him much after that." *Damien had paused, deep in thought.*

"Was it March? Yes, a year ago March was the last I saw of him. I met him in Manhattan and we had a few drinks. We've written a few times since then, but it hasn't been the same. He's different now. He's still my old mate Will, still enjoyable to talk to, I suppose, but he is…more serious, I guess. All this* work *is changing him; it's not healthy." Damien had pulled a disgusted face, spitting out the word "work" as if it were synonymous with something vile, like a nasty parasite or an intestinal disorder.*

"Meanwhile, I hear that the change is exactly what his parents *hoped for. They're sure that when he comes back, he'll be fully ready to take over the business. What a bore that will be.... To make it worse, they fully expect him to be ready to settle down with a nice girl from a wealthy family—someone like Libby." He'd chuckled and then leaned in confidentially, still smiling. "You can be sure he's welcome to her if he wants her."*

I'd made a disgusted face of my own and nodded in agreement. I knew what he meant; even if Damien was sleeping with her, he had no desire to be stuck with her forever.

He'd laughed at my expression and glanced down at his plate, shaking his head. His food sat cold, looking congealed and none too appetizing anymore. "Do you see what you've done to me, Lizzy? You've kept me talking so long that I've barely gotten to eat. Now we're going to be late, and it's all your fault." He'd tsked at me with mock disapproval.

"Right," I had said, falling back into my old sarcasm as I usually did with him. "Because we're always on time wherever we go." I'd rolled my eyes at him. "Just finish and we'll get there when we get there."

I smile at the memory of him finishing the rest of his dinner: With every bite, he'd chastised me good-naturedly as he'd winced and groaned excessively over the flavor and texture of his cold meal.

But one of the things that sticks out from the conversation is his own use of sarcasm, back when he'd mentioned Libby. "A nice girl from a wealthy family," he'd said, with exaggerated emphasis on "nice."

He knows as I do that Libby is *not* nice, not at all. She makes time for him because she'll settle for his money if she can't have William's. He makes time for her because she's willing to keep him physically entertained—the same as he does for Glory and who knows how many other girls. Still, he'd rather accompany me to a ball or a dinner or any other social event. I am, he says, his intellectual entertainment—the girl who keeps him busy outside of the bedroom.

But Damien is not the issue here, it's Libby. *We* know that she's horrible, but somehow the adults have no idea. William's parents are eager for him to join with her, and would be happy to have her as their daughter-in-law. I guess it's just so amazing how blind parents can be to what goes on with their children. Surely some of them should have noticed her cruelty, but, I suppose that's what happens when the act of "raising" a child is to hire a wet nurse, a nanny, and a governess, and then ship them off to boarding school. I suspect it would tend to blinker the eyes when it comes to one's offspring.

All Mr. and Mrs. Wood know is that Libby is pretty and blonde, and from a very affluent family. She will make adorable grandchildren, always act politely in public, and be a valuable connection for the Wood family. And that's all they need to know, even if she were to make their son's life miserable.

But I know better. She is a conniving little witch and she would surely make my grandfather's life a living hell for their short time together before she hangs. *Or will she? Is she the Elizabeth I am looking for?*

The lack of a paper trail doesn't make sense, though, given her father's prominence in the legal community, it does kind of seem logical that they could cover things up.

The other question is this: If she is my ancestor, did she actually commit the crime? After all, the more I learn about her, the more I doubt her innocence. She seems quite capable of almost anything, and that scares me.

◊

July goes by in a blink, sped up by my busy schedule. They say that time flies when you're having fun, and it's true.

It's a beautiful day in early August, more than a month since my arrival. It is unseasonably mild today, even with the unforgiving sun shining high above. Amos Fishbourne is holding an open-air luncheon at his parent's mansion, an all-day affair. The huge house stands with its gilt-edged French doors wide open so that her privileged guests can move freely in and out; the fair ladies may need to seek shade at any moment. It would be a shame if any were to be stricken with—*gasp*—freckles, and hats and parasols might not be enough.

The grounds are bright and green, despite the distinct lack of rain in the last week. The lawn is trimmed evenly without a weed in sight, and the trees are cleanly manicured into perfect orbs. Amazingly sculpted topiaries shaped as exotic animals dot the landscape, but the obvious pride of the place is a massive hedge maze. It sits upon the better part of two acres, and must have taken years to grow to its current splendor.

As usual, I show up on Damien's arm, today in a pale-pink-and-white walking dress—one of my favorites. It's fitted to show off my curves while the small bustle flows femininely into an almost imperceptible train. Tiny bows and intricate lace abound, along with a row of tiny white pearl buttons down the center of my back. Once again, my hair is held up with pins, piled beneath an elaborate flower-covered hat, so that only two dark tendrils curl from underneath. Following the current fashion, a stuffed bluebird perches in the midst of the fragile pink flowers on my hat, a trend I despise, but one I condone so that I might fit in.

Regardless of the dead bird on my hat, I know I look fabulous. Damien's jaw dropped when he picked me up less than half an hour ago. My friends offer compliments with sincerity in their eyes. Even the jealous looks of the not-so-friendly act as unspoken compliments, truths that callous words cannot dispel.

I am gorgeous today and not even Glory can compete.

This I know because, as we walk into the garden, the first people we lay eyes on are Libby and her ilk. Glory looks washed out in an ill-advised orange dress, one that clashes with her fiery hair. Libby, on the other hand, looks prettier today than I've seen her. The bright lighting of the midday sun makes her flaxen hair shine with hints of gold. Her expression also gives her a more pleasant look. It's soft when I first spot her, deep in conversation with a frail young man I've never seen before. But her face hardens, as do those of the other girls, when they spot me looking at them.

I've told them many times that Damien and I are just friends, but do they believe me? Of course not. They still give me the evil eye whenever they see us together.

Sometimes I worry that Damien, being the jerk that I know he can be, encourages them to think we're dating. If nothing else, Glory was completely right that first day I met her; he fully enjoys the attention that it creates. I'll never understand why he enjoys his women with that subtle tinge of jealousy.

I wonder how he can be such a sweetheart and yet such an ass at the same time.

"Damien. You need to do something about this. I am extraordinarily sick of your girlfriends shooting daggers at me. You do assure them that we're just friends?" He nods unconvincingly. I throw a quick glance their way. Even the pinched and tiny Emily is glaring at me, her dull brown eyes hot with malice.

"Are you really seeing all three of them?" I ask, exasperated.

"Of course not, darling. Just Glory and Libby. I think Emily is just trying to fit in with her betters." He flashes a cheeky grin and says, dismissively, "Anyway, Lizzy, what does it matter?" He tugs my arm. "Come on. Let's explore this hedge maze."

"What does it matter?" I repeat incredulously. "You're bedding two women at a time."

"Only two? You underestimate me, love. There may be a few other girls as well. I don't seem to recall their names at the moment."

"Exactly. And they think you're courting me as well, so they hate me all the more for it." I shake my head. "Yet somehow they still adore *you*."

"Probably the money," he says, unapologetically.

"Well, we know it's not because of your loyalty," I shoot back, exasperated. "Seriously though, they already loathe me. Why throw another log on the fire by letting them think we're together?"

"They can't help it. It's in their nature, Lizzy. I swear, I do tell them we're not an item, but they don't believe me. Would you?" His smile grows. "Besides, it's probably because you're so damn gorgeous." He gives me a wink and eyes my beautiful dress. "Honestly, if you want them to like you, you need to stop showing up like this. Just look at you!"

I don't fall into his trap. I will not be placated by his empty compliments. "I don't want them to like me," I shoot back petulantly. "In case you haven't noticed—and by the fact that you're courting them, I'm going to guess that you haven't—the three of them are evil incarnate. I simply want them to leave me alone. They always look like they're ready to sink their claws into me at any moment. I suppose I should just be happy if they stick to whispering vile things behind my back."

Rant over, I look down at myself and assess my appearance. His compliment might be worth something after all. "But maybe you're right about the dress," I concede. "You think it's too much?"

"On the contrary, I think it's just perfect. Though you know I think you're beautiful any day of the week." He wraps an arm around my shoulder, the tiny golden hairs on his wrist flashing in the sun from under his cuff.

We wander through the maze at leisure, making random turns as we go. Damien and I talk about everything and nothing; Libby and Glory are forgotten. Every now and then, he takes a flask from his pocket and downs a gulp. I ignore it; he does this sort of thing all the time. I don't even bother to roll my eyes at it anymore.

It seems that we've made our way away from the crowd. I can still hear the low hum of many voices and the beat of the jolly background music, but it's faded. I can hear occasional laughs and giggles of a few nearby revelers who are trying to find their own ways out, only to come upon a seamless wall of hedges, but none of them seem too close.

We turn a corner and abruptly find ourselves facing a dead end.

"Nice going," I tease, since Damien has been leading this trip. "I guess we'll have to backtrack. I didn't even notice when the path split." I move to leave, but he gently pulls me back. "Damien?"

"Let's just stay for a few minutes. It's nice and quiet here, away from everyone else."

"Of course. But I thought you liked the noise and attention of a group," I add, puzzled.

"Most of the time I do. But not right now." He turns to face me head-on. "Liz…" His voice is soft, almost a whisper, and his brown eyes won't let go of mine.

He begins to move in towards me, and I catch a whiff of the alcohol on his breath. The strong smell makes me recoil. *Just how much has he been drinking? And how much did he drink this morning before he picked me up?*

I'm suddenly uncomfortable, something I've never felt with Damien before, not even on that first day before I knew him. My eyes shift back and forth, from Damien to the entrance of the alcove, hoping to see a friendly figure emerge. Surely there must be something to distract him?

No such luck.

I focus my gaze back onto him, confused and pleading. This is not supposed to happen. He is supposed to be my friend. My heart pounds quickly in my chest, so similar to and yet so different from the sweet fluttering I feel at James's touch.

"Liz…" Damien says again, his gin-laden breath wafting

horridly into my face. "What I said is true. I did tell them that we're not together. But…what if… What if I don't want that to be true? What if I want to be with you, only you…?" he says, softly and seriously.

My breath catches. This is not what I want.

"No, Damien." I hold my hands up in front of me, toward his chest to stop his advance. "I like you as a friend, that's all. Nothing more. Please accept that." I draw back as far as I can, but the hedges are close. I'm up against them in just a few small steps, their prickly tips poking through the fabric of my dress and into the flesh of my back and arms.

Yet Damien follows me—and he continues to lean in, closer and closer. His hands enclose my small wrists and his eyes slowly shut as his face moves ever so gently towards mine. I'm in panic mode: my body tense, my pulse rushing. I'm unable to move an inch more. But the moment his lips touch mine, his kiss gentle and yet full of urgency and possessiveness, I snap out of it.

I barely even think as my self-defense lessons kick in, years of training taking over even as my mind fails me. I find myself holding him in a wristlock, his hand bent backwards at an extreme angle, while he whimpers from a kneeling position on the ground. His one free hand cradles his groin delicately and his face is stuffed unceremoniously into the unyielding hedge.

Oops. Seeing him in pain on the ground, I think perhaps I overdid things just a bit. I let go of him and back away, still pumped with adrenaline.

Free of my grasp, he tries to straighten out, managing instead only to fall over on his side, his head still partially in the hedge. He looks at me wide-eyed. "What the hell was that?!"

His incredulous tone overcomes my pity, and I answer him in a fury. "What the hell was *that*? What the hell did you think you were doing, kissing me?! Here I am, thinking that you're one of the best friends I have, and you go and do something like that! I told you 'no' and I meant it!"

"Ow..." He groans and shakes his head, exposing the angry red scratches that the branches left on his face, surely matching those along the backs of my arms. "I'm sorry." He hisses in pain as he attempts to stand. "I guess I thought... I hoped... You were...being coy? I just—"

I interrupt him. "Coy?" I lash out at him, still furious, slapping away the hand that reaches up for assistance. "Have you ever known me to be coy, Damien?" I ask scathingly. "What the hell were you thinking!? Where I come from, no means no."

An amused voice rings out behind me. "Where you come from, apparently, young ladies also engage in wrestling like savages." I'd recognize Glory's dulcet voice anywhere.

I groan. How long have we had an audience? I turn around to see Glory, Libby, Emily, and Angelica standing in the only entrance to our little dead end. They look triumphant. Well, the first three do, anyway. They must have followed us in. Still others, hearing the tumult, arrive behind them to find out what is so interesting. Even as I watch, a small crowd starts to gather. *Lovely.*

"Well, isn't it obvious? She was raised by wolves," chimes in Emily, always the joiner.

"I only wonder," begins Libby, "if her father willingly married an ape or if the beast had to thrash him mercilessly until he submitted to the union." She smirks.

That simpering expression on her face is insufferable, and her comment about my mother sends me into a blind rage. I hear a guttural snarl and a loud crack, followed by a cry and a collective gasp. I look around to see what happened, confused by my loss of control. Many shocked faces stare my way. I'm still disoriented and it takes me a moment to realize that I am the source of the sounds.

Libby is a few steps away from me, on the ground, being comforted by her friends. Emily and Glory glare at me with utter loathing and something else, something new... Yes, that's it: fear. Libby's hand is covering her eye and nose, marking the spot that my fist must have struck. I don't remember moving, but I'm five feet from where I stood just a moment ago, and the knuckles on my right hand are sore and red.

I can feel the angry tears coming on; this whole day has been too much. First Damien and now this! I hold the tears at bay; I want to get out of here with my dignity intact. I keep my chin up high and walk slowly at Libby. She flinches back as best she can, frightened. The dark look I give her now should terrify her.

"My mother is dead," I say in a low voice, cold like ice. "I loved her very much, and if you *ever* say another word about her, Libby Hunt, so help me..." I'm so angry that I can't finish my sentence. Besides, what punishment could possibly be fitting enough for this horrible wretch? The hangman's noose is likely on its way; my retribution is hardly needed. Instead, I merely let out an angry exhale and begin to stalk through the ever-growing throng, barging through, even as people try to clear a path.

My last fleeting look back at the scene finds Libby and friends still glaring at me with undisguised hatred, the air thick with their impotent fury. Damien glances back with a wounded look, still gently cupping his injured groin. Our audience ranges from the curious to the incredulous; the whispers move rapidly so that soon everyone knows what went on here.

Interestingly, the reactions aren't all bad. Quite a few young ladies are smirking or even giggling into their gloves, happy to see the mighty fallen. Even Angelica can't hold back a small smile at seeing Libby get her due.

At the moment, though, I'm too angry to really care. It takes only a few seconds for me to break through the crowd piling up in the corridors of the maze, though it certainly feels like longer with their unwavering eyes upon me.

I wander through the maze without pause or care, somehow getting lost only once on my way out. No one gets in my way. Even those who missed the proceedings cannot miss the look on my face, and they quickly let me pass.

Once freed from the high, leafy walls, I walk purposefully to the house and through it, straight out the front door without even one word to my host in apology.

No one tries to stop me. From there, I walk the two and a half miles all the way home without looking back.

Chapter Thirteen

The walk back to the inn clears my head and the light summer breeze revives my senses.

For the rest of the day, and then through an almost sleepless night, I can think of only two things. First, I am so upset and angry that Damien would do this to me. I thought he was my friend. Second, I contemplate the damage I've probably done by losing my temper. Surely everyone will find out about my outburst, and it's likely that many parents will forbid their children from associating with me, even if some of those children aren't bothered by it.

After all, Libby is the epitome of a polite society lady, isn't she? And Damien may be a cad, but he is a rich cad, one of this town's most eligible bachelors. Me? I'm just a newcomer, now also known as a scandalous and disgraceful savage who's managed to assault them both.

Sleep finally comes and calms me, but doesn't resolve anything. How will I find Elizabeth Wood now, when I'm an outcast from her society?

I try not to let my troubles affect my mood when I make my

morning visit to the farm. I avoid bringing up the events of the previous day; I don't even want to think about the predicament my explosive temper has put me into, nor my sadness and anger at losing a friend.

Perhaps I avoid the subject for another reason as well. James did warn me about Damien, after all. I ignored his entreaties not to trust him and look what has happened. Might James not throw those four dreaded words at me? *I told you so...*

I try to be my usual self, but he notices, of course. He also picks up on the redness and swelling of my hand, left over from the slightly painful, if satisfying impact against Libby's face. But he doesn't push me when I tell him I'd rather not talk about it, nor does he question me when I decide to stay late today.

Why shouldn't I stay late? No one will visit me anyway.

But I'm wrong; I do have visitors. I'm taken aback when I return home to find that while I was gone, I was inundated with calling cards from quite a few people. There is one card that is conspicuously absent: Damien's, which is usually a given. No surprise there. Fine. I'm not ready to face him anyway.

I sigh. *I guess I won't be getting a nap today.*

I enter my room and pull Lanie from her embroidery, a beautiful floral pattern. She helps me change out of my dingy work dress into one of my walking dresses, a pale green frock that perfectly matches the color—though not the depth—of James's light eyes.

I visit all over town, a quarter hour at a time, exactly as is proper, only to find that my tussle with Libby has turned me into something of a celebrity. Oh, some of the older folks disapprove, as I thought they would, politely but undeniably expelling me from the impressionable presence of their star-struck daughters.

However, several of them have actually listened to their daughters and they know the anguish Libby has put them through. They've dealt with their girls coming home in tears, flinging themselves upon them, searching for the respect they've been denied. They've lived through the times that those same girls, ecstatic at their luck, go on and on about the glorious attentions Damien has bestowed on them, only to see their pain when he is seen lavishing that same attention on others. So even though they perhaps disapprove of the actions I took, many seem to approve of the results.

My biggest supporters by far are Aurelia and her mother. I sit in their parlor, entranced by the artwork on the walls and the stories the images tell of strong, powerful women. Amazons and Valkyries appear in heated battle against cruel male oppressors. The three Graces, windblown and beautiful, sit above the world, inspiring all who look at them. The three Furies, as hideous as their counterparts are lovely, take vile retribution on a group of screaming men in another painting. Even Odysseus' Sirens make an appearance on the walls of the sitting room, singing sweetly from their rocky enclave as a ship is dashed upon the boulders, her pitiful crew dead and drowning in the swirling waters below.

I'm curious as to why Mrs. Goodwin's ideals of feminism include not merely bringing women up into equality, but rather lowering men down into the vacated lower class of human. When I ask, she's more than happy to tell me her story, though poor Aurelia gives me a look, having already warned me not to get her mother started on the subject.

"My bastard of a former husband," her mother tells me almost cheerfully, "was a very strict man with very old-fashioned notions about women." I am horrified as she goes on to tell me how he used to hit her so hard that he almost killed her on multiple occasions and caused her to miscarry two pregnancies. I listen in shock and horror until she finishes, "I certainly do not miss him now that he is dead, my dear."

He died somewhat suspiciously about five years into their marriage. She was suspected, of course, but no evidence ever turned up and no charges were ever filed. She was apparently not the only one who disliked him, because no one seemed to miss him enough to bother.

After his death, she inherited his fortune and moved away with it, from their marital home in Manhattan to Thorne Hill, a much quieter town in which to give birth to her only living child, Aurelia. That's when she decided to stand up for herself and others like her, leading demonstrations for women's rights and counseling abused women.

Sadly though, not many of the high-society women appreciate what she does. Her work with the lower classes is viewed as something to look down on instead of something to respect. So she is just as impressed with me as Aurelia is, and she laughs out loud when I recount what I did to Damien. Then she applauds mightily when I tell her about the incident with Libby.

"Sweetheart, that girl has deserved a punch to the face for years now. She gives all women a bad name. Thank you."

And while she's the only mother to thank me, she's certainly not the only person. No, the hatred towards Libby goes deep in many of these girls, so long her victims. She has been a thorn in most of their sides for far too long, and their mothers certainly don't mind seeing her out of the way for a while. I've managed to bring her low, and they can appreciate that, if nothing else.

◊

The week goes by more slowly than usual. Without Damien by my side, my evenings feel subdued, even boring. My mornings with James have always been the highlight of my day, but they become even more so now.

It turns out that without Damien's dry wit and saucy remarks, an evening can go on forever. No one, not even Aurelia, (who spends a lot of time with me, but leaves often enough when her dance card calls for it) and certainly not Angelica (who, free of her friends, is much more pleasant), nor any of the young men (who, after a few slow starts manage to overcome their new-found fear of me and endeavor to engage me in a conversation or a dance) can keep me as occupied as Damien can.

It's the end of that long week, a Saturday afternoon, when I hear a knock at the door and Lanie answers, as usual. Expecting it to be the bellman with a calling card, I'm taken by surprise when I discover it's Damien. I stand up from my chair and Lanie backs away and goes to her room, instinctively realizing that I'll want privacy now.

Damien looks completely disheveled, as though he hasn't bothered to wash himself or change his clothing in days. Nor has he bothered with his customary top hat; his blonde hair, in need of a cut, curls wildly around his ears. His face is covered with stubble that's darker than his hair. He probably hasn't shaved all week.

Most surprising however, is the look in his chocolaty brown eyes. They are sad and desperate, but also hard. I've never seen him looking like this before. I abruptly realize what is causing the difference. For the first time I've ever seen, Damien is stone-cold sober.

His first act upon seeing me is to fall to his knees and beg for forgiveness.

"Lizzy, I am so, so sorry. I was a fool. I was a stupid drunkard who abused his relationship with his magnificent best friend. And you *are* my best friend. At least you were before I screwed up so piteously. Wood may have held that title once upon a time, but what is he to me now? He never even writes, but *you* are here. And I hope to God that I haven't lost you, too.

"You told me that friendship was all you wanted, but I'm such a fool that I could not accept it. I'm so arrogant that somehow I thought you could want me even after all of my hideous indiscretions. But I can accept it now. If being your friend is the only way to have you in my life, then friends we shall be. That is, of course, you can find it in your absolutely glorious heart to forgive me for being such an insufferable beast."

I stare down at him, not coldly, but giving nothing away yet. I came to terms with his drunken mistake days ago, during yet another evening of wishing for his company.

I suppose I've known for a while that he is *my* best friend here, too, though it took a week without him to realize how much his company really means to me.

After all, I spent that week in the presence of my other friends, people whose companionship I can enjoy while he is at my side; but honestly, I was often bored out of my mind without him. Besides one other true friend, Aurelia, who is lovely but could not be with me all the time, the girls and I talked of boys and clothing; the young men flirted and posed for me like peacocks. None of them have the depth that he does, the spark of life that makes him irresistible. Even dear Aurelia doesn't have that. None of the others know me as he does, and what do I know of them? I have spent weeks with them, talked and danced with them at endless balls and dinner parties, yet I know very little of any of them.

But still, as James once warned me, I should not trust him, not fully. I eye him warily. "You promise? Just friends?"

"Anything you want, Lizzy! Anything at all!" When I begin to look as if I might relent, he gives one of his huge grins. "After spending so much time in your delightful company, I must say that I'm bored to tears by these other ladies. They can't hold a candle to you, darling!" He winks outrageously, getting some of his old cheek back. I can't help but laugh at him, especially since he literally just voiced my own sentiments. "How can I spend another dreadfully dull evening without you?" His eyes, no longer desperate, widen greatly, taking on the longing look of a puppy.

"You silly fool!" I say, still laughing. "Yes, I forgive you. But honestly, don't you have any other friends? Gentlemen friends, perhaps? Surely not *everyone* bores you senseless?"

Standing up and brushing off his pants, he looks taken aback, as if the answer to my question is incredibly obvious. "Of course, love. But all we do is drink, play cards, and bet on horses. And then, of course, chase after girls. I've done plenty of the former and as for the latter, it's really so much easier just to skip that step and go straight for more interesting company to begin with." He smiles.

"Besides, it really hasn't been the same since Wood left," he says thoughtfully. "Sure we would drink and carouse, as you well know, but it was more than that. God, what conversations we had! It is lovely to have *someone* to converse intelligently with, hence my friendship with you, my dear. Most of my companions wouldn't know a witty conversation if it came up and slapped him across the face."

He pauses, thinking. Weighing out what he's about to say. "Come to think of it, the two of you would probably get on quite well. You share a lot of opinions—on my love life, for example. I told you he never did understand why I can't settle down with just one woman. Remind me to introduce you when he finally comes home." Damien looks at the ground and then adds softly, "Heaven knows he deserves a chance to meet someone better than Libby."

"I'm sure he's a wonderful man, but I doubt I'd be interested," I hedge. For obvious reasons, I refrain from telling Damien exactly why I'm so uninterested. He doesn't need to know that William is my ancestor. Elizabeth Wood may share my name, but I am not *that* Elizabeth.

"I still can't believe those two were ever an item," I add, shaking my head in disbelief.

"Only for a short while, darling, though if you recall, Wood's parents still think it's a great match. But I think you'll find that Libby is getting very impatient waiting for him. If I'm not mistaken, she seems to be seriously trying to trap me now, and everyone knows I'm only second best. Well, when it comes to monetary assets anyway." He chuckles. "As though that will ever happen. You and I both know that I'm not the marrying type."

"That's never stopped you from sampling the wares, though, has it?" I tease.

"And *that*, right there, is why I was a fool to think you would ever want to be with me. You know me too well, I think."

"Luckily for you it doesn't mean that I don't love you anyway. But as my best friend and nothing more." I stand on my tiptoes and kiss his scruffy cheek.

He smiles wistfully at me. "Of course, Lizzy." He perks up. "By the way, I almost forgot in all the hubbub to congratulate you."

"Congratulate me?" My eyebrows crinkle in confusion. "Whatever for?"

"For the marvelous job you did on Libby, of course. I may have been impaired by my pitiable injuries—"

"Fully deserved..."

"Indeed." He winces. "Fully deserved, but still very unfortunate injuries, but I did manage to see your little bout of fisticuffs. A lovely punch, there, I must say, as well as I've ever done. Believe me, she has got one stunning black eye. Though by now it's surely an exquisite shade of yellow and green."

He turns serious. "I know I deserved what I got, and Libby... she deserved it, too. That was just cruel what she said." He hesitates. "I didn't know about your mother. When did it happen?"

"Ten years ago," I answer softly. "I was eight. She had cancer. She just... She got sick one day. She started getting headaches, wasn't very hungry anymore." I sigh sadly. "They were things that seemed minor at first. But we found out that it wasn't minor at all. She had a tumor in her brain. Her symptoms got worse and worse. And then she was gone, just a few short months later. I still miss her every day."

For once, Damien is completely solemn. "I'm sorry. No one should have to go through that." He offers his arms for a hug and I accept.

"Thank you," I acknowledge sincerely. I give him another kiss on his cheek. "Now, enough of this sadness. What should we do this evening?" I stop to look him up and down, wrinkling my nose. "After you get cleaned up, of course. What on earth have you done to yourself? You look awful!"

Chapter Fourteen

Sunday morning, the day after Damien's apology, I decide to tell James about what happened in the hedge maze. I know now the real reason why I'd kept silent: I'd been hoping to stay friends with Damien and I didn't want James to think too badly of him.

Things being patched up between us, I decide that it should be alright to let it come out now. I don't like keeping secrets.

"Gracen did what?!?" he explodes.

I was wrong.

"He was drunk," I explain patiently. "He tried to kiss me."

"I'll kill him! Where is he?" His green eyes flash dangerously, hard like the gemstones they so resemble. I've never known him to lose his temper easily, but he's furious. I try to jolt him out of it.

"James! That is enough! He's apologized and it will never happen again. He promised."

"That's right, it will never happen again! And I don't care if he sang his apology from the rooftop of the theater! He can't be trusted. Didn't I tell you that?" James is so livid that his whole body is shaking. "I'll punch him in that pretty-boy face of his, see how he likes that. I promise you that he will regret touching you against your will."

"James. Calm down, please," I placate. "Trust me. He already regrets it, I assure you."

He closes his eyes and pinches the bridge of his nose, taking a few deep breaths before looking at me. At least he is actively trying to control himself now. "How can you be so calm?"

"Listen to me. It happened more than a week ago. He made a mistake and I have forgiven him, and so should you. Or at least stop worrying about it. He is still my friend, and I will be very cross with you if you try to hurt him any more than I already have." I smirk, remembering him cowering in the maze. "Believe me—I did quite enough damage to him already."

He gives me a small smile from hearing that. "Really?" He narrows his eyes, looking doubtful. "And what damage could you possibly have done?" he asks teasingly, running his eyes up and down my small frame with obvious skepticism.

I smile in relief that his temper has cooled. "Well, now that you've calmed down, I can show you if you'd like."

He laughs. "You really hurt him?" he asks disbelievingly.

"In more ways than one. Almost everyone saw it happen, or at least saw the aftermath. He'll never live it down." I flash him a grin.

"Well then, I have got to see this."

"Fine. Come here, I'll need your help to demonstrate." I gesture for him to come over, and he stands in front of me. I can feel the heat pouring off of his body. "Closer. Hold onto my wrists. Gently."

Suddenly it gets very difficult for me to concentrate. James eases in closer to me and my body goes into overdrive reacting to his touch. Goosebumps rise on my arms and I feel charged with electricity.

"Like this?" he asks softly. He also looks strained. His eyes have changed, no longer rock-like but smoldering as if they were made of green fire. They search deeply into my own eyes.

"Yes," I breathe. "That's perfect."

Still speaking softly he asks, "Now what?"

Flustered, I say, "I... Well... This should be authentic, you know, for the purposes of the demonstration. So... You should lean in and...kiss me."

Those pale green eyes hold mine for a beat longer and I can feel his breath on my face, fresh like the mint leaves he chews on the same way I used to chew gum. My heart beats erratically, coming to a fever-pitch as his face comes closer still, his eyes closing automatically. It's strange—the whole thing is so similar to and yet so different from my experience with Damien last week.

After what seems like an eternity, his lips finally touch mine. I vaguely remember that I'm supposed to be doing *something*, but in this moment it escapes me. All I can concentrate on is him. On his firm lips against mine. On his scent—not just the mint of his breath but the smell of *him*—the musky scent of his sweat, the clean smell of freshly mown hay, the not unpleasant odor of the horses and cows he's been around all day. I can hear his breathing and feel his heartbeat—fast and wild like mine— through my hands that reach unconsciously to feel his strong chest through his rough muslin shirt, even as his hands travel from my wrists up my arms, moving to my back, and shiver with the sensation of electricity that his touch trails along my skin.

Finally, we pull apart, and James cups my cheek gently in his hand, stroking my jaw with his thumb. He looks into my eyes and says very seriously, "Well, if that's what you did to Gracen, then I guess you really showed him." He smiles a wicked smile, and runs his hands back down to my wrists, ever-so-lightly touching the length of my arms on the way down and driving me wild.

I laugh though, and let him lean in to kiss me again. But this time, I keep my wits about me enough to remember what to do. His eyes, closed again for the kiss, fly open in shock as my hands flip around and grab him firmly back. I raise my eyebrows at him and shoot back my own wicked smile before flipping him around into the same wristlock I used on Damien.

Luckily for him, before dropping him, I modify the groin strike, coming close—but stopping just short of touching the fabric of his trousers.

He's taken completely by surprise, one moment standing and the next forced to his knees. He'd had no reason to suspect that someone of my size and strength could bring him down. I see him grimace in pain and I quickly let up and drop his wrist.

"Now *that* is what I did to Damien. Only he got the full experience with no sugar coating. My knee did *not* stop so early for him." I smirk while James winces in empathy, still wide eyed.

"Where did you even learn that?"

"Back home. My father always said that a girl should know how to protect herself from unwanted attention. He made sure I learned self-defense."

He looks at me in awe. "You are amazing, Elizabeth Franklyn."

"Why thank you, James Percival. I know." I smile innocently.

He laughs. "And so modest, too."

We get back to work. Our dispute—and our subsequent embrace—is lost in the comfort of our daily routine. But I can't forget it; it doesn't matter how long we leave it unspoken. I don't know how he can ignore the electricity that still tingles between us each time we get near each other, but he doesn't bring it up again and I can't either. *What if it was a mistake for him? Does he regret it?*

By the time he drops me off with a light kiss to my hand, as he always does, I'm beginning to think that I imagined the whole thing.

I wake up from my latest dream, disoriented, hot, and excited. This dream was different than the new normal for me, which is a wild rush of images from the past and future. I didn't see the familiar faces of people from this time and a time that's more than a century away from me, images of the places that I've been, both here and there. Nor was it my long-running nightmare, the horrific dream where I watch Damien being brutally murdered in a hundred different ways by a woman who must be my own ancestor, her face eerily similar to my own.

No, on this night, for the first time since meeting him in person, James has appeared in my dreams as the lone subject. He'd been absent, I suppose, since his living self more than makes up for his dream presence. But this was different... I had always yearned for him before, but I only saw imperfect glimpses of a perfect face. I didn't know then who he was or if he truly existed at all. I would wake up filled with a mixture of longing and curiosity; I'd wonder who he was and why he appeared to me so often.

This time, though, the dream was vivid and intense. I could see him fully and look upon him, not merely in brief flashes. I could feel everything as if it were real: his bare chest pressed against me, his hands on my body; his mouth pressed firmly against my lips, my face, my throat. I could taste him and smell him and feel his very essence. Those brilliant eyes stood out unlike I'd ever seen them before in dreams or in reality. They were blazing and smoldering, backlit with a green fire that glowed behind them, and they burned into mine with the heat of a thousand suns.

Now I lay awake, gasping for air and wanting more. Never have I been so disappointed to open my eyes before. Feelings I have never felt so strongly in my life had surged through my body at his imagined touch. Without it, I feel an overwhelming sense of loss. Everything that just happened was only in my mind, but it had felt so real that, for a time, I truly thought it was.

And foolishly, I want so badly for it to be real that tears slide silently down my cheeks as I slowly fall back to sleep.

I wake again, and this time it's morning. Everything about last night's dream stays with me, all of the excitement and heat, all of the sorrow and loss. The strong desire I felt—and still feel—for it to be real has brought new urgency to a topic I should have been thinking of all along: my future here in the past.

Rationally, I know that the best course is to stay far away from James, as I should have from the start. Without being distracted by him, I could concentrate fully on finding Elizabeth Wood. I've been dawdling, and I know it. Yes, I'm searching slowly, but I know in my heart that I'm not looking as hard as I could be. As I should be. I've become too happy and comfortable in my life here.

If I use all my contacts and leads, if I leave James alone, and instead concentrate solely on my work, I should be able to make some real progress. And with my mind occupied only on my task, I should have no problem finishing my sleuthing by next June. It's what I should have decided on from the beginning.

The problem is that I have no idea what I'll do without him. I am completely and utterly in love with James Percival. I've known that since my first day here, even if it took longer to admit it. I can't just leave him alone and go about my research, pretending that he means nothing to me—not when he means everything.

How do I reconcile that with the fact that I need to finish my research and go back home where I belong? I can't stay here and marry the man I love—like a normal girl. I'm a time traveler from the future; I am anything but normal. I eventually need to go back home.

Chapter Fifteen

I promise myself that I'll get back to work and find a way to leave James alone.

Soon. But not quite yet.

In the meantime, I do my best to prolong and enjoy every moment we spend together.

The perfect opportunity for that comes up when James arrives one Sunday morning with two horses, the pretty chestnut mare with the glossy coat, and a large Appaloosa, his shoulder higher than the top of my head. The mare is even equipped with a sidesaddle that he must have recently acquired. So used to sharing a mount, I'm confused. *Is there some reason he doesn't want to ride with me today?*

But the confusion is quickly cleared up.

"Good morning, Liz," he says in his friendly, mild voice. "I have a surprise for you today."

I smile brightly in childish delight, quickly forgetting as usual that I ever made such a stupid resolution as to stop seeing him.

"A surprise?" I answer excitedly. "What is it?"

"If I told you, it wouldn't be a surprise," he admonishes, as though it were obvious. Which, of course, it is.

"Fine," I harrumph, feigning annoyance. "But will you give me a hint?" I look up sweetly and bat my eyelashes in a pleading manner.

He boosts me up onto the mare and remounts his steed. I feel naked without his strong body behind mine, unstable even, though it's been only a few months since I've ridden true sidesaddle alone.

"I suppose I could do that," he acquiesces. "Here it is: We are not needed at the farm today."

"We're not? So where are we going?"

He just smiles mysteriously, a gleam in his eye. "This way!" And off he rides across the meadow towards the brook, looking back to make sure I'm following behind.

We ride east for a while, then south. As always, we travel the well-worn paths and trails through the forest and fields, instead of the main cobblestone streets through town. The one stretch of main road we take goes over a wide wooden bridge across a flowing river, larger than the babbling brooks and tiny streams that the horses wade through. We pause often to rehydrate them, since even a minimal effort under the ever-rising mid-August sun brings glistening sweat to their hides.

We take our time, not pushing the horses and happy to let them drink their fill. It's enough to spend time together riding slowly side by side, taking in the forest scenery and lulled by the rocking motion of my mount's walk.

Nearly two hours pass before we arrive at our destination: a narrow, rocky point that juts off the shore into Long Island Sound, hooking back towards the mainland as it goes. The white foam and brown surf washing up on the rocks gives way to deep blue farther out. It makes my heart soar to see it, my old friend, the sea.

This is the first time I've seen the ocean since I've come to the past. Living so close to the shore, I usually spent half of my summer vacation at the beach. As I grew up, my time at the beach was spent less and less on sand castles and jumping in the waves and more on sunbathing with my nose deep in a book, always ready to look up should one of my friends spot a cute boy from school.

But I've been too busy this summer to think of the beach, too far away from its calming sounds and familiar smells, even though I'm almost the same distance away from it as I was before. But things seem a lot farther away when they have to be reached by foot, horseback, or carriage.

We take the horses up the middle of the point, keeping to the areas where vegetation clings so the animals have plenty of traction. We eventually come to a secluded spot—as if any spot in this area could be more secluded than another—on the end of the point, a narrow strip of rocky beach that overlooks a huge yellow hotel across the waves. There is a small patch of scraggly-looking trees that we tie the horses to. They relax in the dappled shade.

"Where are we?" I ask in awe as he helps me down.

"This jut of land is called 'Elizabeth's Hook.' I thought you might appreciate it."

I should have recognized Thorne Hill Point, once called Elizabeth's Hook, so named for the woman who once owned the land. We used to come out here when I was a child, before Mom died and Dad stopped taking us places. I would sit and watch the boats go by for hours. I could just stare across the water at the fishing boats, speedboats, sailboats, and yachts, sneaking peeks into the lives of the people onboard.

Sometimes my dad and I would walk along the rocky shore and he'd point out all of the different creatures in the tide pools. Tiny periwinkles clung to those dark rocks with suction so strong that the breaking waves couldn't move them. Hermit crabs scuttled around, pulling into their rented shells when I would reach my chubby little hand in to pick them up, fascinated by their tiny claws. Alex was young then, little more than an infant, and he would play in the sand just at the edge of the surf, too afraid to toddle in any farther. Mom, of course, would keep vigilant watch over us all.

In my childhood, the beautiful yellow hotel along the sea is gone, to be replaced by newer, more modern hotels and massive seaside mansions. Everyone wants a piece of ocean-front property in the future.

I remember that once we even stayed at one of those fancy waterfront hotels, and not for any particular reason. Some of the best things were the ones we did just because. I was seven; Alex was four. It was a Saturday. My mom wanted to go to the beach—not that tiny stretch of pebbles that was our spot on the Point, but to a real sugar-sand beach. We had our choice of public beaches and private, as members of the yacht club through my grandparents, but Mom wanted one particular stretch of sand and she'd have no other. So we climbed into the gas-guzzling SUV we'd had at the time, and went to that beautiful strip of sand and shells in front of the hotel.

We parked in the hotel lot and climbed the barrier. Mom

and Dad were over with Alex and I was climbing it myself when the guard stopped us to tell us it was a private beach, for the hotel guests only.

Having a seven-year-old's sense of proportion, I thought for sure that we were going to be arrested on the spot. But Mom and Dad just looked at each other and shrugged. We proceeded to head back over the barrier to the hotel, where they checked us in for the next two nights. We enjoyed that sandy beach for three days, and the plush comfort of the hotel at night.

But all that was before my mom died and we stopped going on family outings.

I sigh softly, thinking about how I'd love to be able to tell James my family stories like this. But I didn't exactly plan ahead for moments like this one, with altered anecdotes ready simply for fun and amusement rather than meant to wheedle out certain facts. I'd surely end up telling him something that would be impossible to explain, or worse, give me away as the liar I am.

No, instead I smile and pretend I know nothing of the place, which is, of course, as much of a lie as if I'd told him my story.

"Elizabeth's Hook? Really?" My voice sounds false to me, as it always does when I have to pretend. James doesn't seem to notice, as he usually doesn't. I still wonder if he doesn't see right through me, but he's never once mentioned anything about it.

"Yes, really." He says indulgently, no hint that he's heard the change in my voice. "It's named for one of the founders of Thorne Hill. This place once belonged to her."

"It's beautiful, James. I love it. Thank you for bringing me here."

"You're very welcome." Without seeming to think, he puts his strong arm up over my shoulder. I lean into his warm body, relishing the comfort and protection he offers, and glad that he forgives me my small lies. We stand like this for a while, taking in our surroundings.

The small, muddy waves break weakly on our pebbly beach. Figures across the water stir on the hotel's sandy shore. Sunbathers maybe, worshipping that warm golden orb. Even from here, where the people look no larger than colorful bugs playing on the beach, I can make out the ladies in their huge bathing gear, covered almost from head to toe. So different from the teeny bikinis I wore in my time. No one enters the water yet, so early in the day, but huge bathing machines sit in waiting behind the beachgoers in a long row.

I'm quite eager actually, to see one of those silly things in action. They are nothing more than large, wheeled, wooden boxes, but women enter them to strip down a bit more before entering the water. Big burly men, employed by the hotel, will roll them into the waves. The ladies will climb out of the bathing machines and into the sea, hoping to remain out of sight while so scandalously underclad. It is such an utterly Victorian tradition, ridiculous and extravagant in every way.

Closer to us, boats large and small can be seen on the murky New England waters. At this hour, many are probably fishermen, though I think I spot a few enthusiasts, just out to enjoy the beauty and tranquility of the sea.

I want to stay in this moment forever, but too soon James pulls away from me. I don't want to let him go, but I can just about convince myself that this won't be the last time yet.

He makes his way back to the horses and reveals something that makes me realize that I haven't eaten breakfast yet—a picnic basket. He pulls a light blanket from a saddlebag and we set up on a driftwood log overlooking the water. Quicker than any Boy Scout I've ever met, he starts a perfect fire and makes us a pot of tea to go with our breakfast. The meal itself consists of his own hearty bread and creamy, flavorful cheese to spread, and a bowl of fresh, tart blueberries.

I can hardly believe that it's been less than two months since we've met. But in that time, we've spent every day together, getting to know each other, teasing and serious, talking and silent. So today when we eat our meal in silence, it's nothing like that first time. The stillness is not painful and awkward, but calm and peaceful.

After we eat, we sit side by side, content to listen to the sounds of the surf and the seabirds, instead of each other, in this almost sacred spot. Here, somehow, our usual chatter seems as if it would be rude and out of place. Neither of us feels the need to check and see.

I lean once more into the crook of his shoulder, and he immediately responds by placing his arm back around me. I fit into this spot as if it had been made especially for me, but it's certainly more than that which pulls me over and over again into his embrace. If only I could spend the rest of my life never moving from his side.

But of course that's impossible. Soon I'll spend my last minutes snuggled into his warm shoulder. I nestle in all the tighter now for it. We spend hours just like this, watching, listening, just as I used to do as a child. The boats go by and the people across the way duck and play on the beach and in the waves. We eat lunch as we did breakfast, more bread and cheese on our driftwood log.

After lunch I feel hot and languid and I make a split decision to follow the examples of the sunbathers on the sandy hotel beach, who have finally made use of their absurd machines. I pull out of his warm hold and speak to him in the hushed tones this day seems to call for.

"I want to go swimming," I say.

"In your clothes?" he asks, confused. "You haven't got a bathing outfit, have you?"

"No. But I'm so hot. I won't even make it back to the inn without something to wake me up. The water looks so cool and inviting; it ought to do the trick." I turn my back on him, facing the hardy dune grass. "Will you unbutton me?"

I hear and feel nothing but his breath, slightly faster than before. I turn my head back around and find his jade eyes wide with…fear? Surprise? I'm not sure.

"Well?" I say. "Will you help me or won't you? It will be difficult to unbutton myself."

He gulps and then nods slowly, his eyes never narrowing or leaving mine. Taking this as a yes, I twist back around. I feel his fingers, very tentatively, push a few loose hairs off of my neck before slowly and gently unhooking the first button. Even in the midday heat, his touch causes goose bumps to erupt all over my body and a shiver to run down my spine.

His hands work slowly, uncertainly. I don't try to rush him.

When the last button is unhooked I stand up and let the dress fall to the ground. James hurriedly averts his eyes, even though I'm still fully covered by an excessive amount of underclothing. I'm unsure for a moment of how I should swim, but his aversion to my body helps me to make my decision. Though it helps to think of how much I loathe getting dressed over wet clothing. I reach behind me to untie my ruffled petticoat from around my waist.

"Wh-what are you doing?" he stammers, peeking quickly at me and away again just as fast.

"I'm getting undressed, silly," I answer primly. "Since you obviously won't help me any further."

The petticoat slides down, revealing the next layer. James sees nothing of it.

I struggle with the ties of my corset next, but as I expected, I get no more help from him. His eyes stay firmly on the distant shore and don't stray again, and for once his cheeks are the ones flaming, not mine.

When I finally finish, the corset gets thrown unceremoniously on top of my petticoat, and the rest of my underclothing soon follows. He knows nothing of this, still staring stubbornly into the distance.

I take my time on the pebbly shore, picking my way through washed-up shells and sharp stones. I'd prefer not to fall onto the rocks, especially without the protection of my clothing.

I make it safely to the surf, then walk, and finally swim out to where it's deep enough to tread water, so that the small dark swells cover my bare skin. I feel free in the cool water, no longer constricted by the calm and quiet feelings so prevalent on the shore.

"I'm in!" I call loudly to James. I don't feel the need for soft voices in here. He is now looking resolutely at the dunes, having rotated as I made my way into his view. "You can look now!"

He says nothing, but eventually turns to face the water again, his cheeks still bright red. I laugh at this and his face takes on a wounded expression which causes me to laugh all the harder.

Gaining my composure, I call up to him again. "Please don't be mad at me! The water feels so refreshing. Why don't you join me?"

"Are you crazy?" he answers. "I can't go in with you! You're not wearing…" he drifts off, unsure of my attire since he didn't see me undress. He glances over at the pile of my clothing.

"Anything!" I supply helpfully. "I'm not wearing anything at all."

His blush returns, so crimson that I imagine that half the blood in his body has been rerouted to his face to cause the effect. Then I blush myself, as an errant thought crosses my brain, regarding where the rest of his blood might be headed to.

I laugh, embarrassed, and swim awhile in the cool water, which helps me clear my mind. I close my eyes and relax while enjoying the bobbing motion of the light surf while I float. I let myself drift slowly with the waves, opening my eyes only occasionally to get my bearings and make sure I haven't floated too far from shore. It must be at least fifteen minutes before I look back at our little picnic spot. James is still standing by the log, staring obstinately away, his back to me. I can't help myself; his stubborn propriety is so cute that I start laughing again.

Feeling thoroughly refreshed, I start swimming into shore. "I'm about to get out now!" I call teasingly, as if he might accidentally see me somehow. I get my feet under me and begin walking in. I stumble suddenly as something sharp pierces the bottom of my right foot. I cry out and fall to my knees, getting a face full of water in the process. I cough to clear the salty brine from my mouth and nose.

Before I catch my breath, James is standing hip-deep in the water beside me, helping me stand.

"Are you alright?"

I nod, but wince as I put weight onto my foot. "Ouch." I quickly stand on my other foot instead. He moves to my right side and hugs me to him, holding my weight so that my foot doesn't have to. He is suddenly oblivious to my state of undress, but it has become just as suddenly very obvious to me, despite the pain I'm in.

When I still have trouble walking, especially once we're out of the water, he scoops me up in his arms. My foot drips bright-red blood onto the gray and brown stones. "Just great," I moan when I see it, wincing again.

"Are you sure you're alright, Lizzy?" He plants a gentle kiss on my wet forehead. "Your foot is bleeding steadily. What on earth did you step on?" I just shrug.

When we get to our log, he sets me down on the picnic blanket. A small red spot immediately forms on the cloth beneath my foot. Despite his outward calm, he must still be uncomfortable with my nudity, because without even seeming to think, he strips off his own shirt and wraps it around me.

I am obviously not hurt too badly. It takes me a moment to pull the shirt close around my body because I am too busy drinking in his. The ache in my foot dims as my eyes take in his bare chest. I have felt the muscles under his clothing before; his body felt strong and hard, and so he is. Perhaps he doesn't have the sculpted six-pack that is so popular back home, but his chest is broad and his stomach is flat. A smattering of hair creeps across his upper body, and to my great surprise, I like it. He is a man, not a boy.

But my attention is drawn back to my foot as James tears a strip of cloth to bind it. "I haven't any alcohol to clean it," he says solemnly. "Just a bit of fresh water. Hopefully you won't get blood poisoning. We'll need to get you back to see a doctor. It may require stitches."

He pours water over it and then wraps the strip of fabric around and around my foot, putting plenty of pressure on it, but not so much as to cut off the circulation to my toes. I grunt a little as he ties it off, but actually, the pressure makes it feel better. "Thank you."

"You are very welcome," he says, smiling and finally looking up from my foot. His smile freezes. I almost laugh. The shock has worn off, I take it. He's just noticed that I am wearing nothing but his unbuttoned shirt. I begin to chuckle again at his silliness even as my own cheeks redden.

"I'm so glad that you seem to be alright," he starts in a strained voice, "but...let's get some clothes on you, shall we?"

He helps me into a standing position without looking once in my direction. I balance on my one good foot as he collects my clothing for me. He has no idea of what is what, and hands me my garments well out of order, groping about without seeing as he tries to find one of my hands to deposit the fabric. I pull on my pantalettes and then tug his shirt off to hand back to him. He blushes furiously, though I quickly tug my chemise over my head. I am now more fully clothed than in most of my old summer outfits, but his flush doesn't go away.

I pull on as much as I can without help, but I need him to

tie my corset and to button my dress back up. He bears it well, doing it all without comment this time, but I can tell from the heat coming even from his fingertips that he still feels embarrassed.

We ride back home differently from the way we got here. He still thinks I might be weak from my minor ordeal, so he insists that we ride tandem. I can't think of a good reason to disagree, especially since I never want to be free of his arms. So he packs up our picnic items and stows them on the mare, then leads her alongside the big Appaloosa that we ride together.

It's a long trip, and he rides slower than before with our combined weight bearing down on the sweating horse. The sun sits high in the sky, broiling us whenever the treetops open up enough to let it through.

I didn't think I was so bad off, but I droop like a wilting flower in his arms, first cold, then hot.

When we get back to the inn, James carries me up to my suite and instructs Lanie to tuck me into bed, having already sent a messenger in search of the doctor as soon as we set foot through the front door. He stays with me until the doctor arrives. I try to protest, but my objection isn't as serious as it could be. I do feel weak and feverish. Perhaps I need a doctor after all.

Chapter Sixteen

I recover slowly over the next two weeks, not leaving my bed for much of anything. It turns out that whatever it was in the water had infected my foot. Blood poisoning, they call it here. I spend days tired, aching, and feverish, with poultices wrapped around my injured appendage. Each morning, James sits faithfully by my side for hours. Once he leaves, the afternoon brings other friends and well-wishers, usually staying no more than a half-hour each. They may be my friends, but they have other calls to make, after all.

Each evening brings Damien, who rivals only James in the length of his stays, not leaving my side until I fall uncomfortably into the arms of sleep.

As soon as I begin feeling better, I tell both of them to leave me and get on with their lives—farming and partying, respectively—but neither listens and I'm touched by their willingness to give up hours of their days to bring me comfort and company.

Though I'm more or less an invalid, these weeks are some of the best times of my life.

Of course, the best of times can't last forever. I spend so many hours in bed that I can't actively try to do anything, let alone something I don't want to do. But an opportunity comes up just the same. It comes from Aurelia, who both reminds me of the opportunity and then offers me the means to take it: the opportunity to leave my beloved James behind.

Being more than halfway through August, there is only one thing for the Thorne Hill elite to do: leave home and spend the rest of the summer in their fabulous mansions in Newport. Everyone is going—or at least everyone who can afford a second home on or near the sea cliffs.

Aurelia and her mother are among those who can afford the pleasures of a summer home in Newport. During one of her daily visits to my sickbed, she mentions that she and her mother would love to have me accompany them as their guest. They'll even wait for my recovery—as long as it doesn't put them off for too long, anyway.

I'm flattered, and unsure of my decision at first. I know what I'd be leaving behind, but didn't I already decide it would be for the best? I know that I can't stay with James forever. *The sooner I cut myself off the better, right?* It will only hurt worse the longer I stay. I love him more and more with each passing day.

Damien is the one who clinches my decision. I only have to mention the offer when he exclaims that he would have invited me himself if he hadn't been sure that I was already going.

When I'm still unsure, he begs me so pathetically that I can't help but say yes.

What should have been my first thought, though, is that it's my responsibility to follow along after them. It shouldn't have been a question. These are the people who can lead me to

William and Elizabeth Wood. It's been hinted that William himself might even show up. I'm not going to find either one of them on a farm, no matter how much I enjoy my time there. That means heading to Newport and leaving James and everyone associated with him far behind me.

◊

James is not happy.

I tell him about my plans while at the farm, only two days after I've recovered enough to renew my outings to that happy place. By this time, the Goodwins have already postponed their journey twice on account of my health, each time a few days more. We'll be leaving the day after tomorrow.

"Do you really have to go?" he asks again, a sad, defeated look about him. He already knows the answer to this. I've told him.

"I've told you, yes," I respond, as brightly as I can. "It's a good opportunity for me. I should get out of town, meet new people…"

"You know it will be the same people you always see, don't you? That's how these things work. Everyone you already know is just moving the party eastward."

"I'm sure plenty of people come from all over. You don't know. Have *you* ever been?" I bite my lower lip and look down at my hands clasping each other in my lap, already ashamed of that question. Of course he hasn't been. When I look back at him he's composing himself from a look I can't place. Pain? Anger? I don't see it long enough to be able to tell.

"I'm sorry…" I sigh. "It's just that I've heard that there are plenty of people coming that I've never met. Besides, I've already promised Aurelia that I'd go with her. She and her mother were kind enough to offer me a place to stay. I can't back out now."

I don't give him my most powerful argument: how important it is that I take care of what I'm here to do rather than indulge my imprudent fantasies with him any longer.

He sighs. "I'll miss you." He looks so forlorn that I reach out to him. I enfold him in my arms like I used to do for Alex when he was young and scared or upset.

But this experience is so different from that, changed from innocent and comforting to something more by James's mere presence. His body feels warm against mine; his masculine scent is like fire to my senses, spreading through me and warming me. I breathe in deeply, hoping to store it away so I might remember it while I'm gone. I'll miss him, too. More than he can know.

"I'll be back before you know it," I say as cheerfully as I can manage, which isn't very, knowing that I don't mean it. I have to do my best never to come back to the farm at all. I break the hug but take his hand, hating to release him so soon. It feels so good to hold him; I wish I never had to let go. "Besides, you'll barely notice I'm gone. You'll be so busy getting ready for the big harvest that you wouldn't even have the time to spend with me if I were here."

"You know I'd make time for you, right?" he asks, suddenly concerned. "That's not what this is about, is it?" He really seems to think this is about him not making time for me when that couldn't be further from the truth. He always makes time for me, when instead he should be making time for his work. And making time for someone he can actually be with in the future.

REBECCA DAVIS

His future, not mine.

"No," I tell him gently. "I know you would. But this is something I have to do, alright?" He doesn't answer, and for a moment we just look into each other's eyes. I try to conceal the pain in mine while his take on a desperate gleam. I know he's about to say something I can't hear from him right now.

No, that's not right. I can't hear it from him ever.

"Elizabeth, I—"

My heart beats faster.

His face moves towards mine ever so slowly. "I just—" He breathes in raggedly.

My heart is breaking. I can't let this happen. I want it so badly, more than anything I've ever wanted in my life. But I'll never be able to leave if he kisses me now. If he tells me he loves me.

I break the mood.

"You just what?" I say teasingly, albeit slightly out of breath myself. "Can't wait to get a full day's work done without me tagging along like an annoying kid sister?"

"Liz," he admonishes gently. "I'm trying to—"

I cut him off. "I know." I sigh and look back down at my hands. "But you know I can't let you."

He closes his eyes and takes a deep breath. I've hurt him. I know it. When I peek back up at him, I can see the pain written on his face, as clear as day, the tears building up in his eyes that I'm sure he will never allow to spill over while I'm here. I want to leap into his arms and kiss him, to say I'm sorry, and tell him over and over how much I love him too. Instead I stand up, kiss him lightly on the cheek, and let him think the very worst of me.

For what can he think but that I've finally come to my senses? That this is because of our class differences? What can he think but that because I'm rich and he's not, I'd let the best thing that's ever happened to me slip through my fingers?

I move to leave. "I'll be in town for another day. Do you still want me to come?"

His green eyes are stricken, but they meet mine without flinching. "Always," he answers, so softly that I barely hear him.

I smile sadly back at him, then turn and walk out the door.

I make it to the cover of the woods before I begin sobbing uncontrollably. I don't even hear the footsteps coming up behind me, so I startle when I feel a hand gently rest on my shoulder.

"James…" I can't control my tears, so I just turn to face him only to find Gus behind me, looking concerned.

"It will be okay, Miss Liz," he pats my shoulder, his soft voice soothing.

I cry, "Oh, Gus!" and fall into his comforting embrace, sobbing into his shoulder.

He waits until I cry myself out before speaking again.

"So he told you, did he?"

I nod miserably. There's no point in hiding anything now.

"I was wondering when he'd get around to it. I've known from the first time I saw you two together."

"He didn't—he just tried to tell me. Gus, I couldn't let him."

He smiles sympathetically at me, his once unpleasant face so much more appealing now that I've gotten to know the kindness behind it. "Come on, I'll walk you home. We can talk about it if you want to."

I nod again, sniffing.

We walk in silence for a few minutes. He's letting me choose if I want to discuss it or not. I decide I don't have much left to lose. "You must think I'm horrible."

He turns to me, honestly confused. "Now, why would I go and think that?"

I give a miserable little laugh. "I know how you must see me. Poor little rich girl, breaking a good man's heart, simply because he's not wealthy enough to provide a life of high style, right? Really, I can't imagine you'd see it as anything but a cruel game."

"Miss Liz, I don't see that. I see a young girl whose heart is broken because she can't be with the man she loves. Any fool can tell how you feel about him. It's there in your face, every time you look in his direction."

The tiniest smile pulls on my lips. "Am I so transparent?"

He nods, grinning kindly. "Even Michael can tell." Transparent indeed.

I give a little half laugh, half sob. But then I shake my head. "But it doesn't matter, Gus. That he loves me back, it only makes it worse, don't you see? It can never be. It was bad enough when it was only my own suffering, but now *he* is suffering as well."

He looks at me kindly. "You know as well as I do he's been in love with you the whole time. There was never any chance for either of you."

I just nod, sniffling into a proffered handkerchief.

"Is it them?" He gestures toward the buildings looming in the distance. "Society?"

I just shrug, not willing or able to go into my real reasons.

"You can't let them dictate your choices, Elizabeth. Sometimes you just have to follow your heart."

The tears well up again and spill over. "I wish it were that simple! But there is so much more to it than that." I pause for a few deep breaths, deciding just to tell him as much as I can. "I'm here for a reason, Gus. An assignment, you could call it, I guess. But once it's finished, I have to leave here. I don't have a choice. That's why I can't let him tell me that he loves me. I can't hear it from him or I won't be able to leave. But I have to! I have. To go. Back!" My voice escalates with my pain until I'm yelling into the trees, and I have to stop walking to sob against Gus's shoulder once more.

We finally continue and walk the rest of the way without speaking. By the time we reach the inn I've calmed down enough to think things through. I turn to Gus one last time. "Please, will you give James a message for me?" I manage to say, one single tear streaking down my cheek.

"Of course. What is it?"

I take a shuddering breath. "Please tell him that I'm sorry, but I think it's best if I don't come tomorrow after all. Would you do that?" My eyes are pleading.

He looks me in the eye and nods his head sadly. "You have my word." Then he turns and walks away.

"Thank you," I whisper to his retreating form. I don't know if he hears me.

I make my way inside, holding my head high until I reach the privacy of my suite. Once I'm there, I lose it completely. Lanie is out visiting with friends until early afternoon. When she does come in, I pull myself together enough to tell her she's off for the day. She doesn't need to see this.

But she does anyway. Instead of leaving, she instructs the

concierge to tell any callers that my illness has returned and that I'll take no visitors today. Thankfully, almost no one is left to come calling anyway, since most of the crowd has begun their journeys to Newport.

Lanie stays by my side, makes me some tea, and forces small amounts of food on me. During the worst of it, she strokes my hair and speaks comfortingly. I'm deeply touched, even though it can't help; my heart is broken and there's no use trying to mend it. It will stay that way forever.

I spend the rest of the day there, crying miserably until I fall into a fitful sleep. James stars in my dreams once more, but this time all I see is his face, crumpled in pain, over and over again. I didn't think I could hurt worse. But watching him suffer is a hundred times more painful than my own suffering. I wake the next morning feeling as if I haven't slept at all.

Chapter Seventeen

Three more days go by before we leave, at the insistence of the Aurelia's mother. More delays due to the "resurgence" of my illness. I honestly wish we'd just go already. Three long days pass with no visits to the farm and no sign of James. Damien has already left. Thankfully, I have Lanie, and she is my rock. Even so, three days feels like forever, but finally we leave for Newport.

We ride in comfort in the Goodwin's private train compartment for most of the way. Sadly, though, Lanie has to ride in a separate train car with the Goodwins' servants in second class. Too bad, because I could use her company now, caring and attentive as she is. Aurelia doesn't know of my heartbreak and I can't really tell her, not without bringing forth more questions than I'm willing to answer.

Only one servant rides with us in our small but elegant compartment, to cater to us during the trip—one of Mrs. Goodwin's maids. She doesn't talk much. Not that she could if she were allowed; Aurelia's mother talks nonstop.

I spend my time pretending that I'm still slightly under the weather. Aurelia, when she gets a word in edgewise, takes the time to check on me and see if I'm okay. But mostly I just sit quietly and think. Every now and then a tear comes to my eye when my thoughts slip over to James, but I brush each one away contemptuously. I have important things to do here. The more I concentrate on my project, the sooner I can wrap it up.

I still have ten months left before I can go home, but right now all I want to do is leave this pain in the past where it belongs. I'm not sure what I'll do with my time when I finish, but I don't care.

Like in the sorrowful days before we left, time passes much too slowly in Newport. I don't really know what to do with myself now that I don't have the farm to go to every day. I won't allow myself to give into the sadness anymore, so lounging lazily in bed is not an option.

I sit politely for breakfast and tea with Mrs. Goodwin each morning. Unlike my previous acquaintance with her, while living under her roof, I find that she is sometimes a little off. Some days she is coherent and full of hope for the future of her women's movement; some days she comes to breakfast smelling of sherry and gets into a dark funk. When this happens, she rambles on and on about how men are all that is wrong in the world. I tell her the truth—that I'm sure things will start looking up for women in the future. We may not be equal even in my time, but most of us are a heck of a lot closer.

In an effort to keep busy, I take up writing. I mostly write letters to James, even though I never send them. Not one. I suppose it's really more of a diary than anything else, but each time I sit down, I write as though I'm speaking to him. I find that it helps me to get my feelings for him out and onto paper, even if he'll never read them. What else can I do? I won't give in to melancholy, but I can't stop thinking about him.

Even with the writing, I have so much extra time in the mornings. Everyone here stays out even later than they did back home, dancing and partying until the sun rises pink and orange over the Atlantic. Try as I might, I cannot stay awake until the crack of dawn with everyone else; I'm too stuck in my routine. I inevitably have to have Damien bring me back to the Goodwin mansion by 1:00 in the morning, at the latest.

Of course *he'd* never call it a night so early. He brings me home then heads back out to party the night away.

Because of this, I wake long before most of the people here. I take to walking the cliffs in the early morning silence before breakfast while the others sleep.

There are miles of cliffs overhanging rocky beaches, just like when I used to come here with my friends on school trips. The cliff walk hasn't been built yet, but there are well-worn paths in the ground from where loners and families and lovers stroll along the edge to watch the mesmerizing flow of the sea.

There are fewer homes here than in my time, but I recognize some of them. They look brand-new, paint gleaming in the morning light, not that I ever saw them looking worn. I spend hours wandering the sea cliffs, admiring the immense summer homes, clambering up and down the rocky faces, and wading in the cool New England surf among the washed-up seaweed. I'm always very careful with where I place my feet. After all,

James is not here to carry me out now....

Sometimes Lanie comes with me; she's as used to early mornings as I am. We frequently talk quietly as we stroll together, but some days are meant for silence and so we walk comfortably side by side without a single word.

After one such walk, and a particularly long, painfully slow morning listening to Mrs. Goodwin rant at the breakfast table, I take an early nap.

When I wake, I decide that rather than risk getting caught by her again, I should sneak out the back way. True, Aurelia is surely awake by now, and she can act as a buffer to her mother, but I need more stimulating conversation than even she can provide today. There's only so much discussion of last night's outfits that I can take.

I make my way to the Gracen mansion to find Damien. It's a beautiful day, and I enjoy the solitary walk in the early afternoon sunshine. He stays in the guest cottage, away from his parents' prying eyes, so that he can come and go as he pleases. I knock on the door once, twice.

I'm about to walk away disappointed, when he finally answers the door in just his pants and an unbuttoned shirt. His blonde hair is mussed and he glares past me at the sky through squinted eyes, as if he's angry at the sun for daring to shine on him.

"Good afternoon, sleepyhead." I smile pleasantly. "A little hungover, are we? Did I wake you?"

"No...ugh, yes." His returning smile is a pained one. "But you know I'm always happy to see you. Come in, love."

I follow him into the guest cottage. Every time I enter, it amazes me. His parents' Newport mansion is one of the largest here. It's overwhelmingly huge, but it's also very tasteful and beautiful. The guest cottage is a smaller version of that splendor. It's a cottage in name only; even as a guest house, it's far bigger than James's two-story farmhouse, closer to the size of my own family home in modern times.

I look around me at the antique furnishings. Deep, rich wood tones contrast with pure whites of all the fabrics, kept clean and perfect by an army of servants who maintain both this and the main house. Fresh flowers in crystal vases are placed strategically around the sitting room, spots that do most to show off the beautiful colors. White sheers hang in the open windows, blowing languidly in the light breeze and softening the harsh sunlight just enough to make the room seem to glow.

Damien pours himself a drink, his own "miracle" cure to ease the pain of a hangover. I had thought—foolishly it seems—that after his drunken mistake and sober apology that sobriety might become a new habit.

But, no. Instead, he began drinking again, and more than ever. While he's with me, he never gets drunk anymore. He never even gets more than a light buzz, remembering his awful blunder at all times. He's always a gentleman with me, and a good friend. But I hear what happens after I'm safely at home. That is when the wine and booze start to flow freely, and when crazy things start to happen.

Scruffy, unkempt Damien looks out of place here against the pristine setting of the cottage. In his wrinkled pants and beer-stained shirt, he looks like he'd be more at home in a seedy pub.

Unable to stop myself, I think of the cozy farmhouse kept immaculate by James's own hands, his well-worn work clothes that he scrubs meticulously clean each night before he'll go to bed. He could never be like this, living a grand life but taking it all for granted.

"You look so serious all of a sudden, Lizzy. Whatever's wrong?"

I look up at my friend, startled, having gotten lost in my thoughts. "Sorry." I shake it off. "It's nothing, really. I'm just thinking." I feel guilty for thinking such things about Damien. He is who he is, and who he was raised to be. It's not my place to judge him. After all, he has his good qualities, too. He's a good and loyal friend, someone whom I can tell almost anything. He can make me laugh like no one else can. He's my best friend.

And I need him to be that best friend now. Not only do I feel guilty, but James has been pushed to the front of my mind. And suddenly I want very much to talk about him with someone.

I've told no one—not even Lanie—about all the particulars of my heartbreak. Will it make me feel better to get it off my chest?

I bite my lip, indecisive. "Damien? If I tell you something, will you promise to keep it a secret?"

Still concerned, he's serious for once. "As you wish, darling."

I sigh. "Maybe it's crazy to ask this of *you* of all people, but, have you ever been in love?" He just nods, thoughtful, ready to hear more.

I continue, becoming agitated. "With someone you can't be with?" He surprises me by answering with another nod. "And maybe they even love you, too, but it doesn't matter, because you don't belong together no matter how you feel about one another?"

"Yes. Actually, yes I have," he finally says, surprising me again. I had no idea. He's kept as much a secret as I have. He's still so serious, not his usual self at all now. "But I thought you were going to tell me something. That seems like quite a few questions but nothing more, Liz."

"You're right. It's just that… I feel that way, Damien. I'm in love. Madly, passionately, painfully in love. Please, this is the part that no one else can know. He's… He's a farmer. His name is James." I let out a deep breath. I've finally said it out loud. "I suppose his name really doesn't matter. I'm pretty sure—no, I'm *sure* that he loves me as well. But there's no way we can be together. Do you understand what I mean?"

"Yes, Lizzy, I do." He sighs. "It's different, though, for me. You see, this girl I love, she also loves me back. She just doesn't love me as much as I wish she did."

"Oh, Damien!" My heart goes out to him, my empathy for his situation taking away some of my own pain to make room for his. "You've never told me. It seems we've both been keeping secrets. I'm sorry to hear that you have to live this way, too."

I give him a hug before posing a question that suddenly has become very important to me. "But…*how* do you deal with it? What do you do to make it through the day without her?"

He laughs bitterly, unlike any sound I've ever heard from him before. "Liz, look at me. I *don't* deal with it. I go out and drink myself into a stupor every night so that I don't *have* to deal with it. I use alcohol to wash her from my brain, even for a short while. I bring other girls home night after night, trying to replace her, to drive her from my mind." He finishes in a monotone, looking straight into my eyes. "But while I'm with them, all I can think of is her."

The fervor and self-loathing in his face turns to sadness.

"Honestly, the only thing that helps me deal with the pain is to spend time with you."

The corners of my mouth turn up just a little. "Really?" I ask meekly.

"Really. I've told you before; you're my best friend, Lizzy. If anyone can cheer me up, it's you." He gently touches my face, pushing an errant lock of hair behind my ear.

My smile widens. "Well then, we'll just have to cheer each other up, right?"

He finally smiles back. "Yes, I suppose we will." His voice changes immediately, animation where there was listlessness. "Now that that's all settled, I have a brilliant idea."

He jumps up, suddenly back to his old self again like our conversation never happened. "Wait here." He presses his lips coolly to my hand and runs off down a hallway, his bare feet slapping on the wooden floor.

He returns a few minutes later, fully dressed in clean, pressed pinstriped trousers, a clean and fully buttoned shirt, and a handsome pinstriped vest. His pale hair is combed and covered by his favorite silk top hat and his feet are securely ensconced in shiny leather shoes. Only his scruffy chin remains to remind me of the sad man that was sitting before me only moments ago.

Damien grabs my hand and pulls me up off the settee. "Come. Dance with me."

I laugh delightedly, surprised that laughter can still come so easily. I should have known to count on Damien. He's helping so much already.

Ready to acquiesce, I make only one protestation, "But we have no music!"

"Should that stop us?" He takes hold of my other hand and pulls me into the dance position. "We'll make our own music."

And with that, he starts singing a silly music hall tune he calls "Champagne Charlie."

We twirl around the room, dancing and laughing, all evidence of our earlier somberness forgotten. An odd choice, I think, but even the topic of the song, so similar to Damien's tale of drowning his pains in girls and drink, can't bring us down again.

The mood has turned light and silly, due mainly to Damien's dreadful singing abilities. His voice, so sultry and eloquent when he wants it to be, cannot hold a tune at all. He struggles to keep singing through his laughter, and I giggle uncontrollably.

Until I hear a noise behind me, from the hallway that leads to the bedrooms.

I don't want to look, to be distracted. Let the maid work around us. I want to keep dancing in my best friend's arms, where we are safe together in a way we aren't when we're alone, protected with happy feelings from the painful thoughts of our lost loves.

But Damien has seen the interloper, and I can tell by his look it's not the maid. He tries to keep his face neutral, but I can see the change in his eyes, the acknowledgement that the moment of safety is over.

I turn around to see Libby, herself tousled and fresh out of bed as Damien had been only minutes before. I know immediately from whose bed she has arisen, and that she is another attempt to drive the mysterious woman out of his thoughts.

Her own blonde hair is mussed from sleep, and the petticoat she's wearing is rumpled and half undone, still visible as she flees down the hallway. For she has turned away from us, and she tries to rush down the hall and back to the safety of the bedroom, away from the cozy scene before her and away from the prospect of being caught. But she's too late. I saw her profile as she turned to run and I'd recognize her anywhere.

And even more than being offended by our closeness, self-preservation must be the reason she ran. She could hardly know that in my time, premarital sex is not the end-all that it is here. Sure, there can be major consequences—parental anger, pregnancy, and disease to name a few—but barring that, unmarried couples live together all the time. Shows like *Sex and the City* and all manner of chick lit books practically encourage women into one-night stands. So even though I might not do it myself, I won't judge her for it.

But here in 1875, such an act can have all the consequences of its future counterpart in addition to the complete ruination of a girl's reputation and future prospects for marriage. A man may have as many partners as he likes, but a woman should have no one but her husband. Such unfairness rankles, but there is nothing I can do about it except let Libby be.

Because, of course, the last thing Libby would want me to find out is that she is sleeping with Damien. After all, we've been enemies since our first meeting. She knows I spend a lot of time in his company, and even thinks that I feel I have some claim over him. She has no idea what I might do with the information. I might blackmail her, I might simply tell everyone; the possibilities are endless.

But I already know I won't do any of those things despite the hatred I feel for her. If Libby Hunt is the future Elizabeth

Wood, then I have to be prepared with the knowledge that she is a potential murderer. Even if she's not my ancestor, well, I've seen Libby in action. She's got all the charm of a venomous snake. No, I don't want to cross her either way.

Oddly, I also feel kind of sorry for her. I can only imagine how she must feel. She came out of Damien's bedroom to see the man she was only recently so intimate with dancing happily in the arms of a hated rival. Even if her only goal is his money, well, that still had to hurt. She must have felt the truth, that despite their time together, she will never be the one he wants. I'd have run, too, if I were her.

I look to Damien. His expression is one of guilt and chagrin. I feel like I should be disappointed in him, but I can't. Not after his confession earlier. I wish it didn't have to be like this. I wish that he could live happily with the woman he loves instead of destroying himself to try to forget her.

"You should go." I motion towards the hallway. "Regardless of how you feel about her, she's your responsibility."

He nods and starts down the hall. Before he gets far he turns back to me. "Thanks." He kisses me on the cheek and turns away once again.

◊

"Elizabeth. So *wonderful* to see you again," Libby says sweetly, although I can hear the sarcasm dripping through like acid.

It's later that same day and we're all attending a dinner party at the Wood family's mansion. Like all of the greatest houses here, it overlooks the rocky shore I walked across early this morning. Libby stands on Damien's arm tonight, her free hand clasped over his. *Good. He's taking his responsibility seriously.*

She stands proudly beside him; whatever Damien said to her earlier about our dancing together has placated her for now. Though certainly not enough to be civil to me, of course. That would take a miracle.

I decide to play nice. I still feel a little bad for her.

"Libby. It's so nice to see you as well. You know, I was just thinking of you earlier today." I pause, letting her think that I saw her at Damien's. Her eyes widen slightly in alarm. Alright, so I don't feel *that* badly. I can't let her off quite so easily as to allow her to think that she's safe. It's all I've got. But instead of a clever barb, I continue nicely, "I was thinking of that gown you wore last night. It was absolutely stunning. Where did you get it?"

She's taken aback by my sincere tone, and even Damien looks at me oddly, not understanding my meaning. I motion just slightly with my eyes for him to help me out here.

"Yes, Libby, darling," he manages after a quick look of comprehension. "You looked quite splendid. Still do, in fact." He smiles his charming smile.

She looks at me uncertainly for a moment, but he takes her hand and bestows a kiss upon it, and she melts as easily as chocolate. Flustered, she speaks to me in an almost pleasant voice. "New York, of course. That's where all the best clothing in the country is made." She pulls herself together, shifting into her superior tone. "You should come shopping with us. Well, if you can afford it. The ladies and I are leaving for Manhattan about a week after we return from Newport."

I'm about to decline when we are interrupted by the hostess herself (and my great-to-the-fifth-power grandmother), Mrs. Wood. "Oh, Libby, darling, wait just a week more, won't you? I've just heard that my William will be in Manhattan a fortnight after we return. I'm sure he would adore seeing old friends while he's there! Maybe you can convince him it's time to come back home; I've had no luck whatsoever with my letters."

Libby drops Damien's hand so fast you'd think it was suddenly made of molten lava. Her full attention is immediately upon Mrs. Wood. "Of course we will postpone our trip, Mrs. Wood. You know I've been waiting in agony until I should see my dear friend William again! How wonderful that he should be in town so close to our own plans! It's no trouble at all to change them, I'm sure."

It seems that no matter how proud she was upon walking in with Damien, she'll be only too happy to trade him in for a bigger fish. I think I've officially stopped feeling sorry for her.

But forget Libby. This information could be the break I've been waiting for. Newport has been a complete wash so far, with no sign or word of William Wood until now. I *must* go. It seems I'll be taking another little trip soon after I return.

As if reading my thoughts, Damien takes my advice to forget Libby as well. He doesn't seem too brokenhearted about her lack of attention. The moment she dropped his hand, he moved away from her side and came straight to mine.

He, too, seems excited about going to Manhattan, adding his own good feelings to the conversation. "My dear Mrs. Wood, what wonderful news! I may just decide to join the young ladies on their shopping trip. It's not every day one gets a chance to see an old friend like Will!"

Mrs. Wood is delighted by the reaction to her news. She is obviously overjoyed that her son is so universally loved.

I use the calming influence of her presence to agree to the trip, taking Libby by surprise. "Libby, thank you so much for inviting me along! I haven't been to the city in such a long time. And do you know, I've never had the privilege of meeting the young Mr. Wood." I look up into my great-great-great-great-great-grandmother's clear gray eyes and smile. "It would be such a pleasure to finally meet your son, Mrs. Wood. I have heard so many wonderful things about him that I'm sure it will feel like meeting an old friend."

She smiles back, flushing with pleasure. "My dear, I'm certain he will be very happy to meet you as well. He truly is such a wonderful young man, so popular with all his acquaintances. It saddened me greatly when he left us. Of course I understood." she amends quickly, "It's very important that he learn all about his father's business. But it is so nice to have one's children close to home."

Libby looks fairly certain that William won't enjoy meeting me at all, but I won't let her spoil this. I've sacrificed everything for this chance. Glancing sidelong at her, I make a quick promise to myself that I won't interfere when she makes a play for William. If she's the Elizabeth who I came here to find, then I merely need to know the truth, that's all. I will not try to change things, no matter what.

"Splendid, ladies, just splendid!" pipes in Damien. "My dear Mrs. Wood," he begins, "do tell us exactly where he is staying and we shall take him by surprise. We won't let him get even a moment's work done, you know, and we certainly won't stop badgering him to come home with us for even an instant."

She beams at Damien and pats him on the shoulder. "Oh, dear Mr. Gracen, we do miss you at the house, as well. You never visit us anymore. You could call on us sometime, even without William at home, you know. It would be almost like having my son with us again. Isn't that right, George?" She directs her last question at her husband who has just joined us.

"What?" he asks moodily. "Oh, yes, I suppose. Just stay away from my little Maribelle, Gracen."

"Sir!" Damien feigns shock. "You know me better than that! I would never—"

"You most certainly would. I know you too well, my boy. But if you can keep your hands to yourself, you know you're welcome any time, son. Come, let's have a drink and a cigar and leave these ladies to their gossip." Mr. Wood puts his arm around Damien's shoulders and steers him into the men's smoking room, leaving me alone with the two women.

I'm about to say something to Mrs. Wood when she speaks first. "Please excuse me, ladies, I've simply got to mingle with all of my guests. You two have fun!" She smiles and, in a flash, she's gone. I look around to see if there is anyone else at all that I might speak to, but everyone seems to be involved in a conversation. Libby and I are left to one another's attentions.

"So," I begin calmly, "New York. I can hardly wait." I smile blandly, my face betraying nothing. "And won't it be nice to finally meet the famous William Wood?"

She smiles sweetly in return, a better actress than I am. One could almost think she meant it. But while her tone and look speak sweet sincerity, her words give another message. "Alright, *Lizzy*, you can stop the act now. We both know you were going to decline that little invitation until you heard that William will be there." I can't deny it and I don't try. "So I'll make this *very* clear. Stay away from him. He's mine." Her clear blue eyes take on a look of icy intensity, daring me to challenge her.

And of course, I do. I know I shouldn't, but she brings out the worst in me.

I feign an expression of confusion. "I'm sorry; I think I might have missed that. You said that William is yours?"

She just looks back haughtily without speaking, finally averting her eyes.

"Right," I continue. "See, this is what confuses me. I was under the impression that you think Damien is yours. Or, I suppose it's more accurate to say that I thought you were attempting to make him yours."

Still no answer. She continues to avoid my gaze.

"Let me guess… Damien is your backup plan, just in case William doesn't come home, right? Or, God forbid, if William chooses *not* to marry you when he does?"

This finally elicits a response.

"Oh, he'll marry me," she whispers harshly, defensively. The sugary voice has disappeared now that I've found her weakness. "Don't you worry about *that*. He'll be a good little boy and do what his parents want him to. And *guess* what they want?"

She pauses dramatically, triumphantly. "They want *me* as their daughter-in-law. Not you, some no-name, new-money, nobody. I have the wealth; I have the connections. They'd never let him even think to marry a little piece of rubbish like you," she finishes viciously. She composes herself, smiling once again. "That is, if he'd ever even look at you in the first place." With that, she turns and walks away.

Chapter Eighteen

After the Libby incident, I only visit with Damien later in the day, hoping to avoid finding him with company. It doesn't always work. Once I come across him with a young lady from Manhattan whom I immediately dub Barbie. She is tall, blonde, and voluptuous. Unlike Libby, she is decidedly not shy, strutting past me in very little clothing to hang all over him while he looks at me instead, obviously miserable but unable to stop himself. She's surprisingly nice, though, and we actually have a good conversation before I make my way back out. It turns out her name is Sandra.

Another time I find him with a curvy brunette. She's running away by the time Damien opens the door, leaving only a fleeting view of her long dark locks and a generous backside. I'm not sure, but I think it's Paulette, a girl we met from Boston. She's really sweet in person, and loves books as much as I do. I hope, if it is her, that I haven't scared her away from talking to me at another party.

But then something happens that makes me vow never to come over unannounced again. Finding Sandra and Paulette was awkward; seeing Libby at Damien's was worse. But when Glory's emerald eyes stare back at me in surprise I draw the line. Libby and Glory are not strangers. Not to him, not to me, and not to one another.

I leave quickly after walking in on that scene, but I decide that maybe it's time for an intervention.

"Why do you do this to yourself, Damien?" I ask later, when we sit by ourselves on the sofa after sharing a light supper. "You said yourself it doesn't help."

I don't know how I was expecting him to react to my question, but this was not it.

I've only seen three sides of Damien before. The one I know best is the fun and charming one—confident, happy and full of life. But I've also met the sober and penitent Damien, the man who begged so ardently for my forgiveness. And then most recently, I met the sad and defeated side—the one that still pains me to think of.

This Damien is angry.

"Do you know what, Lizzy? You're right. It doesn't help." He stands up and begins pacing feverishly across the shining floor. "The alcohol dulls the pain, but never takes it away, no. It's constantly there, pounding in the back of my head, throbbing to the beat of my battered heart.

"And no matter how different the girls are—their manner, their dress, their looks, their voices—they always remind me of…her. Every time. There is always something—a gleam in the eyes, a hint in the smile, or the precise shade of her hair— something in them that brings her to the front of my mind and opens up the wound as deep as it can go.

"But you know what, Elizabeth, *I'm* trying. I am trying. I try every day to push her from my heart, to keep her away where she can't hurt me anymore. What are you doing? You lean on me. That's all you do.

"You know I love you and I think it's fine and great and wonderful that you need me. You of all people know it's the only bloody thing that helps me, too, so I don't mind at all. I'm happy to do it for you. But what else is there, Elizabeth? How else do you stay sane? What are you *trying*?"

I just stare at him, stricken. He's right. I had thought that I was handling things rather well, but he's right. He is the most effective balm I've found for my aching heart.

"Exactly. There is nothing. You do nothing else but wallow. You walk the cliffs alone, dreaming of him. How often do you concentrate on anything your friends say? I see that look in your eyes. And every moment that you are bored, every time your mind drifts off, where is it?" He pauses, continuing in a softer voice, though still heated. "I know exactly where your mind goes. To your James's farm, reliving the memories of your time there."

He sighs, his anger finally spent. He asks dully, "Does it help, Lizzy? Does it help to think about him all the time like you do? If it doesn't, then why do you do it to yourself?"

Tears stream freely down my cheeks. I may not spend *all* of my time wallowing, but he is right enough. I sob quietly.

"Oh, Lizzy, I'm so sorry." He gathers me up tightly in his arms and the tears that flow gently from his own eyes drip onto my face and mingle with the moisture already there. "What have we done to ourselves? What's to become of us?"

If his question isn't rhetorical, it doesn't matter. Neither of us answers it.

We don't go out this night. In the end, we fall asleep holding each other, keeping the pain at bay.

And in the morning, when I wake before him and look upon his features, I see that the despair on his face has been replaced with the same contentedness that I feel.

I know it's a bad idea, to lean on Damien even more after all he's said, but neither of us can seem to help it. Over the next two weeks Damien and I spend almost every waking moment together. I eat breakfast with Mrs. Goodwin and then head out the door to meet him and we walk the cliffs together. When we attend a party or event, neither of us even thinks of showing up with someone else.

Even so, I do try harder to think of what I came here to do—to put James out of my mind and truly enjoy my time here. It doesn't always work, but it's better.

And so is Damien. He drinks less, and now goes straight home after dropping me off at the Goodwins'. While we both agree that we'd be more comfortable together, propriety stops us from spending any more nights in each other's arms, innocent though they may be.

But even without my presence overnight, Damien has stopped bringing girls home to his bed. When I ask him about it, he gives me a silly answer. He says that if he spends enough time with me all day, the feeling of my presence can last throughout the night.

I call the idea ridiculous until I realize that the same principle works for me, too. I suppose it's almost like storing his energy within my heart. It seems to radiate through my body in waves of tranquility, to calm me while I sleep.

No matter how silly it seems, it helps to stop the nightmares about James, though I still suffer dreams of extreme longing. I would have thought that my nightmares starring Damien himself would come more often, brought on by the increase in his presence, but somehow it has the opposite effect on those, too.

So when it's time to head back to Thorne Hill, I guiltily ditch the Goodwin ladies' private compartment to ride with Damien in the Gracens' own personal train car. Like everything owned by the Gracens, it is over the top extravagant, yet in a somehow understated way. Dark wood paneling, pale blue curtains, tiny hints of crystal and gold. Lanie rides with us, and while she isn't involved in the conversation, it's a comfort to have her with me as well. We travel in the utmost luxury, and I can almost forget about James for the duration of the very long ride.

But it's much harder to forget him once we arrive back home.

I look out my window on our first morning back only to see him standing beside his chestnut mare at the edge of the woods across the meadow, watching intently.

He's waiting for me.

But I don't go to him.

Chapter Nineteen

Manhattan. The Big Apple. The City that Never Sleeps. Or at least, that's what it will be called in my time. In October of 1875, Manhattan is a different world. The buildings are shorter, no longer seeming to truly brush the sky as they always did. The Empire State Building is missing, the impressive view from its blustery decks just a drop in the ocean of my memories. The majestic Twin Towers, so far from being destroyed on one horrible, fateful day in the future, are not yet even a spark in the back of an architect's mind. The Brooklyn Bridge, such an icon of the city in the future, is under construction, its massive form beginning to rise as if out of nothing.

While the fast-paced city does move to a much quicker beat than the smaller towns of the Connecticut countryside, it is still much slower than I remember. The yellow cabs are gone, replaced by horse-drawn carriages, the drivers atop their high seats searching the dirty streets in front of them for a waving hand.

Ah, yes, the dirt and grime. It's not so bad in the parts of town we tend to keep to, with the wide main streets lined with stores and markets and fancy hotels. But only a few blocks back, smaller retail shops abound, places where the owners live above their stores instead of in nice apartments in a better part of town.

And not so far beyond those, the slums begin, with second-hand shops and seedy taverns, with apartment houses with almost nothing but vermin inside. I don't get to see those areas, but I know they are there, even if my companions pretend they're not. We stay far away from those places, but they are there, hiding far behind the fair facades of Fifth Avenue.

We remain instead fairly close to where we're staying, the Royal River Hotel right off of Madison Avenue—a grand affair just like every other place in which this crowd tends to spend their time. The most fashionable dress shops, the fanciest restaurants, and the finest tearooms are all open to us. Lavish townhouses belonging to the wealthiest people in the city are ours to wander during the whirlwind of balls and parties that take place in this last month of the Season.

While we move about the bustling city in our carriages, I stare out the window and think about how August and September are gone. More than two weeks have passed since our return to Thorne Hill, before we set out to New York. For two weeks, I'd watched out my window as James waited for me. He spent an hour every morning at the edge of the woods before turning and fading into the trees. No matter how much I tried to sleep in, staying out later than ever each night, I could not avoid waking promptly by seven. I could not stop myself from checking the forest's edge for that beloved face.

I always found it. He refused to stop waiting for me.

Despite the time I spent with Damien those weeks—most of each day, every day, just like in Newport—the nightmares returned. Regardless of the time I spend with him now, they remain with me here in the city. Seeing James's face so near to me and yet so far brought them crashing back and now they won't leave.

I feel lost most days here in Manhattan. Not lost in the sense that I don't know my way around—while the city may be different than I am used to, the familiar grid is what identifies it as what it truly is. No, I just feel lost without *him*.

The chairs in the waiting area are plush and lined in plum-colored velvet. The shop windows are dressed in beautiful blue curtains that are covered with tiny, pink, embroidered flowers with minute seed pearls sewn at their centers. Yards of fabric of all colors surround me, from creamy whites and dainty pastels to deep greens, blues, and burgundies. Tucked away in a back corner are the grays and blacks, the mourning colors that almost no fashionable young woman of this era would bother to wear otherwise.

I sit politely on one of those padded chairs, wishing that it was as comfortable as it looked.

Shopping used to be fun. I'd try on clothes, talk with friends, laugh at some of our worst fashion picks. The mall was huge and always full of things I wanted and could usually afford to get.

Even in 1875 Thorne Hill, shopping was interesting. I'd ask the dressmaker to describe what was going on so I could watch and learn as the dress took shape right before my eyes.

Today, it's maddening. Of course, James is on my mind,

waiting in the back of my head for my willpower to slip and bring him to the front. Which is when the ache begins. To top it off, I'm really missing my family and old friends today. Shopping without Donna and my other friends just isn't the same. And New York City was always something I did with Mom and Dad and Alex.

But they're not here either. And what is my distraction today, to keep my mind from wandering all over the place? Four girls, three of whom I despise. They are all that I have to keep my mind busy. And those three hate every strip of fabric, every amazing pattern, every bead and every ribbon that I choose.

I take their advice at first, heeding the voices of experience, but I soon learn that they're just playing with me. I should know that. Why else do they adore the teal silk with the eyelet lace trim when Emily picks it out but not when I did ten minutes earlier? Why do they hate the pattern I choose for a beautiful modern dress, lightly ornamented and with only the slightest bustle, but when Libby admires one that's almost identical they go crazy for it?

Even Angelica, who has been nice to me in the past, who has complimented me when we were alone together, doesn't say a single word in my defense even when I can see she's in love with some of my ideas.

So that leaves me with only one option: ignore them. Which, of course, leads me back to my original problem.

However, a new solution finds me when it's finally my turn on the dressmaker's stool. Thankfully, he's a talkative man, and soon he is chattering away while his assistants measure and he cuts panels of that amazing teal fabric for that fantastic new dress design I found.

Of course, the girls sit aside and sneer at my choices as if I'm not there, but I concentrate on the dressmaker's voice, focusing only on understanding his words. It's difficult, because he has a strong French accent. But that's good for me; it makes it a better distraction from all that I'm choosing to avoid.

It doesn't take long for my companions to grow bored, and they eventually make their way out of the shop to where Damien is chivalrously waiting for us in a small tearoom across the street. No amount of pleading could get him to enter this women's sanctum for so long.

It takes a while before the dressmaker finishes with me, finally assuring me in his thick accent that I won't be needed until the final fitting in a few days. Even when he's through, I stay for a few minutes more, happy to listen to his voice to keep my mind from wandering—happy to avoid the ladies from Thorne Hill for just a little more time.

When I can stretch my visit out no longer, I head outside with the same enthusiasm I would have heading to my own funeral. I cross the street to find Damien and the ladies in a frenzy.

"Whatever is going on out here?" I ask, interrupting the babble of conversation from which I can glean nothing. Too many voices are talking at once.

Angelica is the one who answers me properly, willing to talk to me now that the others are preoccupied. "Oh, Elizabeth, you just missed it! William Wood was right here; we were talking to him for almost ten minutes! He only just rode off, see: That is his carriage just there." She points to a small brougham about a hundred yards away from us.

My first view of William Wood. All I can see of him is a black top hat rising above the back of the seat. I stare blankly after the small carriage, too shocked at my rotten luck to even look disappointed.

"Sorry, my darling," Damien comforts me, unruffled as usual. "I told him he'd want to wait to meet you, and that you'd be out momentarily, but he couldn't be persuaded. Apparently, he has a very important appointment to get to." He smiles and pats my shoulder affectionately before his attention is sidetracked by a street vendor and he goes over to haggle.

Still I stare after William.

"Don't worry, Liz, you couldn't have known." Libby smirks. "But you'd think he'd be polite enough to wait a few more minutes to meet the *sensational* new girl in town, hmm?"

She and Glory laugh while Emily adds, "Well, it's a good thing! We don't need her trying to steal *him* away too…"

I react even though the comment wasn't directed at me. "I don't know what you're talking about," I say blankly, finally turning away from the bustling avenue.

It's Glory who speaks up this time, and she's no longer laughing. Her bright green eyes are hard. "Don't play innocent with us, *Lizzy*. Somehow you've managed to get Damien wrapped around your little finger, the fool, but don't think you'll do the same with William. He and Libby—"

"He and Libby were over before they even started," I interrupt impassively, looking at Libby for a moment before adjusting my gaze back to the distant street, but William's top hat has been lost in the shuffle. "Damien told me exactly what happened between her and William. As his best friend, he'd be in a position to know, don't you think?"

I look over to Glory, annoyance finally creeping into my voice. "I haven't stolen Damien from anyone. I know better than anybody that he belongs to no one. And I'm not going to try to steal William. If Libby can manage to land the poor man, she's welcome to him, God help him. So please just bugger off."

They give me nasty looks that change instantly into huge smiles when Damien returns to us, fresh flowers in his hands.

"Here we are, ladies." He hands each of us a red rose, one at a time, finishing with me. Then he kisses me on the forehead. I don't bother to glance at the others, knowing how much they'll have hated to see that.

"Dear Lizzy, don't look so down!" Damien cries after I accept my rose without so much as a smile. He looks at my face, concerned. "*Are you alright?*" he mouths.

I nod slightly, letting him know it's not what he thinks, and then answer publicly. "It's just that I wanted to meet your friend. I've heard so much about him."

He breathes a sigh of relief, happy that my problem is more minor than he'd thought, and that it's something within his power to fix. "Didn't I tell you? He's going to meet us for dinner on Friday evening. You'll get to meet him then."

Friday can't come fast enough, though my anticipation does have one helpful side effect: It keeps my mind firmly in the right place. Between the shock of my just missing William and the eager tension I feel awaiting our meeting, I can finally concentrate on the project I came here to do.

The days go by slowly, each feeling longer than the last. We shop more, we go to our fittings and pick up our new gowns and dresses, and of course we attend the never-ending stream of dinner parties, operas, theatre, and more. Every evening, there's a new group of people to meet, and a new sight to see.

Some distract more than others; the opera is long and boring, sung in Italian, and completely incomprehensible to me. The guests at dinner range widely from tediously dull to completely captivating, but society in Manhattan is much more diverse than back home. Many of the guests have fascinating stories to tell.

The play we attend is wonderful, a production of Shake-speare's *Hamlet* like I've never seen it before. The actors have such depth that I can feel the pain and confusion of the young prince. I weep openly over the death of the lovely, mad Ophelia, and the tragic murders marking the end of Denmark's royal line are more poignant than ever.

Damien, as usual, keeps me linked to sanity during these public hours, my port in a storm of uncertainty. It's he who gets me through the long days and endless nights. It's his hand that squeezes my arm to remind me to be polite to a man I might want to scream at, his calm voice in my ear to wake me when I want to sleep away a dreary show.

I also lean on him more than ever because of his link to William. I can't help it; anytime I get him alone, I throw questions at him. I can see his curiosity, can see him itching to ask me why, why do I care so much about this man I've never met? But he doesn't ask, just patiently answers my questions about what sort of man he is, what kind of girl he's interested in, and if he's definitely opposed to marrying Libby—among dozens of others.

The days trudge along, but Friday night finally arrives.

I want to make a good impression on my great-great-great-great-grandfather, so I wear my new teal gown with the lace edging. It's long-sleeved, sleek, and modern. The tiny bustle behind me ruffles its way to the ground in tiers of gleaming fabric, ending in a short train. Though the neckline is at my throat, sealed with a delicate cameo button, and the fitted sleeves flare ever-so-slightly past my wrists, taut skin peeks naughtily through cutout shoulders trimmed with lace.

We enter our meeting place, a gorgeous little restaurant on Madison Avenue. For our small group, there are no less than six waiters, all exceedingly courteous and eager to please in every way. Every door is held open, every coat or wrap is taken without a word, every chair is held out for every lady to daintily take her seat.

The restaurant is stunning, so much so that I'm at a loss for words from the moment we enter, happy to simply look around and silently admire. They bring us to a private room, the table set perfectly for our party. Place cards designate each chair exactly as Damien has told them, each card embossed in gold and written in perfect calligraphy.

Gold-plated crystal chandeliers light the room, just enough for that perfect restaurant atmosphere. The table is covered in a floor-length cream-colored tablecloth and set with gilt-edged white china. The wealth of silverware beside each place setting is so profuse that I give a silent word of thanks to my etiquette instructors for drilling me so thoroughly. Without that training, I'd be horribly confused by it all; it looks like we're once again in for a full seven-course meal.

The hand-carved mahogany chairs contrast beautifully with the pale cream of the table cloth. The floor is gray marble and the walls are wood paneled in the same dark tone as the chairs. Works of art are hung on the walls, not crowded together as in the Goodwins' home, but widely spaced and well-lit like in a museum or a gallery so that one can appreciate each well-chosen piece.

It's in this beautiful setting that we sit and wait. And wait. And wait some more.

We wait because our dinner companion, the ever-elusive William Wood, is late. So of course, not wanting to start without the guest of honor, we wait.

We wait for more than an hour before we begin to eat without him. A seven-course meal takes a long time from start to end. Well over another hour passes before we finish. He doesn't show.

The others may claim to have seen him, but I'm beginning to think this man doesn't actually exist.

We pull on our coats and shawls, just getting ready to head out into the brisk autumn night when someone enters our private room. We all look to the opening door in unison, like a group of prairie dogs reacting to the sound of an approaching predator.

It's not him.

Not that I would know by looking at him; I've never seen so much as a portrait of William. But the reaction of the others is quite enough—their sighs and looks of disappointment are a quick indication that I'm not seeing the man of the hour.

No, the young man turns out to be a messenger, waylaid by an injured horse. He carries a note for Damien. I peek at it over his shoulder even as he reads the first half aloud.

> *Gracen,*
> *Caught up in an unexpected meeting. Won't be at dinner.*
> *Please give my apologies to the ladies. Meet me at the bar*
> *later? Perhaps one o'clock? Send a reply back with my*
> *messenger.*
> *—Wood*

Chapter Twenty

I have to get to that bar.

Damien sent the messenger back to William half an hour ago, letting his friend know that he'd be there.

Now I'm in the coach with Damien, heading back to the hotel for the night. The other four ride separately in their own carriage.

I ask to look over the letter again.

"Sure." He hands over the folded piece of paper without question or hesitation. This time, when I study the light-handed script, I'm struck by a strange feeling. I'm sure I've seen similar handwriting before. I wrack my brain, determined to place it.

Ah! That's it! It reminds me of my mother's swirling scrawl. I remember reading some of her love letters to Dad; her handwriting wasn't so tight or rushed, but it was definitely similar. *Yes....*

With my mind cleared of that conundrum, I look back at Damien, ready to continue my plan.

"He doesn't say which bar." I say casually.

"There's no need to, love. There is only one bar in the city we ever go to. It's kind of our place."

I pause a moment before asking tentatively, "May I come with you?"

His eyes widen in surprise. He hadn't thought of this possibility. He shakes his head. "Lizzy, I'm sorry, but no. Not this time."

I hate myself for whining, but I do. I can't help it. "But why not?"

He looks into my eyes, seeming unsure of how to answer. Finally he replies.

"Well for one, the place we're going to is hardly upscale. Wood and I go there to get away from things. The clientele can be… a bit rough around the edges."

"I'm hardly worried about offending my feminine sensibilities. I can handle it."

Flustered, he continues, "How should I put this? The women who go there are not…proper ladies. They're not like you."

"So?" I say, rolling my eyes. "I've seen the 'lower class' before, Damien." He fidgets uncomfortably, not knowing what to say. I've never seen him like this, even upon arriving to find a girl in his cottage. "I'm not sure what you're getting at," I tell him, though I'm beginning to get an inkling. But it's too much fun seeing him squirm for me to stop now.

"The only women who frequent that bar are, well…ladies of the evening," he says hesitantly, then looks at me wide eyed, willing me to understand. Seeing my quizzical look he continues, "They come there to look for clients…" He is clearly at a loss for words.

Of course, now I do understand, but this is too funny. He's actually embarrassed. His cheeks are flaming as bright as mine ever have, visible even in the darkness of the coach. It seems impossible, but somehow I manage to keep my face innocently curious when I ask him, "What do you mean?"

The deer-in-headlights look he gives me then is all I can bear. I can't help it—I start laughing.

"What?" His injured expression makes me laugh all the harder.

"The look on your face!" I manage, in between bursts of laughter. "I've never seen you look so frightened! Like you were going to have to explain the whole business to me!" I deepen my voice the best I can and affect an English accent, trying to impersonate him in several stuttering and ridiculous attempts at describing things. "Well, you see... A prostitute...er... A girl who... er... Men pay for... no..." I can go on no longer. I'm laughing so hard that my stomach hurts and I can't sit up straight.

"You knew!" He splutters. "How am I to know that you know what a prostitute is? You're *supposed* to be a lady."

I keep laughing. "As long as I'm not a lady of the evening!"

He unwillingly cracks a smile. "No, certainly not," he says with mock sternness. "You're far too innocent for that, even if you are a devious little pretender."

I catch my breath enough to stick my tongue out at him.

"*Supposed* to be a lady," he repeats and shakes his head, starting to laugh himself.

I give him my best curtsy. It isn't easy, sitting inside the coach, squeezed into a tight bodice and surrounded by yards of excess fabric, but I have to.

We arrive at the hotel, still laughing. The doorman helps me out of the coach, looking at us oddly as we struggle to stand up straight on the sidewalk. Damien leans one hand on the side of the building, the other clutching his stomach as the muscles contract and double him over with laughter.

Libby and Glory, just stepping down from their own coach, shoot daggers our way. Their eyes are rock hard with fury.

I don't give them a second thought until I'm safely ensconced in my room. It's then that I put myself in their shoes and realize that I can see what they might get upset about. To an outsider, it probably does look like there is something between us. After all, we do spend most of our time together. But surely any fool can see that our relationship is only that of a pair of very good friends.

Right?

Almost as soon as the door shuts behind Damien's retreating back, I begin to rush around like a maniac, assembling an outfit that will bring me within reach of William Wood. If the only way I can get through the door is dressed as one of Damien's ladies of the evening, then that's what I'll do.

Lanie's asleep, thank goodness, so I rummage through my wardrobe and trunk, shoving aside yards of colorful silks, velvets, cottons, satins, and brocades. I search through everything, hoping against hope to find something right for this. But my searching is in vain; none of these fancy dresses will do. You won't find many expensively garbed girls in a low-end bar.

I finally give in and sneak guiltily over to Lanie's wardrobe. I dig out one of her few work dresses, as well-worn as I can find, promising myself that I will replace it tenfold if anything happens to it. I pull it on quickly and keep searching, racing against the clock so I can follow Damien to the bar.

Her feet are bigger than mine, and I know that I didn't bring any work shoes, so I don't bother searching. Instead I pull on the oldest pair I have, white button-up boots that are still slightly scuffed from walking through the city this morning. They still look too nice. I wipe the bottoms of my other shoes on the white leather, rubbing in all the dirt and dust with my bare hands. It's an improvement. I pull them on and they look even better under the shadow of the worn, ankle-length hem of Lanie's old work dress.

I search through a wicker basket containing my shawls and scarves, though I'm sure I won't find what I need. No, none of these expensive linens or silks will do the trick. With regret, I go back to my wardrobe with a pair of scissors. I wince as I cut and tear a long, wide strip from the bottom of one of my dresses. It's a rich chocolate brown color, spun from the finest cotton. It's not my favorite dress, but it's still a shame to ruin such a lovely piece of work. I drape the fabric around my arms and shoulders like a shawl.

Next, I open the top buttons down the front of my borrowed dress and fold in the sides in an attempt to enhance my meager cleavage. My chemise gets in the way so I cut it, too, and tuck it under with the buttons.

I look in the mirror. The outfit looks good enough, but my hair and makeup is far too fancy for this mission. I don't think I have time to wash my face clean, so I apply more makeup right over what I've already got on. My hands slip a few times because of my haste, smudging and thickening the black kohl around my eyes more than I had meant to, but I don't change it. It's probably better this way. I put on a thick layer of dark crimson lipstick and I heavily overdo the blush.

Next, I pull my hair out of its tight pins and bindings and

let the gentle waves hang to their full length down at my waist, something I never do.

With that done, I'm finally almost ready. I bought two cloaks the other day, and I grab them both and layer them one on top of the other. On the bottom, with its hood down, I put a plain black wool cloak with a pewter clasp, no frills or baubles, that I had originally bought as a gift for Lanie. On top, I put the other, a dark gray wool cloak lined with green velvet, and with an intricate silver clasp set with small emeralds. This one I wear with the hood all the way up to hide my face.

I head down to the front entrance to wait, careful to make sure the long cloak covers me completely. I don't want to be recognized, and I really don't want to be thrown out of the hotel.

I get quite a scare when I turn a corner only to see Libby and Emily walking my way. Engrossed in conversation, they don't see me. Panicking, I back up into the hall I just came from. Their voices get closer. Thinking fast, I take my key out and pretend to place it in the first door I come to.

My heart pounds as they walk by and I fiddle with the key, acting as if I can't get it to work. Emily and Libby go by, ignoring me.

I let out a sigh of relief.

I make it to the entrance without further incident and wait quietly in the lobby, ever watchful.

A few minutes later, Damien walks by, changed out of his dark dinner suit but still well dressed in a pinstriped ensemble with a top hat and a black calf-length overcoat. I follow him out the door.

I get ready to hail a cab to follow him, but thankfully he turns left, away from the hotel, and walks along the sidewalk.

I trail behind, staying far enough from him that if he were to turn around, I'd be just another face in the darkness.

He doesn't, though. Damien leads a life with few worries and certainly has no reason to think he'd be followed.

He leads me on quite a walk into a less prosperous part of town, past the retail shops and onto a road just a few small steps away from the smelly tenements that house the poor and destitute. I pause as we walk through the ever-filthier streets only to flip my cloaks around, hiding the beautiful, expensive one and revealing the plain.

Just as he told me, the bar he enters is dark and dingy. The tables are made of rough-hewn wood and are none too clean, though a man with a rag stands near the bar and wipes it down. The windows are dark with soot from what can only be many years' worth of fires. It is definitely not the kind of place that society women frequent. The only ladies in this place are here on business. They eye me warily, but don't challenge my entrance.

I try to situate myself so I can see Damien's friend, but their table is tucked up into a corner. The room is not square, and many walls jut out in odd places. Sadly, William is already here, hidden from view by such a wall. Damien, though, sits where I can see him, which means that he can also see me as I stand by the entrance. I pull back into a corner table on the opposite side of their wall, practically back to back with William Wood. The barman makes the rounds. He brings Damien and William each a tankard of ale. Being pretty much the only drink on the menu, I get one, too. It sits in front of me, untouched after the first bitter sip.

Knowing I'd look suspicious otherwise, I brace myself and

put my trust in my disguise. I remove the cloaks, careful to keep the expensive gray one hidden, lest it get stolen. Then I settle in to listen intently.

Eavesdropping may be a repugnant practice, but it's all I have tonight. Having failed to meet my ancestor any other way, I'm stuck in a corner, dressed as a common prostitute, and listening in on my best friend's conversation.

"William Wood. Damn, it's good to see you again."

"You, too, Gracen. What have you been up to?" It's not much, but these are the first words I hear William speak. His voice is comforting and familiar, deep and smooth with that easily recognizable upper-crust accent common to all the affluent people of the area.

"Oh, the usual. Parties, dances, Newport… Typical life. You?"

William lets out a breath. "You have no idea. Working for a living is a lot different than my old life, but most days I enjoy it. I've been meeting with people all week—including my father—trying to expand…" he pauses a moment, "…operations and such. If it weren't for my father's connections, I probably wouldn't get very far."

"Sorry, mate, but it sounds extremely dull. Expanding operations? How do you stand it?"

"You keep busy, my friend. Going back to my old life now would probably seem dull to me."

"I doubt that. You'd have my company, after all." I can hear the cheeky grin in his voice, which makes me smile. "We never did let things get boring before."

William chuckles and the sound somehow reminds me of summer. "You're right, of course. We did have some fun, didn't we?" I grind my teeth in frustration, wishing I could see his face. He sounds happy, I think. But is there a hint of something else in his voice? I'll probably never know.

"That we did. Remember that time…"

They head off into a world of memories and I listen, fascinated, to their tales of friends and enemies, good times and fights, girlfriends and exes. Some of these I've heard from Damien before, but with William's added perspective, they take on new life. Others are new, and these I listen to with added pleasure, almost hypnotized by the simple sound of their two voices playing off of each other.

Having been lulled by their friendly repartee, I almost jump out of my seat when I hear the question I've been waiting for: "Is there anyone you're courting these days?" But soon I relax back into disappointment when I realize that William, not Damien, asked the fateful question. Nonetheless, I'm curious to hear the answer. He still hasn't told me her name.

"Yes and no. But you'll be happy to hear I've finally taken your advice."

William scoffs. "I was always giving you advice. Which piece did you actually listen to?"

I can hear the smile in Damien's voice. "Women," he answers simply.

"What? You've finally gotten into so much trouble that you decided it would be better for your health to be with just one woman at a time? Or…" His sarcastic tone lightens, "…did the eternal bachelor fall in love?"

"Go ahead and laugh, Wood. Yes. I have fallen in love."

I move even closer to the men, daring to scoot my chair out

and sit with my back to them so that I won't miss what he says.

"I am truly amazed, Gracen. Who with?"

"No one you'd know."

"Come on, won't you tell me?" I silently second that, urging him on.

"She's the most amazing girl I've ever met. She's smart, funny, and so beautiful it hurts to look at her." He pauses when the barman stops by to refill his drink. I curse the man, impatient to hear more.

"She's unlike any girl I know," he continues. "She's strong and brave and she's not afraid to say what's on her mind. She can be stubborn and willful, and, though she doesn't show it often, she has a fiery temper that will make you stand back in awe."

Wow. No one's ever extolled *my* stubbornness and bad temper as virtues before. I'd never even thought of such a thing, really. Damien is truly in it deep.

"You still haven't told me her name, Gracen. Are you sure I don't know her? She sounds a bit like a girl I've met before…"

"No, you don't know her. I'm sure of that."

"Well, I'm glad to hear that someone has finally tamed you. I wish you the best."

Damien sighs heavily. "No, it's not like that. I wish it was, but she doesn't want me. She's in love with someone else. A farmer, if you can believe it. No, Lizzy is my best friend and that's all she'll ever be."

I choke as I inhale a sip of my drink instead of swallowing when I reel from the shock of what he's just said. *Can I really be so blind? How did I miss that?!?*

I can't tell for sure, but I feel a pair of eyes on me. Is he

watching me, the back of a woman coughing across from him?
I hunch down in my seat, trying to control the spasms, trying
to make it clear that I don't need help. The last thing I need is
a Good Samaritan to call attention to me, but in my current
disguise, I really needn't worry. Not many people will come to
my aid while I'm dressed like this. But then, Damien being
Damien, he just might.

I manage to get my lungs under control quickly enough to
hear part of William's horrified response, "Not Libby!?"

Damien laughs darkly. "God no, not Libby. Lizzy. Libby is
way too much trouble, and besides, she still has her eyes on you,
Lord help you, you poor bastard.

"No, her name is Elizabeth Franklyn. She came to town, what?
About four months ago now." Something in his tone makes me
turn around, just a small peek at his face. In the darkness I can
see him smile, hear it in his voice. My heart goes out to him.

"I remember meeting her on her very first day in town, and
by the end of that day I knew she was different than the rest
of them. She became my best friend within a couple of weeks.
And not long after that, I kissed her."

William speaks, anxious for his friend. "What happened then?"

Damien laughs again, the sound tinged now with the happiness that nostalgia can bring. "I'll just say she was definitely
not interested, and she let me know quite firmly." He chuckles,
remembering. "God yes, quite firmly indeed." I'm still in shock,
but I can't help but laugh with him at the memory. So long
after the fact it's easier to see the humor in it. *What an idiot he
was that day.*

"I don't regret it for a moment, though," he adds so softly

that I have to strain to hear him over the other voices in the bar.

"Perhaps I'm a bit dense, but is this girl from our circle? Because I'm not sure I understood you before. You said she doesn't love you because she is in love with a…farmer?"

"Oh, she is one of us. Her family is from Watch Hill, and I myself have seen her spend money like water. But I told you, she's different." He shakes his head lightly. "As for the farmer, I find it hard to believe myself. Don't ask me how she met the man, I've no idea." His good humor is gone again; he's begun brooding. "All I know is that she can be with him no more than I can be with her. You have no idea what it's like to watch her mourn him." He sighs. "And the worst part is that she needs me to keep her sane. She needs me and I—I need her, each of us warding off the pain of our separate broken hearts. Only she doesn't know that she is both the malady and the cure." He exhales despondently.

A strong hand is placed atop Damien's, my second glimpse of William. I barely notice. I'm too caught up in what I'm hearing.

"I'm so very sorry, Damien," he condoles. I can tell that he means it. It's good to know that William is a compassionate man. I know I'm sorry, too.

"I won't die of a broken heart anytime soon, mate." He takes a deep breath, pulling himself together. Always mercurial, his good humor reappears as quickly as it went. Peeking over my shoulder, I can see him as he gives his tablemate a wicked grin. "What of you? Does Libby have any competition I should know about?" he asks slyly.

"I do hope you're joking. She's not truly waiting for me, is she?"

"Oh, yes. Even your parents still think she'll be a good match for you. She thinks your money is a good match for her. All in all, everyone is happy. Well, except for you, of course."

"Then she won't be happy when she learns that she is the last woman in the world I would ever marry. There is a lot more to me than my inheritance and my connections, but she doesn't care anything about the rest. The money might be good enough for her, but I have more important considerations."

Well. At least my eavesdropping seems to have brought *some* good news. She can't be related to me now.

"You know, Wood, once upon a time, I might have disagreed with you. I didn't used to care if women only wanted me for my money. After all, I only wanted their company for one reason."

"Trust me, I know that, my friend."

"But it's different now. I love Lizzy, and she loves me. Not the way I want her to, but she does love me. And not because I'm rich but because I'm…me. Even with all my flaws, she loves me. And now that I have that, I realize how important it is."

Oh, Damien. I want to go to him, comfort him. I inch back to my own table and a tear glides down my cheek, a regretful tear for so many things. Because I can't love him the way he needs me to, not while I'm so in love with someone else. Because even if I could, I wouldn't be free to be with him any more than I am with James. And worst of all, because I know he won't live to find someone else to love him the way he loves me.

I'm so lost in my reverie that I don't notice at first that some-one has come up beside me. I sense him now; how long has he been standing there? I still don't look. How can I face Damien now, after all he's said? My eyes downward, I involuntarily throw a glance behind me at his table, only to find him still engaged in a conversation that I have since tuned out.

Nervously I look at my visitor, working my way slowly up to his face. A dirty, brown work jacket is the first thing I see, followed by a long dark beard streaked with gray. Inside that tangled bush of facial hair lies a leering mouth set in a scarred and craggy face. His rheumy eyes don't waver from their course; he stares unapologetically at the pale skin exposed at my breast.

This is an unforeseen event. I suppose I should have expected this to happen, walking into a bar dressed as I am, but somehow, I managed to overlook this possibility when I came up with my brilliant plan.

The man sits down across from me, still leering. "Well, hello there, missy. Ain't you a spot a' light on a dark evenin'?"

I peek back again at Damien with more urgency. He's still talking to William, paying no attention to the young girl across the way.

"I'm sorry, sir," I say quickly, "I'm waiting for someone." My heart rate increases and adrenaline pumps into my veins. Will he leave me alone?

"Really? 'Cause I been watchin' you. You been waitin' fer over an hour now. Seems like yer 'pointment's late, little lady. And me, well, *I'm* someone. Now, why don' we go on upstairs? I tell ya, I bet I can have ya back down here afore yer man even gits here."

My heart pounds faster. I smile tightly at him. "You know, I'd really love to help you out, sir, but as I said, I'm waiting for someone. Someone *else*," I add pointedly. "Perhaps if you come back tomorrow I'll be available…"

The man is drunk and now he's getting angry. "Now listen here, I gots money now an' I intend to have ya tonight!" He stands up and comes around the table to my side. With every word he says, he slams a grimy finger down on the rough wood beside me. "I don't take no lip from no whores!"

I gnash my teeth together. I don't think there's any way to get out of this without causing a scene. I'm not even sure if there *is* a way to get out of this. I stand up slowly. I can't risk a glance behind me. *Is Damien watching, listening?* I can't let that direct my actions; I need to get away from this man.

"You know, you're quite right, sir," I say softly, sultrily, trying to placate him. "Perhaps I have time for you tonight after all."

I stand up, and instead of moving away from him where he can follow and box me in, I move closer to him. I can smell the whiskey on him, mingling with atrocious body odor, which smells like a mixture of old garlic, bile, and dung.

His hand reaches toward me, lightly sweeping into my loose hair but he's too drunk and I easily brush it back out of his grasp. His anger has melted away with my acquiescence, and he doesn't fight it when I put a hand on him to spin us around and back him into my little corner. He doesn't seem quite sure about what to do with this but he does seem to like it; he grins, showing almost vacant gums studded with a few brown teeth, and goes along with me easily.

He's not so agreeable a moment later when my knee slams up into his groin as hard as it can go, nor when my foot stomps and grinds on his toes through his soft, cheap boots, making a crunching sound. His grunt is louder than I might have hoped for, but the pain deters him from more than a weak grip on my arm which I quickly shake off.

I turn to make my escape, pulling my cloaks on quickly.

And then I lock eyes with Damien.

There is no mistaking the shock on his face; his eyes widen and his jaw drops almost comically. But I don't stop, not even when another head peeks around the wall to see the cause of his friend's condition.

Perhaps I was eager to see William before, but I don't even have time to register his face now as I immediately turn away and pull my hood up over my head. I practically sprint for the door, not waiting to see if he or anyone else follows. Thankfully, no one calls for me to stop—no one else seems to notice or care about the wretched old man or the prostitute who knocked him down.

The return trip to the hotel seems to take much longer than it should, probably because I make a few wrong turns in my haste. Eventually, mercifully, I make it back to the safety of my room. I clean the dirt and makeup and tears from my face with the water in the basin, turning it brown. I change into my nightclothes and throw everything I wore tonight but my beautiful new cloak and Lanie's dress straight into the garbage. Moments later, I return to the wardrobe and throw those out as well, emeralds and all. I guess I owe Lanie ten new dresses, but I don't care.

I go to bed, my mind reeling with unpleasant thoughts and unanswered questions. I lay awake for hours before finally, in the deepest hours of the morning, I fall into a troubled sleep.

Chapter Twenty-one

Damien and I are under mutual agreement that I was not there that night in the city.

It's more difficult for me, I think, than it is for him. After all, I know what happened. I know without a doubt what I saw and heard.

Damien, at least, has the luxury of being able to doubt what he saw. It was dark, he was drinking, and I was on his mind. For him, it might have been anything from a trick of the light, to a girl who resembled me, to a full-fledged hallucination.

It's been more than two weeks since the incident. It's been difficult, pretending that I didn't hear what I did. It's hard not to let it change my behavior. I used to hold hands with him without a second thought. I used to snuggle into the warmth of his body when he draped his arm over my shoulders, easily give him a hug or a friendly kiss on the cheek. It's harder to be normal when the meaning of all of our actions seems to have changed.

In the first few days, in New York and on the train home, I found it very challenging indeed. I kept away from him so fervently that he thought I was angry again. I realized that not only was I giving myself away, but I was also being unfair. After all, he has changed for me. He has shown that he can control himself, that he can simply be my friend even while he hides a deep passion within. *So what if he loves me? Don't I love him? If it comforts him to be with me, how can I keep from him a thing that I can give so easily?*

Thus, relations between us go more or less back to normal.

Life, too, it seems, goes back to normal. Nineteenth-century normal, anyway. The Season is coming to a close; the last major event is tonight.

I dress carefully, in a beautiful gown I commissioned especially for this evening. The style is old-fashioned, even for this time period, more Regency than Victorian. The gown is empire-waisted and the fabric is an almost iridescent green silk—the exact color of James's eyes. Lanie piles my hair atop my head into an elaborate updo topped with delicate cream feathers that point into the air like antennae. I take great pains with my face and finish it off with a small mask which covers the area around my eyes and over my nose. The same pale green of the dress, the mask is intricately shaped like the fragile wings of a perfect Luna moth.

Yes, to honor the end of another good Season, there is to be a masquerade ball.

We file into the ballroom, Damien and I. The whole scene is a barrage on the senses. There are dozens of people here, more than I've ever seen all together in town like this, more like a city event than any other we've had in Thorne Hill.

The colors are the first to overwhelm me; the variety tonight is breathtaking. Masks and costumes abound, and people are not shy this evening. Even the older guests remove themselves from the normalcy of natural tones and dainty pastels. In just a quick glance around me, I see gowns of ruby red and deep purple, dresses covered in stripes and polka dots, suits of all fashions in blue and crimson—and one memorable tailcoat in a strange burnt orange hue. Everyone has gone all out to have fun tonight.

After the swirl of colors, the next thing to catch my attention is a burst of smell. It's well past dinnertime, so the hors d'oeuvres are cleverly organized as after-dinner sweets and passed out by servants throughout the room. The scents of cakes and pies and tarts tantalize me from all directions. I inhale deeply the warm smell of apple crisp, a homey aroma coming off of miniature pumpkin pies, and the sweet perfume from a chocolate cake smothered in thick raspberry jam.

And then there are the sounds. The light hum of the guests fills the room as they talk to friends and acquaintances. The sounds of the shuffling of feet, the tapping of heels, and the swishing of ball gowns echo across the shiny black marble floor.

Of course, the most impressive of the ballroom sounds is the music. Stationed in the corner are the musicians: not merely a quartet or trio for this evening, no, but a small orchestra. Violins, cellos, flutes, clarinets, and more play in perfect harmony. The music is sometimes deep and moving, but just as often it is light and fun. Either way, the dancers know exactly what to do and move with each other in beautiful, precise motions. Having gone to so many dances, I recognize many of the songs that are played and hum along. Damien hears me and smiles.

Aurelia is next to me, on the arm of Amos Fishbourne. They've been courting for a month now. Even her mom approves. They are still full of that glow of early love, complete with bouts of staring into one another's eyes and ignoring everyone else present. I give Aurelia's arm a small squeeze of greeting and leave them to it.

Damien and I make our way around the room, saying hello to people, trying to guess who is under each spectacular mask. Some only cover half of a person's face, like mine. These are the easy guesses, though even easier are the masks which the wearers hold up by sticks. Sooner or later, their arms tire, their hands fall, and their identities are revealed.

Some though, are actually quite difficult. Many people wear full-face masks instead, some even going so far as to use a mesh covering over the eye holes so that no trace of flesh shows through to give their secrets away. It's these people that must be identified by voice and mannerisms alone, a task much harder than it sounds when so many people in the room are still a mystery to me.

Beside me, Damien is dressed as a young dandy in canary yellow trousers and a golden tailcoat. His yellow top hat sports a golden band that perfectly matches his coat, and a massive yellow silk flower sits in his breast buttonhole. Only his mask contrasts his bright and silly outfit.

The mask covers only the top half of his face, leaving his small blond mustache and strong jaw line open for all to see.

But the mask is deep, glossy black, accented by an evil looking brow line and a hint of devil horns. The effect is dramatic: the dark mask paired with that overly bright outfit. He looks like he might be a wayward demon trying—and failing—to look as innocuous as possible.

We dance and talk and eat. I'm often whisked away from my escort by masked strangers, off to decipher the identities of another new dance partner. What makes the task even more difficult is that everyone is here for this occasion: young, old, married, or single, and each is happy to stand for a dance simply for the fun of the guessing.

So it happens that I am accosted by a man in a dark blue cloak with a blond beard covering a strong chin that I recognize—it's Damien's father. His steady leading is much like his son's. Apparently, this is where Damien learned to dance. We make small talk for a short while before he throws it at me: "Have you had a dance with young Mr. Wood yet? He arrived in town this afternoon. He claimed he was coming to the ball."

I stumble and have to collect myself. Flustered, I'm not sure how to speak for a moment. "Um, no. I haven't. But you can be sure I'll get an introduction, thank you."

My next partner boasts a pair of dark green eyes under the mask of a wise old owl. We talk a few moments before I place him, and I smile when I realize that these eyes belong to my own ancestor, Mr. Wood, William's father. He confirms what Mr. Gracen told me; his son is here tonight. But he refuses to tell me what costume he's in. He says that he doesn't want to spoil my fun.

A few more dances brings me back to the yellow demon

without any trace of William, but this time I'm not worried. I may not see his face, but I'll find him for sure this time.

"Damien," I ask, "have you seen William? Where is he?"

"Lizzy, my dear lovely little moth, in case you hadn't noticed, most everyone here is in disguise. I've not seen him and I might not at all unless he points himself out to me."

"Well, surely he will. You promise you'll introduce him to me?"

"You have my word, my darling."

And off I go again, into the arms of another masked man, and another after that.

The night wears on and still I don't meet William. I feel discouraged, but then, I have danced with three men whom I haven't been able to identify at all. All three wore full-face masks with their eyes blocked out and no hint at all of their identities showing.

One man is short and stout, wearing the face of a clock. I almost laughed out loud when I saw his costume. It reminded me of Cogsworth, the clock from the Disney movie *Beauty and the Beast*.

The next has a figure like my father, tall and lean like a beanpole. He is dressed as a fencer. Nothing more, just a white fencer's uniform, a foil at his hip, and a dark mesh mask across his face.

The last was the most intriguing, and if I had any choice, he is the one I'd choose to be related to me. Surely there are plenty of good genes in that man. He has a strong figure, solid and muscular. His bearing is regal, as is his costume. He wears tall boots and a crisp, blue military-style jacket with a bright red sash reaching from his broad right shoulder to his taut left hip. Golden medals adorn his strong chest. A small gold crown sits on his brow. To top it all off, he dances every bit as well as Damien does.

But his mask is frightening: a big, gray leering skull. It's like he is the king of the dead. I don't like it. He didn't speak much during our dance. A few trivial remarks about the weather and the dance is all he said. His death's face intimidated me so much that I didn't try very hard to make conversation. But when we broke apart, I could feel his masked gaze following me as I walked away.

Hours later, I'm tired. Damien is off, having been swept away by a very persistent doe-eyed girl dressed as a swan. I stand alone for the first time in quite a while. And I am annoyed. No, I'd have to say that I'm seriously pissed off. Even after hours of mingling, dancing, and guessing, William has remained as elusive as ever. *What is it about this man that makes him impossible to find?* No one will tell me what costume he is wearing, but they all swear that he's here, that they have danced with him or spoken with him. I'm starting to think they must be suffering a group hallucination except for Damien, who, as of twenty minutes ago, still had no idea.

I decide some fresh air is in order so I head outside. Picking my way through a winding path, I come to a gazebo that is covered in vines. This summer, the vines had virtually dripped sprays of pretty white flowers, but now, with autumn in full swing, they hang listlessly. The flowers are gone and the leaves are brown and crinkly and starting to fall. It's a warm night for late October, but there is still a strong chill in the air and a brisk wind that comes and goes. I wrap my arms around myself, but I don't move to head inside. It feels good after the stuffy interior of the ballroom and helps to ease my frustration.

I'm not long outside before I hear footsteps. Damien, I guess, checking on me as usual. He must have lost that poor girl after only one short dance.

But I'm wrong. It's not Damien at all, but the king of the dead who comes up the path, still looking tall and dashing and scary as hell.

I start to move away, to head back down the path, but he stops me with a word. "Wait," he says simply. And I do.

I don't recognize his voice, muffled behind the mask as it is. Again, I wonder who this man is. Could he be my ancestor? William Wood at last? Perhaps Damien finally found him and sent him to introduce himself?

I wait. Nervously, cautiously, I wait.

He reaches up and takes hold of his mask, neatly pulling it off of his face in one quick motion.

My heart stops.

Chapter Twenty-two

It's not William Wood. The man behind death's mask is James Percival.

"What? How? Why?" I manage softly, in shock.

I haven't seen him up close since we parted that terrible day in August so long ago, but he is still as handsome as ever. He has waited for me every morning since then without fail, but seeing him from a distance does not do him justice. His face is smooth, still tan from countless hours in the sun. His hair is neatly trimmed and styled. His pale eyes match my gown perfectly, and they look into mine with uncertainty. He's nervous, I realize.

It could be the nervousness that gets to me. Or maybe it's just the fact that I've missed him so much it hurts. Regardless of which, when my pulse starts up once again, I can't help myself. I close the gap between us quickly and wrap him in my arms.

He responds in kind, and the feeling of being hugged by him is like coming home.

I pull back to look at his face, and I see it coming, if only for a split second. I don't stop him this time. His eyes search mine for only seconds, questioning. Finding what he was looking for, those eyes slowly close and his lips move in to meet mine. As if attracted by magnets, our lips come together. There is nothing in this world that could stop it.

The kiss is everything our first was and more, so much more.

A spark, bright and vibrant as the sun, takes hold of me at the touch of our lips. Electricity, hot and crackling, makes its way through my body, but there is no pain. My hands move of their own accord, taking in the feel of his body. My palms tingle with the sensation as they run through his hair and down his neck and back.

My brain is not working. All my questions have disappeared; all my doubts have vanished. I don't care how or why he is here, only that he is. We were meant to be. Forget time, forget everything. There is no one for me but James, and no one for him but me.

It could be minutes or hours later. It feels like a perfect eternity and yet also like it could never last long enough. But the moment ends when I feel a change. His body stiffens and he looks over my shoulder.

"What?" I say, turning a moment too late to see more than the dark bottom of a skirt moving around the corner. It could belong to anyone. "Who is it?"

He looks at me, into my eyes, and smiles. He relaxes. "Nothing. No one important."

"What are you doing here, James?" I ask, my curiosity returning.

"Isn't it obvious? I came to find you," he answers simply. "You wouldn't come to me, so I decided to come to you."

I sigh contentedly, for once not caring about anything but us. This is wrong, but I don't care anymore. It feels too right. I hug him to me tightly.

"Oh, James," I burst out. "I'm so sorry that I shut you out. I wanted to be with you more than anything but…"

"Shhh," he hushes, putting a finger to my lips and smiling tenderly, the skin around his eyes crinkling. "You don't have to apologize. What matters is that we're together here, now." He runs the back of his hand gently down my cheek. "Are you happy?" he asks softly.

My relieved grin and the love in my eyes is enough of an answer, it seems. He kisses me again, once, twice. Soft, light pecks this time, one hand on each side of my face.

"I love you," he whispers.

My heart soars.

"I know," I reply cheekily, smiling, before adding in a much softer tone, "I love you, too."

His grin widens—a feat I might have thought impossible a moment before. "Still the same old Lizzy," he murmurs, absently brushing a few stray tendrils of hair away from my face. "Modest as always."

We stay this way for a time. He strokes my hair and face. We say, "I love you," over and over. We smile stupidly at one another, lost in the fervor that is love, finally confessed. My mind stays happily in the present, stubbornly refusing to voice any objections to the current situation.

And then he turns serious.

"Elizabeth," he says softly.

"Hmm?" I answer lazily from my cozy spot against his chest, not bothering to open my eyes.

"There's something I've wanted to ask you for a long while now. Since before you left, actually."

That gets my attention. I look up at him.

Still holding my hand, my young farmer-king lowers himself slowly to one knee.

Oh, God, I think. I'm not even religious but, *Oh, God.*

"Elizabeth Franklyn...I can promise you nothing more than to love you more than anyone has ever been loved, and to bestow that love upon you for all of time. But still, I ask you, will you be my wife?"

For the second time this night my heart stutters to a halt. My breathing stops. There is nothing more I want in all the world than to say yes. *Forget time,* I remember thinking earlier. *Forget everything.*

Can I really do it? Can I go against everything to follow my heart?

I stare into his pleading eyes, so full of hope and love. And then, without conscious thought, I hear myself say one simple word: "Yes."

Chapter Twenty-three

Never one to be patient once I make up my mind, it's barely a month later when I'm standing in the back room of a tiny church on the outskirts of town, wearing a simple but beautiful white dress. Lanie is at my side, helping me with my hair and draping a delicate veil across my face. She'll be standing up with me as my maid of honor.

The weeks have passed slowly. I have gone back to spending my mornings with James. I have been using the rest of my time to slowly ease myself out of society. I've decided that it's best if they think that I've left town altogether, so I have been making my goodbyes to all but Damien and Aurelia, who stands with Lanie as a bridesmaid. I decided to risk letting her in on my secret.

Their dresses are—what else—my favorite peacock blue. Though simpler even than mine, Lanie has never worn anything as extravagant in her life. It makes me smile to see her surprise at her own elegance every time she catches a glimpse of herself in the mirror. Poor Aurelia, on the other hand, is not sure what to make of such a plain gown. But still, she takes her job seriously and I love her for it.

Waiting down the aisle with James are, of course, Gus, Thomas, Walter, and Michael. All of them are his "best men," after he couldn't decide whom he wanted to stand with him. Each is decked out in his Sunday best. None would allow me to purchase him a new suit for the occasion.

James, on the other hand, *is* wearing a new suit, having managed to trade away his kingly costume for it. When I asked him how much it had cost him to purchase that mask and outfit, he told me with a loving smile, "Please don't worry about it, Lizzy. It was worth every penny and more." When I'd asked why he had chosen such a frightening mask, he'd just laughed and said, "It was all they had left in the shop."

It's a beautiful early December day. Almost everybody I care about is here today to witness our wedding.

Almost everybody.

When I hesitatingly told Damien what had happened, he smiled weakly and told me that he was happy for me. We've spent many an evening together in the last few weeks, and though I know he is upset, he's trying not to show it. I can tell though, by the way he doesn't smile quite so easily. By the way those smiles don't reach his eyes anymore.

It upsets me that I am causing him such pain in the midst of my own happiness. I am being selfish beyond all reason in more ways than one, but I just can't help myself. I haven't seen him in two days now, which upsets me even more. And he promised me that he'd be here today, my own best man.

But he's not.

I peek out, but no one else has arrived at the little church. We start in mere minutes.

At this thought, I have yet another moment of panic. My mind is completely at war with itself. Am I seriously going to do this? Getting married is the stupidest and most selfish thing I could possibly be doing. Who knows the consequences that this will have on the future? And yet, every time I see James, every time I look in his eyes, I know that we are meant to be. Fate has seen fit to bring us together. And since he can't come home with me, I will have to stay here to be with him.

When the wedding march begins, played by the church organist, Lanie walks down first, resplendent in her new dress. Her hair is pulled into a simple bun and wrapped in a wreath of tiny white silk flowers. She holds a bouquet of larger silk flowers—white daisies—in her hands. Aurelia follows slowly, and much more gracefully, behind her.

I am much the opposite of my attendants. Where their hair is bound tightly, mine is pulled back into a loose ponytail and secured with flowers. Long dark tendrils float around my face. Where their flowers are white, mine burst with color. I incorporated the blue of their dresses into my silk carnations, paired with pretty yellow daisies. Wild roses add a dash of pink to the mix. Where their dresses are colorful, mine is pure white. Unlike so many of the ornate gowns I've worn in the past months, this dress has none of the excess frills. It is fitted over a corset, but there is no hint of a bustle or train even with both being so trendy nowadays. Flounces and bows, ribbons and lace were all purposely left off. I'm marrying a farmer, not a prince. The only hint of wealth is the row of tiny pearl buttons running down my back.

It's my turn to walk. I take a deep breath and smile. It is

my wedding day, after all. I breathe deeply. *Forget time. Forget everything.* I meet James at the end of the short aisle. He can't stop staring at me, his green eyes wide with love and wonder. He takes my hand and leads me to the altar.

◊

"You may now kiss the bride," the priest intones kindly.

James looks into my eyes and again I can't believe it's over. I must be crazy, because I feel like the luckiest girl in the world, not at all like the girl I know I am, one who is self-serving and shortsighted, willing to give up her entire family who needs her. But James somehow makes me feel like everything is perfect anyway. He kisses me, gently at first, but with more intensity once our lips touch and the electricity begins to tingle through us once more.

Lanie gives a titter and the boys let out a few guffaws before we part. Aurelia is just smiling at us, knowing what it's like. I am blushing and James is beaming like a fool. I feel so much love right now.

And then I glance up and see Damien at the door of the church. My breath hitches in my chest. My heart, so full before, now feels as if it might burst.

That is, until I see him clearly. He's not quite as disheveled as when he came to me to apologize so many months ago, but it's a close thing. He's staring openly at James with a disgusted look upon his face. A betrayed look. My heart aches for him. I know what I've done to put that look there.

He spots me watching him. I smile encouragingly. I try to

invite him in with that look, show him that all the love I have for him is still here. He doesn't smile back, just stares emptily at me for a moment. He gives a resigned sigh, an almost imperceptible shake of his head, and then turns and walks out the door without a word.

I try to go after him. I step away from James and the others, head towards the door, but Damien quickly gets lost in the bustling crowd outside. Before he disappears from sight, I see him pull a silver flask from his coat pocket and bring it to his lips for a long draw.

I want to cry, but know I need to be strong. I can't do anything for him right now. I'll talk to him soon and help him through this. So instead of letting the tears fall, I take a deep breath and let it out shakily before turning my attention back to my new husband. And I smile. Even if it does take a while before that smile becomes real.

When we get to the farm, I'm surprised to find welcoming faces. The guys' families are all here, piled into James's little farmhouse. I've never met any of them before but that doesn't stop them from enveloping me in huge familiar embraces.

There is food everywhere. Thick venison stew filled with root vegetables bubbles merrily from the stove. Mashed turnips and baked pumpkins, each stuffed with bread and cheese before cooking, steam away. Roasted duck swims in grease. Hearth baked yams and fresh, crusty bread let off aromas that make my mouth water. Gooey fruit pies line the windowsills, with syrupy filling made from this summer's berries that we canned earlier in the year.

I meet everyone throughout the day. Gus brings over his wife, Margaret, and all seven of their children, ranging in age from fifteen to three. Each and every one of them gives me an affectionate hug. Walt and his wife, Clara, bring their three girls up to meet me. Two of them, it turns out, are identical twins. Even Walt's mother, no longer spry at 79, gives me a warm smile and a surprisingly tight squeeze. Tom's two sons are adorable in matching outfits. The elder is perhaps seven, his younger brother five. Not only do their outfits match, but as they eat from the huge selection of food, matching dribbles soon appear on their fronts. Their mother smiles indulgently, giving me a quick, 'kids will be kids' look. Michael is happy to introduce me to his brother and sister, and especially his father, who has made quite the recovery since the summer months.

Soon my corset feels unbearably tight as I sample the massive array of food that my new friends have brought. James is never far from me, and I laugh quietly as he inconspicuously loosens his own belt. He looks at me and grins sheepishly, as if embarrassed to be caught in the act, but I lean in to give him a hug and a kiss. "I do love you," I say with a smile.

It's late in the evening when I see something else that makes me light up with a delighted grin. Michael has been eyeing Lanie all day, and she him. Until now they have been exchanging shy smiles and not much more. It seems that one of them has gotten up the courage to start a conversation. They sit together, deep in discussion, oblivious to the rest of the party. I make a silent wish that they find happiness.

Later that night, James and I head off to bed blushing, shooed away by our rowdy friends with cheeky grins and knowing winks. Alone at last, we look to each other almost uncomfortably, suddenly unsure. We both know what is expected of us. We both want it; I can tell. And unless I'm much mistaken, he's as terrified as I am.

"I had a bit of an adventurous youth," he admits nervously, "but I never actually…"

"Me neither," I say, and we go back to our awkward silence.

But gazing into each other's eyes, a kind of spell suddenly comes over us. It happens in an instant: One second we are sharing a look, the next we are melded into one another so thoroughly that nothing can part us. It is intense, to say the least. That familiar electricity takes hold, sending flashes of tingling blue current through every aspect of my being.

Our hands move of their own accord, removing clothing as they go. The buttons on my dress and the laces of my corset prove to be the largest obstacles, but even those don't stop my new husband for long. After all, he's had practice.

This time, he doesn't turn away from my body. No, his pale eyes seem to glow as they take in every inch of me. "You are so beautiful," he breathes. He inhales deeply before taking my mouth to his once more.

We sink down onto our marriage bed.

Chapter Twenty-four

The months pass in a flurry of domestic bliss. I resume my old role at the farm: tending the animals, tidying up the house, and cooking. I am still learning, so I spend a lot of time in the kitchen. I am happy to do it; there is barely anywhere I'd rather be than by the hot stove and hearth during these frigid winter months.

James and the guys are busy outside for large portions of each day. They spend their time out there cutting trees, splitting logs, hauling and stacking wood. During the first weeks after harvest, they did this for James's home—I guess my home too, now—and for each of theirs. We should all have enough wood to get us through the winter. Now they do it for others, merchants mostly, earning money and keeping busy while our fields lie frozen under snow and ice. The wagon wheels have been traded out for sleigh runners, which glide easily over the snow that has come fast and deep these past weeks.

One day each week, they put in extra hours. It only makes me love them all the more when I find out that they're volunteering that time to supply needy families with firewood as well.

I've decided to keep Lanie working for me, knowing that she'd probably end up on the street or back in her abusive home without this job. Besides that, though, she's my friend, and I like having her around. She's the easiest to confide in when I'm particularly missing Damien, who I haven't seen since the wedding, or even Aurelia, who is busy planning her own wedding for the spring and hasn't had much time for visiting.

I've made up a room for her upstairs, and she keeps me company in the kitchen on the long, cold days when the boys are out working. When they come home, she and Michael often make their way to a corner by the wood stove in the living room, heads together in deep conversation. By this time, of course, James is home, too, and I certainly don't mind being ignored by the others, lost as we are in our newlywed bliss. But it warms my heart to see the pair of them together, and I can't help but smile at their cozy exchanges.

And so it is that Lanie and I are cooking dinner one afternoon in February when a wave of nausea hits me like a ton of bricks. I gag, trying to hold back, but to no avail. I make a run for it and manage to make my way outside before the contents of my stomach decide that they'd rather come out the way they went in. Lanie follows me out into the cold and rubs my back as everything I've eaten, presumably in the past year by the look of it, makes a hasty exit. She helps me to my feet and wipes snow from my skirts as I dab my mouth with the towel she offers.

She puts a hand to my forehead. "No fever," she reports. "You need to lie down, and then I'll make you some nice ginger tea. It will help to settle your stomach."

I agree to the tea, though grudgingly. Because my stomach

is already settled, or so it seems. As soon as it became vacant, the nausea ceased. "Probably something I ate," I say to her. "I feel much better now. Let me help finish with dinner."

But, of course, she makes me sit down anyway. She prepares our evening meal herself, making ginger tea for me and a huge pot of elderberry tea for James and Michael, who are the only two to come back for dinner while the others head home to their families. "To help ward off illness," she tells us as we sit down to eat. And she makes them drink it all.

I eat little dinner at first, but feel better once I do.

That night, there is not a hint of nausea, but I do wake up more than once to make use of the chamber pot. It is hideously cold out from under the covers, but the tea must have run right through me and I have no choice but to climb out from my warm cocoon into the chill air. James snuggles me close when I climb back in each time, warming me up quickly, at least. He was worried about me earlier, but after my assurances that I'm alright, he seems to have calmed down.

In the morning I'm fine. That is, until I smell the eggs cooking. The aroma, which has always smelled so good to me before, makes me gag. A new wave of nausea takes hold, but I manage to keep my stomach this time. Lanie eyes me suspiciously, but says nothing. She does make me another pot of ginger tea, though. I skip the eggs at breakfast.

Still not feverish, I go about my business. Queasiness hits me at random times throughout the day. Sometimes it's in reaction to a smell or flavor, other times for no discernable reason at all. Lanie refuses to let me near the food preparation lest I infect the lot of them. I complain that I feel fine most of the time. Surely without a fever, I'm not in any danger of spreading contagion? Okay, I probably made that up. But still, I sit in the corner and talk to her while she works, trying to remember the sewing lessons I learned in home-ec class so that I might repair a few pieces of my husband's torn wardrobe while I'm otherwise useless.

The next day begins much the same, except for one small thing. Lanie hands me a cup of ginger tea without a word. Then she asks, "Would you like to help cook today?"

"Of course," I say, almost indignantly. Haven't I been pressing her to do just that for the past day and a half?

"Well," she says, "it occurs to me that you are not actually sick."

"I agree," I reply. "I've been saying that since it started."

"But," she continued, "I think I know what's wrong. Or rather," she amends, "what is causing it. Here." She thrusts her hand out at me, palm down. In it I see the edges of something small, knitted in homespun wool.

"What…?" I begin, but before I finish, she drops the item into my own hands. Items, actually. Two of them.

"I made them last night after I realized," she says with a barely contained grin.

Without a word, I contemplate the implications of what she's given to me. In my hands are two tiny woolen baby booties.

I'm jolted out of my shock by the urge to vomit.

Lanie grabs a basin for me, and when I'm done I turn to her. "You can't be serious."

She nods.

"Pregnant? No, I can't be." Alright, I could be. I guess I knew it might happen when I married James, but knowing and being are two very different things. I think back, disbelieving. My cycles have always been irregular, no clockwork here. Twenty-eight days, thirty-five, forty. How long has it been? Eight weeks? Nine? I'd had my period not too long after our wedding. Not a fun time for most women in this era, but not so bad for me since I'd stashed my menstrual cup away in my luggage, unwilling to do *everything* the old-fashioned way. Nine weeks may be longer than average, but not so long that I'd think anything of it if it weren't for my bouts of illness.

Unfortunately, I can't just pee on a stick and know the truth in minutes. I must wait. Surely my period will come soon and the matter will be settled. *Surely?*

The days pass, and then weeks. I continue to spend my time in fits of nausea. Foods that I used to love make me feel ill. I am more and more convinced that Lanie is right, but still I hesitate. James is concerned for my health and finally, despite my protests, calls in the doctor who sees me on a warm March day while James is out cleaning up the fields.

He barely examines me before telling me in his pinched voice, "There is no malady here. You are with child, young lady."

"Are you sure?"

He looks at me as if I were an imbecile and only deigns to respond with a one-word answer. "Yes."

He hands me a brown glass bottle with a cork in the top from inside his bag. Liquid sloshes around inside. "Take this for your morning sickness. It will make you feel better," he says brusquely.

"You should expect the baby in September." Then he turns on his heel and walks out.

I look over the label on the bottle. "Laudanum," it reads. I cringe and take the bottle outside. After popping the cork, I tip it over and watch as the contents spill over the snowy ground, melting the snow in brown spiral patterns as I swirl the bottle through the air. There is no way I'm drinking down a tonic made from opium.

My baby would probably come out with eleven toes, I think. And then I stop. *My baby*, I start again wonderingly. I smile. *Our baby*. I am excited and scared and unsure—sentiments I'm pretty sure are close to universal for a pregnant woman—but I am also horrified that I let this happen. How could I have let this happen?

On top of that, my back aches, I feel nauseated, and yes, damn it, I have to pee again.

And yet, for all of that, I may just be happier than I've ever been in my entire life.

Chapter Twenty-five

James walks in not long after the doctor leaves.

"Well," he says anxiously. "Are you alright?"

I smile at him. I can't help it. "I'm better than alright," I tell him. And then I place the booties Lanie made into his hand.

He stares at them for a beat, confused. Then he slowly looks up to meet my eyes. His are full of wonder.

"Does this mean…?" he asks. I nod before he can finish.

The next thing I know, his arms are around me. My feet are in the air and we are twirling around the room. I laugh and he sets me down to stare into my eyes once more. The wonder is still there, but also excitement, pure joy. His face splits into the biggest grin I've ever seen.

"We're going to be parents!" he laughs, delightedly. And then, in a tone of awe, "I'm going to be a father."

I stare right back at him and correct gently, "No. You're going to be a great father.

He just beams, and I beam back. With reverence, he moves his hands down to my belly. Because of my stubbornness, I am probably farther along than most women when they tell their partners. If I remember correctly from school, pregnancy averages forty weeks from a woman's last period until birth. That would make me nearly twelve weeks along. There is a barely perceptible bit of extra roundness to my lower abdomen, but James places his palms right over it, so gently it makes me want to cry. *Was there ever a man who loved his unborn child as much as this?*

I wrap my arms around him and we hold each other for a long time.

$$\Diamond$$

By summer I feel huge. My barely-there bump has turned into what looks like a basketball stuck under my dress. Or maybe "tent" is a better word than dress to describe what I generally wear now. I swear there is more fabric in just one piece of my clothing than in a circus tent.

James, of course, thinks that I am beautiful. Lanie agrees with him, but then, she is the one making my dresses these days. I'm just tired of feeling like I may never wear anything without an empire waist again, because I refuse to wear the corsets anymore, even if most women do for their entire pregnancies in this era.

All the same, I do feel beautiful, too. Huge, yes; tired, yes; but I also love the feeling of life within me. Our baby moves so often now. I never tire of watching my belly move with the kicks and somersaults of the child within.

I do, however, find it a bit annoying when he or she takes to bouncing on my bladder as if it were a trampoline, usually in the middle of the night.

James, too, could watch my ever-expanding midsection for hours. The first time I placed his hand on it and he was able to feel the nudge of the baby within, tears came to his eyes.

There are, as always, a few dark spots on the horizon. Tomorrow is my birthday. I will not be going home. They'll be waiting for me, my dad and Alex. My friends will be expecting me home from my trip. I tell myself that I haven't finished my search. And of course, that is true in a way, but I can't help but know that it is not the whole truth. William still has not come home, sure, but neither have I been looking. I've found my purpose here and my search seems so irrelevant now that I've just stopped trying.

My other source of stress is Damien. I write to him nearly every day, and unlike my unsent letters in Newport, these make their way to their recipient each time. Like those other letters though, I never get any reply.

I would stop writing him, or perhaps at least stop sending them, at the first sign that he wanted me to. But he doesn't let me know anything anymore. So I keep writing. I need him to know that I haven't forgotten him and that I still love him. And that I miss him so much.

I've even tried more than once to visit him, usually after I drive James crazy talking about him. He'd send Lanie and I out together in the cart so that I could meet with Damien and maybe, just maybe, feel better about what I did to him. But after the sixth time of visiting when he "was not in," even though that last time I saw him there in the window, I couldn't stand it anymore. That one glimpse of him, watching me from halfway behind a curtain, is the last time I've seen him since

James and I got married.

But until he sends me a message back, telling me to knock it off with the letters, I'll write. After all, how long will he be around to write to?

◊

My nineteenth birthday arrives much differently than my last. I'm not sure that I'm even the same person who woke up a year ago in the 21st century. So many changes to my life have changed me, too.

In the privacy of our room, while James is out working, I take the time machine from a compartment hidden at the bottom of my jewelry box, and actually look at it for the first time in nearly a year. I can't help but marvel at it. So small and sleek and yet so full of power. It is so different from the bulky machines of this era. Again, I'm reminded of my smartphone, and that thought blows me away. I haven't posted a selfie or Googled a single thing since leaving 2018.

Strangely though, I no longer think it so crazy that the world could change so much in so little time, from the Victorian age to the 21st century. After all, look at the changes in me in just one year's time.

I wish for a moment that I could use it as a phone, to send my dad a message, tell him how much I love and miss him. I almost—almost—consider a walk down to the old stone walls, to make a quick trip home to see him and Alex, and hug them both tightly.

But I can't. Because if I go home now, they'll never let me come back.

◇

The months continue to go by. I do what they let me do on the farm, which isn't much. I still write to Damien every day. I write to Aurelia once a week, and read the letters she sends to me. She got married, as planned, in the spring. I was even at the wedding, back from afar to attend, or so everyone was told. My belly was small then, and hidden easily enough.

Damien wasn't there.

I think someone told him that I would be. James stayed home, too, even though I'd asked if he would come with me. But he was too busy with the farm, so I went alone. I didn't hide my wedding ring though. Most of the girls admired it, even if it was a bit small for their tastes, and asked after my new husband. I just told them he was busy working his own business and left it at that.

I was very happy for Aurelia, truly, and yet a darkness hung over the whole affair. Damien, my very best friend, wasn't there.

Chapter Twenty-six

Once again I am in the position of time both flying past and yet, paradoxically, creeping slowly along. Creeping because I am beginning to feel that this pregnancy will never end. Flying because Damien is getting closer and closer to an end of his own.

It is late August when I wake feeling like something different is coming. It is a nervousness that I feel deep in my being. *Is it the baby? Is it Damien?*

The baby should be coming soon. As big as I was in June, I am much bigger now. Think: beach ball. Lanie has had to let out all of my dresses again and again. I've been feeling what my midwife calls "false labor" for a week now. "Your body is preparing for birth," she tells me patiently each time I send for her in vain. It feels real enough to me, but what do I know?

That afternoon, James and the guys come in early. A big storm is building up and they all want to be home when it breaks. Michael is the only one who doesn't leave. He is practically living with us at this point, and, as usual, he stays for dinner.

After the meal, I still feel like something is happening.

"What's wrong, Lizzy?" James asks for the tenth time. "Is it the baby?"

I smile at him reassuringly, though I don't feel like smiling. "No, I don't think so. But I'm worried about Damien. I keep getting the feeling like something is wrong." I hesitate, but only for a minute. "Will you take me to him?"

James kisses my forehead before lowering his face to kiss my lips. "I would," he says, "but I really want to finish this cradle before the baby arrives. Can Michael take you?" I'm confused, since he's been so nervous about leaving my side these past few days, but I agree nonetheless. Anything to get me there. Soon.

◊

We are on our way, and I feel more nervous than ever. Something's wrong, I can tell.

I urge Michael to hurry as we speed toward Damien's house. When we arrive, I ask him to wait for me. He moves the cart to the stable to take shelter while I head towards the house. I knock on the door and the old butler, Lennon, lets me in. This is a first; usually I'm told that Damien is "not at home" and I'm sent straight away. Maybe Lennon feels bad, seeing my massive pregnant belly, or maybe it's that the raindrops are just starting to fall from the mass of dark clouds that have been hovering all afternoon.

I give him a quizzical look. "Is everything okay?" I ask.

"Please, Madam, I was only wondering if Master Gracen is perhaps holding a party tonight that he neglected to tell me about. You are the third young lady to enter the house this evening. Miss Hunt has just—"

And that's when I hear the yelling. High-pitched screeches of pure rage ring through the halls.

Chills dart down my spine. I was right. It's happening now. I have to stop it.

I run towards the sound, Lennon close at my heels. My pregnancy slows me down, but I can still run faster than him; his age drags him farther and farther behind me. He trips suddenly and with a cry of pain, but I can't stop for him, not now. I leave him on the ground and keep running.

As I get closer, I start to make out muffled words in what seemed to be just empty shrieks a moment ago.

"...can't believe this, my best friend! You told me—"

Damien's voice is the calm in the storm, loud enough to get through the shouting, yet still unruffled as always. "I told you nothing of the sort, Libby."

"I thought you were mine! Look at me! I'm pregnant for God's sake! I came here to tell you so we can get married—"

"That's not going to happen, Libby—"

"Instead I find you in bed with my best friend!" She growls in frustration. "But you *will* marry me, Damien! There is no question!"

"No, Libby, I won't. I'm never getting married."

"Yes, you are!" she cries in a fury. "You can't think I'm going to do this alone. My reputation will be ruined. I'll end up a spinster, damn it, out on the streets!"

"I'm sorry, but no. I won't marry you. I'm...I'm in love with someone else."

"Do you think I care about that, you bastard? What does it matter?!" There is a short pause. "Wait... *Elizabeth. That bitch.*"

She hisses my name with such venom that I cringe.

I come to a dead end, an empty guest room with no exits. I swear and turn around. Now I wish I'd been to Damien's bedroom before. *Why are there so many doors and hallways and floors in his house? Who needs this much space for one person?*

The voices become muffled again. I follow the sounds frantically, finally realizing that they come from above me. No wonder I can't find them here! The voices fade as I find the closest stairway, the servants' stairs, which are hidden in a small alcove.

The next time I begin to make out the words again there is a terrible urgency that chills me to my bones.

Glory's voice rings out, not dulcet now but terrified. "Libby, please! What are you doing?"

Ever the charming voice of reason, even now Damien isn't afraid. His voice is as composed as if he were merely giving an order to a servant.

"Libby, put my gun down. It's not a toy and this is not a game. We can discuss this like adults. Surely we can come to an agreement. After all, I am happy to give you all the financial help you and the child could need. You see, everything will be—"

I finally find the source, a brilliantly carved door. I grab the knob just as a single gunshot rings through the house and cuts Damien's sentence short.

"NOOOOO!" I cry as I swing the door open and crumple to the floor at the same time.

Somehow they don't hear me, don't see me. The door opens to a sort of entryway, a narrow hall before opening up into the bedroom. I see Damien's legs, splayed out on the glossy wooden floor, but nothing else. I can't see the girls and they can't see me.

Glory is the first to speak. "Libby! What have you done!?"

"Get up, Glory! Quickly, before the damned butler gets here. We need to get out of here! Now!"

I hear a door slam open and shut, and I know they must have left through a second entrance to the bedroom. More doors, farther away, do the same. I crawl through the hall in front of me after I find my legs too wobbly to stand on. I'm afraid to look further into the room, but I have no choice. I have to get to him.

Damien is on the floor, a look of agony on his face and a stain of blood on his chest.

I make my way over to him as fast as I can.

"Oh, no, Damien, no," I moan weakly.

His eyes flutter open. "Lizzy," he whispers.

"Damien, I'm so sorry. I am so, so sorry. Please don't die." Tears are running freely from my eyes, falling onto his ashen face. I grab hold of his hand. He stares up at me, breathing painfully.

"Lizzy…don't be sorry. I…I love you so much…you know that, right?" His voice is a breathy whisper, slow and stammering.

"I know, Damien. I love you, too. You're my best friend," I sob.

"No, Lizzy. I mean… You're her. You're the girl. You're the one I'll always love."

"Damien… I know. I'm sorry…."

"Shhh. Stop. It doesn't…matter now." He winces.

I run my free hand over his hair and down his smooth cheek.

"I…got your letters… I'm sorry I never…"

"Don't you dare apologize, Damien Gracen. How could I ever be mad at you?"

He tries to smile at me, and then coughs. A spatter of blood stains his lips, but I dab it off quickly with a handkerchief.

"Lizzy, will you…do something for me?" he asks.

"Anything!"

"Please, I know you love…him… But, would you kiss me? Just once?"

I nod, my tears flowing even harder now. I take his head in my hands and kiss him, strongly and passionately.

I hold the kiss for a long time, filling it with all the love I've ever felt for him. His lips are weak, but they match my movements, savoring the moment.

When I lift my head he is smiling, tears standing in his eyes. "Thank you," he whispers, and his hand caresses my cheek before it falls dully to the floor.

"No!"

But it's too late. Damien is dead.

It could be minutes or hours later when the sound of footsteps tells me that someone else is coming into the room. I'm still on my knees, huddled over Damien's lifeless body, my head resting on my arms upon his still and silent chest. I don't move when they enter, or even when they touch my shoulder and murmur softly to me. I don't understand or acknowledge them. It makes no difference to me when they leave and their footsteps fade gently away.

After another uncertain lapse in time, more people enter from behind me. I hear them talking, but again their words make no sense to me. They may as well be speaking another language. I ignore them, too.

They try to move me and I resist. I can't leave Damien alone. He needs me. I try to fight them, but I'm weak and disoriented. Eventually I can fight no longer and I let them lift me away from his body and carry me limply downstairs.

They try to talk to me, these people, but stop when I don't respond to their gibberish. I just shake my head blankly at them, willing them to leave me alone. Finally they do.

Time continues to pass in a haze. At last it lifts when a single word cuts through it.

"Elizabeth!"

My name, called out by the only person who could possibly get through to me right now.

"James!" I gasp. He lifts me up, hugs me to him fiercely. "Oh, James!"

The fog in my head has cleared but the tears come back with a vengeance. I can't stop crying and he holds me tightly as my body is wracked by violent sobs. His body is cold and wet from the rain outside, but still I can tell that tears are streaking down his face, too. I feel them as they land on my cheek, warmer than the drops of rain coming off of his hair. But he says nothing. He knows that any placating words would be empty right now. He won't tell me that everything will be okay when I know the truth.

It's happened. Damien is dead. Nothing is okay.

When I'm calm enough, he wants to take me home. The police—they're the ones who pulled me out—want to talk to me first. I do my best, but interrupt myself often with hiccups and sobs. I'm still in shock and not very coherent, but the police seem mollified for now. They tell me to come in tomorrow to make a full statement, and James agrees to bring me.

Michael is waiting by the door, as drenched by rain as everyone else. He looks at me wide eyed when James carries me past. I glance down at myself to see that my swollen belly is covered in Damien's blood. My knees too, from where I knelt by his side, are covered in the rusty red of my best friend's drying blood, and my arms, from resting against his body. I imagine there must even be streaks of crimson on my pale face, from the last gentle caress he laid there.

I don't care, though. I'm still in too much shock to care about the state of me. All I can care about is that he's gone. Gone forever. I drop my head and let it rest against James's chest.

He places me gently in the cart, covering me as best he can with an oiled canvas. It's too late though; I'm already soaked through. As the water drips down my fingers, I feel certain that it is pink with blood. James says a few more words to another police officer, and then he climbs in behind me and cradles me protectively in his arms.

But it's not the same as it once was. After what I've been through tonight, even the refuge of my husband's body no longer feels like the safe haven it's always been.

Chapter Twenty-seven

Everyone, even the midwife, thinks that the stress of my ordeal will bring on labor, even if it is a little early. But August turns to September, and September turns to October, and still the baby doesn't come. The false labor still bothers me often, but I've learned to ignore it as best I can.

While I wait, I try to keep busy. I don't think so much when I'm occupied. I cook. I clean. I wipe up every speck of dust from our little home and scrub the floors on my hands and knees. Nesting has hit me hard, and the house is cleaner than it's ever been. Michael has proposed to Lanie, so she and I huddle together, making big plans for their wedding. The guys, I think, are planning to build them a house for their wedding gift.

But still, the bad dreams come. I'd expected nothing less. More often than not, I see Damien being shot by Libby, over and over and over. But sometimes I feel our kiss, and see him lying there, with that contented smile on his face as he died. And I cry in my sleep, so sad that he is gone, but also strangely glad for him, that he got to die happy. Of course, those thoughts only make me feel worse when I wake up.

It is after one such dream, in the wee hours of an early October day, that true labor finally kicks into gear.

"James." I shake him.

"Hmm," he groans, still sleeping.

"James!" I shout this time, as a contraction wracks through my body.

He is wide awake in an instant. "It's time," he says. It's not a question. He knows. He runs to wake Lanie, who comes in to stay with me. Then he saddles the horse and rides as fast as he can to get the midwife.

As for me, I quickly get lost in the all-encompassing land of labor. Time passes, people come and go, but I barely notice. Lanie rubs my back, I think. But the contractions become the only thing in the world. *Get through it*, I tell myself. *One at a time.* They double me over, but I move with them, sometimes leaning, sometimes laying, sometimes squatting down. I stop myself more than once from asking for an epidural, almost forgetting in the midst of things that I am no longer in my own time.

With no concept of the hours passing, I don't know how long it takes, but eventually contractions change into an overwhelming sensation to push. I do not consciously push, no. Not like you see on TV, with people telling me to, "breathe, breathe, breathe, push, push, push!" My body just...pushes. It takes a long time, I think, but my midwife is not worried. The sun is high in the sky when I finally catch my baby in my own hands while the midwife looks on in approval, warm blankets ready.

They wrap the blankets around me and my baby. My perfect baby. We just snuggle for a time, the two of us, skin to skin. I cry, from hormones, from love, from relief, from everything. Minor contractions continue, and eventually the afterbirth is out. Lanie and the midwife help me into bed. The baby's cord is tied off, and cut, and then finally James is allowed back into the room again.

He enters cautiously. As soon as he sees us, though, his face lights up in such wonder that I start crying again. He doesn't say anything at first; he just looks at us with so much love and pride in his eyes that I reach up to take his hand. "Our baby," he says then. "Is it…?"

That's when I realize that I don't even know. I hadn't even thought to check. I quickly pull aside the blanket to find myself looking at a perfect son. "Jonathan Damien Percival," I say, looking at James for approval. We had chosen Jonathan as a possibility for a boy, after my father, but Damien was not a name we had discussed.

"Would," he says absently, but he is smiling and nodding.

I give him an odd look.

"Hmm? Oh, sorry," he says, shaking his head. "I'm just a bit overwhelmed." He looks lovingly into my eyes. "We have a son!" He hugs us both gently. "I meant to say, 'WOULD you like a cup of tea,' but I got distracted. You must be exhausted."

Tea sounds lovely, but I ask Lanie to fetch it so that we can stay together, our little family. James climbs into bed with us, helping me shift my body to lean on his strong chest instead of the pillow. Our son fusses and searches for my breast. I help him to latch on, and he nurses contentedly. And for now, everything is perfect.

Chapter Twenty-eight

Things are hard. Having a baby is hard, but I am surrounded by friends and helpers, and though I'm tired, it is a joy as well. The hardest part is missing everyone who isn't here. My dad will not get to meet his grandson, his namesake. My brother will never meet his nephew, or teach him to play video games. Donna will never dub herself, "Auntie Donna," to little Jonathan, just as I know she would. I even miss our dog, Penny, whose ears I'll never scratch again and whose tail my son will never pull. I will not see any of them again. And that hurts. A lot. But at least I have the consolation that they're okay, making their lives in the future without me.

Damien though, my best friend, is gone forever. He will never be back, never meet my family, never make me laugh again. I love Lanie, and Aurelia, and James, and all the guys, too. I love my son so much that it hurts. But no one can ever replace Damien. He was too much of a unique personality, and I will miss him always.

But still, time passes. Life goes on.

The farm has prospered. Jonathan has grown so much, and plays happily with the simple toys given to him at his second Christmas, in the year 1877. He is almost 16 months old now, walking, and babbling incessantly with new words every day. Just yesterday, he said "Nanie" as Lanie walked into the room, prompting a huge smile, a few tears, and of course, a giant hug. Which was difficult for her, considering the very large pregnant belly that *she* is now sporting.

Even for my rivals, life moves forward. I told my story to the police after that horrible night so many months ago. As did Michael, and Damien's butler, Lennon. Libby was brought in for questioning after that, but somehow, infuriatingly, nothing ever came of it. She has too many connections in high places and our testimony meant nothing against that.

She moved very quickly after her run-in with the law. No more than a month after she killed my best friend, she was married to a rich out-of-towner. Of course, this other man has nowhere near the money and connections of the Wood family, but he is the "father" to her child—my sweet Damien's child—and her reputation is somehow still intact. I'm so torn now. I'm relieved that she didn't marry William, so she is not my ancestor. And I'm enraged: She is not the Elizabeth who will be executed, even though she is the one who committed the crime. Someone else—someone innocent—will hang for it.

Glory and Angelica are apparently both engaged, to a banker from Manhattan and a local businessman, respectively. Emily is still on the prowl, but I hear that she is not nearly so popular now without the company of her old friends. I would wish her the best, but I don't really care. After Libby managed to walk free, I stopped caring about anyone in town anymore, except Aurelia. But she still tells me the gossip whenever we visit despite my protests.

It's in her house, just before the New Year, when she tells me the latest news. "Libby is telling everyone who will listen that it was you."

I give her a quizzical look. "What was me?"

"Who killed Damien," she replies gently. She puts her hand on my arm. "I know it wasn't. But I'm just warning you. People are starting to believe her, and you're no longer in town to defend yourself."

"Thanks," I say. "But I'm sure it will be fine." After all, I already know that it's Mrs. Wood who will end up with the blame, not me. It seems impossible though. She and William aren't even here, more than a year later. How could she possibly be charged with a crime she knows nothing about against a man she's never met?

Chapter Twenty-nine

The police arrive at our home on a particularly frigid day in January of 1878. The winter wind is gusting outside. Icicles tinkle as they fall down from the roof's edge. And crunching footsteps in the hard snow announce our visitors even before they knock.

"Elizabeth Franklyn?" one officer asks. He doesn't wait for my reply. "You need to come with us."

"Elizabeth Percival," I correct him. "What is this all about?"

James is not here, as is usual for this time of day. He is out delivering firewood in town. Lanie is the only adult here with me, resting her swollen ankles while I prepare lunch. Jonathan plays quietly by my feet.

"I'm sorry, ma'am. But you are under arrest for the murder of Damien Gracen."

◊

I sit alone in a bland cell. The walls are off-white. The one window is barred. It faces a wooden scaffold outside, gallows waiting for their next victim. There is a second cell adjacent to mine, separated by a full wall. Another wall, this one of iron bars, closes up both cells. There is a sort of hallway in front of the bars, and then a door on the right. I watch it now.

Waiting. Wondering. Worrying.

I left Jonathan with a very confused and upset Lanie. He was crying as they took me away, shaking with sobs and reaching for me with his pudgy fingers even as Lanie held him back. A tear runs down my face as I remember it.

I take a deep breath to calm myself. James should have been home for lunch within an hour or two of when they took me. When he finds out what happened, I know he'll get here soon after. I just have to be patient.

There is a commotion out in the office beyond the only door. A few people walk in, I think, but I can't see them. "I'm here on behalf of my client, Mrs. Wood," I hear a man with a nasal voice say. My heart sinks. Not for me, then. I tune him out, daydreaming while I wait some more. But then my head pops up. *Mrs. Wood? Is she here?*

But the only other cell is empty.

The voices get louder and a guard walks in with a man I've never met before, whom I can immediately tell is the lawyer I just heard. He is of average height, small-framed, and wearing spectacles. He holds a leather notebook in one hand and has a pencil behind his ear. He is of middling age, probably in his fifties.

"Mrs. Wood?" he asks, looking straight at me.

"No, I'm Mrs. Percival," I say, laughing a bit hysterically at this irony. *Me, Mrs. Wood? Absurd!*

Then another man walks in the door, this one dressed to the nines. I almost don't recognize him at first, so fine is he in his smart, well-fitted suit and silk top hat, which he removes as he steps into the room. But I would know those pale green eyes anywhere.

"Mr. Wood?" the lawyer asks James in his nasal voice. "This *is* your wife?"

I stare at my husband in shock and confusion.

"Yes, Mr. Hamilton," James Percival says. "Elizabeth Franklyn...Wood." Unlike his normal voice, the one I am so used to, this James speaks with that familiar upper-crust accent, like all of the wealthy people in town—like the voice of William Wood that I once heard talking to Damien in a dirty old bar one night in Manhattan. *No wonder that voice reminded me of summer. It reminded me of James...because it* was *James.*

He tries to look at me. He tries so many times, but can't seem to meet my gaze for long. It's probably because he can see all the hurt and betrayal there. He *lied* to me. For *two and a half years.* He knew I was looking for William Wood since day one, and he lied. So much is rushing through my head right now. My brain is overloading and shorting out.

But I don't have much time to think about any of it, because the lawyer nods and has the guard open the cell and lead me to a private room nearby where we can talk.

"Mrs. Wood," he says to me again. "My name is Albert Hamilton, and I am the Wood family's attorney. Your husband has brought me up to date on your situation, but I need to hear your version of the story. Please tell me all about your relationship with Damien Gracen and exactly what happened on the night of his death."

I just stare at him blankly for a moment. Then I blink a few times. "Please... Mr. Hamilton... May I have a few minutes to speak with James—" I stop, flustered. "Sorry, with...with my husband? Alone?"

James—*William?*—suddenly looks very nervous, but the lawyer agrees and moves out to the hall to stand with the guard.

"Fifteen minutes," the guard calls in.

"Jonathan," I say matter-of-factly, not looking at him. "Is he well?"

"Our son is fine," he replies hesitantly, back now to his normal voice, the one I'm so used to. "He's still with Lanie. Michael is there with them." He pauses. "Lizzy..." he begins.

"What. The. Fuck?" I explode, and slam my hand down on the table loudly to emphasize the last word. My husband, somehow this well-dressed, highborn man in front of me, blanches at my language, and at the fury in my voice. I look him straight in the eyes, those gorgeous eyes that I love so much. "Who *are* you?" It comes out like ice, almost a whisper. I've never spoken to him like this in all our time together. We've had our minor disagreements, but never like this.

He exhales slowly and hangs his head. "William James Percival Wood," he replies slowly.

"How?" I whisper, shaking now. "Why?"

He breathes in and out again a few times. It looks like he's thinking, buying time. "I..." He lowers his forehead into his hands. "It was...something that got out of hand."

I just look at him, the hurt and confusion clear in my eyes.

"I'll start from the beginning..." He sighs.

I keep staring and fold my hands across my chest.

He nods and takes a deep breath.

"It all started after Damien and I left college. I suppose he told you about that?" I nod, and he continues. "We were…in a bad place. We were not a good influence on each other. Gambling, drinking…"

"Girls?" I ask curtly.

"Yes," he says. "Girls. I won't lie to you, Lizzy."

"Oh, that's rich coming from you, *William*," I say acidly.

"I *am* James Percival," he says insistently. "He is the man I became when I didn't like myself anymore. When I no longer wanted the life I was living. I hated the lazy drunkard I had become. And I hated that not one woman I met liked me for me. They always wanted my money, my home, my family connections.

"I remembered, when I was a child, the summers that my father sent me to work on a local farm. He had wanted me to understand the value of hard work. And it was hard, back-breaking work, but I'd loved it. I remembered the pride I had felt in completing a task, and that was something I hadn't felt in a long time. So when I found that same farm up for sale, I knew what I had to do.

"Much as you 'left' town after our wedding, so I 'left' as well. Only my father knew where I went, and grudgingly agreed to cover for me, all the while hoping I'd come to my senses after a year or two of hard labor. Not even my mother, my sisters, or my best friend knew the truth. I all but gave up my old life, except for those annual forays into the city to meet with contacts—friends of friends of friends of my father—about selling and shipping any excess crop yield, and whatever else needed sorting out.

"And then I met you," he says, his manner going soft. "And I fell in love with you almost immediately." He chuckles inwardly. "There you were, walking in the middle of nowhere, carrying your own luggage, wearing the most fashionable traveling clothes, but covered in dust and burrs. You were so adorably flustered to meet me." He smiles fleetingly, but it falters.

"And then…one of the first things out of your mouth was to ask me about William Wood. All I could think was that my damned reputation had preceded me yet again."

I cringe. I knew that had been a mistake the moment I'd said it.

"Why *did* you ask me that?" he says curiously. Seeing my deer in headlights look, he shakes his head and says, "Never mind. It's not important.

"What *is* important is that he wasn't me anymore," he continues, changing the subject back to the original point. "So I treated William as the different man he'd become. As we came to know one another, I truly meant to tell you about my old life. That day you left the farm for Newport, I was going to confess my love and tell you the truth. But instead, you left before I could say it."

I lower my eyes, remembering that awful day. I did leave.

"Then when I found out that you had joined Damien in the city! I couldn't meet up with everyone as I'd planned once I knew you would be there as well. I couldn't let you find out that way. And then, I learned that Damien was in love with you, too. I met him later—"

"At the bar," I cut in. "I know."

"Of course he told you." He smiles indulgently. "Damien would have told you everything. He never could keep a secret."

Unlike you, I want to say. *But then, unlike me, too. I have also kept secrets.* Then I smile wistfully. "He did keep one secret. I didn't know until that night in the bar that I was the girl he was mooning over. He never told me."

He pauses. "That night in the bar..." he begins. Then his eyes widen. "You were there! Damien said so... But I thought he was imagining things... He was right, wasn't he?"

"That was me," I say simply. Then I change the subject. "So, why didn't you tell me later? At the masquerade would have been an appropriate time." I shake my head. "I should have guessed myself, then," I grumble. "That outfit must have cost a fortune."

"I wanted to," he tells me earnestly. "I truly did. But the more I thought about it, the more I convinced myself that it truly didn't matter. You loved me for me, as James, and that's who I was, who I am now. Who cares about the person I had been in the past, when the future was all that mattered? I realize now that I was wrong. I was using that reasoning as an excuse to give in to my fear of telling you the truth. But the past matters, and honesty matters. I was wrong, and I am so sorry."

I squirm and look away. I have not been honest one hundred percent of the time, either. How can I not forgive him, this man I still love? I look back at him. "You do look rather dashing in that suit," I concede.

He smiles, but only briefly. He hesitantly offers me his hand, and I take it. I hold on for dear life. He squeezes gently.

"This," he says, swirling his hand to indicate the room around us, "this is something I never could have foreseen. Libby has gone too far, much too far. We should have put up more of a fight when she was never charged with Damien's murder. *I* should have known that her father, as a judge, would have connections that would see her walk free. But then to put the blame on you? This is something I cannot bear, and I had to bring out all of the firepower I have at my disposal. But I never meant for you to find out this way."

"I know," I say softly. "And I forgive you."

There is a knock on the door and the sound of a tumbler turning in the lock. It opens a crack.

"Please," James—*William*—cries. "Just five more minutes?"

I hear the guard grumble something, but Hamilton must manage to convince him, because the door closes again.

"Are we alright then?" he asks me softly. "Are you willing to be Mrs. Elizabeth Wood for now, until we get this straightened out and you're set free?"

I freeze. This is the first time I hear it spoken like that. My fried brain didn't make the right connections earlier. Mrs. Elizabeth Wood. Just like a newspaper blurb I once read. It had said, *On this day, 20 June, 1878, Mrs. Elizabeth Wood, wife of Mr. William Wood, is to be hanged for the brutal Murder of Mr. Damien Gracen...*

"I'm going to die," I whisper.

"No," he says emphatically. "No. You're wrong. You are innocent."

"It doesn't matter," I say dully. "They will hang me. It's inevitable."

"No," he says again, more firmly. "You don't know that. I will not let them touch you. You have the protection of the Wood family now, and our connections are as impressive as Libby's. Nothing is going to happen to you."

But I am already crying. I am going to die. I know this. My James. My Jonathan. They will have to go on without me. He comes around the table to hug me and I let him.

"I do know," I say miserably. "You've told me your secret, James...William..."

"James," he insists. "I'm still James."

"Fine, right... James. You've told me your secret and now let me tell you mine, even if you'll never believe me. I'm...not from here."

"Yes," he says patiently. "That I know."

"No, you don't know. I'm not from here, but I am. I was born here, in Thorne Hill, Connecticut... in the year 2000."

He looks at me sideways, disbelieving. "That's not possible, Lizzy."

"Perhaps not. It might not be possible...but it is so. Would you like me to name the next dozen presidents of the United States? I've memorized all the way up to forty-five...though I'll skip that one, if it's all the same to you. Or would you like to hear about the next century's great advancements? Electric light is coming soon, already here in fact, though it will get much safer, I promise. Automobiles, televisions, telephones, computers. Air conditioners."

"Liz, I don't think now is the time for joking." But his tone is not as skeptical as it is frightened. "That just isn't possible."

"And I say again, it is." I reach into my skirts, through invisible side slits hidden in the gathers, all the way down to the secret pocket in one of my petticoats. It was almost like I had known I would need it, when I'd taken it out this morning to look at. Jonathan had interrupted me, and I'd stashed it quickly away in my skirts. I glance to the door. It's still closed, but not for much longer.

I pull out the device, the time machine, and hand it to him. It is sleek and modern and like nothing anyone of this era has ever seen. I press and hold the button on the side, and the screen lights up. "Tuesday, January 22, 1878. 2:45 PM," it reads, much like any common smartphone might. He can instantly tell that this is not something he understands. He looks at me, fear and wonder mixed on his face. Then his eyes harden. "I don't care where or when you are from. I don't care what you think you know. You are my wife and I will not let them kill you. We will find a way."

The talk of my impending death should be what catches my attention, but instead I cling onto the word "wife." William Wood is my husband. "Oh, no," I say. "I can't believe I'm married to my—" I stop myself before uttering anything more. *Ancestor. My great-great-great-great-grandfather.*

James looks wary, suspicion dawning on his face. "Elizabeth…" he begins. "We're not…related? Are we?"

"No!" I say, much too quickly. "God, no. Of course not. Ew." I'm babbling now. "That would be weird. Just so…weird. No." This is one lie I will happily take to the grave. *Stop,* I tell myself. I need to not think about graves, either. That's not helping. *Change of subject.* James. William. My great-great-great-great-grandfather. Is my husband. We have a child. *No, stop,* I think again. *That's not a good subject either.* What does that even *make* me? My own ancestor?

This is so weird. And really confusing. And really, really weird.

It's during this strange and frantic line of thought that we hear another knock on the door, lock tumblers turning, the handle twisting. I grab the device and shove it back into my pocket, just as the guard's face appears.

"Time's up," he says gruffly. "Have your meeting with your lawyer so he can get out of here."

Mr. Hamilton comes swiftly back into the room. James—*just James*, I reassure myself—holds my hand as I go into all the details of my friendship with Damien and what happened the night he died—the night that he was murdered. Hamilton is unmoved by my tears, but he is disgusted that Libby was never even brought to trial when there were two solid witnesses. The butler, Lennon, had given testimony against her, as well. Her word against both of ours, and yet she walks free.

He says that if there were really a charge against me, it should have been brought up in the weeks following the murder, not almost a year and a half later, when the butler has conveniently just passed away from a heart attack and can no longer testify in my favor. He says that this case is a joke and he should be able to get it dismissed almost immediately. But I know better.

James goes to his family directly after the meeting to fill his father in on what has happened, having gone straight to the lawyer first. He will have them use their media contacts to keep this out of the newspapers. Neither of us wants the publicity, and I imagine that his parents don't either. I understand now why there is nothing to be found about the trial—about anything really—when I looked in the historic records. We've hidden it on purpose.

Chapter Thirty

Days pass, and turn into weeks. Because bail didn't really become a thing until the 1960s, I am not allowed to leave. I'm not sure if it's better or worse that they keep me in one of the holding cells in the police station rather than ship me off to prison across the state. Surely it must be better, I know. My new family is paying dearly to keep me here. But even with almost daily visits, I get so lonely that I worry I might go crazy.

James brings Jonathan to visit me at every possible occasion, but it is not enough. My arms ache for his warm snuggles in the many lonely hours I spend in my cell. He cries when it's time to go, and clings to me fiercely. It breaks my heart a little more each time I have to break his grip and pull his chubby arms away.

When I'm not sleeping, reading, or planning wild schemes to get out of this mess, I spend a lot of time crying.

Lanie doesn't visit often, having just given birth to her own child. Michael though, brings me tales of his beautiful daughter, Lillian, and that always makes me smile. For a short time, anyway.

But surely, one of my most interesting visits happens about

three weeks into my incarceration.

I sit quietly, trying to concentrate on a book that James has brought me, when I hear the door to the cell room open. The guard comes in to bring me to the visiting room, as usual. What is not usual is that James walks in, followed by a stately older couple that I recognize immediately. A man with brownish-gold hair and tired green eyes. A tall, elegant woman with gray eyes and very dark hair. The Woods.

"Elizabeth," James says, though he is more William than ever with these two in the room. "I believe you've met my parents?"

I barely nod in shock at seeing them here when Mrs. Wood surprises me again by enveloping me in a huge hug. "My dear daughter," she says. And while I can't see her face, I can hear the tears in her voice. And that's all it takes for me to begin crying again, too.

It seems that their son has filled them in on everything. Mrs. Wood had been more than a little upset to find out that her son had been living mere miles from them for years without more than regular letters from "afar"—especially since Mr. Wood had known everything all along and kept it a secret from his wife. She was also mildly disappointed at first that Libby wouldn't be her daughter-in-law, but after hearing what Libby had done to Damien, she changed her mind about that immediately. Mrs. Wood is a proud and loving mother, and she forgave her son and welcomed him home. And that welcome, it turns out, extends also to me, and her grandson, even if I am unable to enjoy her hospitality.

She and Mr. Wood have been told my whole story, and they believe me. No questions asked. Not of me, anyway. *Who knows how many questions they had for their son?* Regardless, they are as sure as Mr. Hamilton is that this case will be thrown out as the ridiculous trash it is.

◊

The case against me, however, is not dismissed, as I had known it wouldn't be. Though Judge Hunt doesn't get assigned to my case due to conflicts of interest, he has cronies throughout the district. We get one of them, a big man with a red face that looks all the redder under his silly white wig.

Libby is fingering me for this, because I "stole" Damien—because I "stole" William. I figure out one day that it had to have been she who stumbled upon us the night that James proposed to me. She would have seen us together, me and William, and her worst fears were realized. This is a matter of revenge for her. As if killing my best friend hadn't been revenge enough.

The trial is brutal. Glory and Libby both testify against me, as I had known they would. They tell blatant lies about my relationship with Damien. That we were always a couple. That we were always sleeping together. That Jonathan is his child, not William's. That they *were* at Damien's home that night: Libby was there for a date, and Glory simply as a companion to keep things more proper, of course. They claim to have left long before I arrived, and as the only one in the house besides the butler, it was me who had shot him.

James, to his credit, testifies well in my defense, but the prosecutor still points out the many hours I spent away from his company. He points out that James wasn't there that night, so who knows what happened? And since there is not yet any such thing as paternity testing to prove things one way or another, there is no way to refute the claim of our son's parentage. How much easier it would have been if Jonathan had inherited his father's extraordinary eyes, but, no. He has my dark hair and Mrs. Wood's clear gray eyes instead. Which I do point out, but to no avail. Of course, I think he looks like James, but my opinion counts for less than nothing here, because this entire trial is nothing but a farce.

The Woods are able to keep the newspapers out of it, but that is the extent of their power over the proceedings here. All their contacts and riches are somehow not enough to block the barrage that is being thrown at me. Emily and Angelica are called in as character witnesses. Even Angelica, sweet-when-you-get-her-alone Angelica tells the court with a straight face that I am a slut who probably killed Damien because I was jealous of his relationship with Libby. Other girls in town, girls who had never been anything but polite to me, come forward as well to call me out. I can only assume that they have been blackmailed by Libby's family, but there is no proof.

Mr. Hamilton, of course, brings up the butler Lennon's account of what happened. But more character witnesses are brought into court to discredit him. I am angry and saddened for his family and his memory. Lennon had been a good, solid man; he was someone Damien had trusted implicitly. But these people make him out to be a doddering old fool who couldn't be expected to know the day of the week, never mind recognize at what hour Damien's lady friends arrived and departed.

Michael, of course, takes the stand in my defense. He was

there that night, and though outside, he witnessed Libby and Glory leaving the house immediately after hearing a gunshot. The defense tears him to shreds. He has always been kind, but he has never been extremely bright. Within minutes of cross-examination, they have him so confused that he's not sure of his own name anymore.

The Woods and Aurelia come in to testify for my character, but even they can make no difference with the horrific bias in the courtroom. Hamilton calls for a mistrial, but the crony judge pays no attention to his arguments.

The Woods' news blackout is actually backfiring now. This circus should be called out all over the front page, but it's too late. The Hunts have realized that and are suppressing it on their own now, and not a word of this travesty of a trial finds its way into the papers.

What would have taken years in my time takes less than six months, whether because of the time period we're in or simply through Judge Hunt's meddling, I'll never know. But my case is lost, as I always knew it would be.

I am to be hanged in a week's time, on June 20th. The day before my birthday. So close to being able to escape. The time machine is useless until the 21st.

I'm so scared. I don't want to die.

Chapter Thirty-one

On the morning of my execution, my guard gives me the newspaper as a last gift. I find the small blurb about my impending
death on the back page of the *Thorne Hill Times*, buried in adver-
tisements, not to be discovered until 140 or so years from now.

*On this day, 20 June, 1878, Mrs. Elizabeth Wood, wife of
Mr. William Wood, is to be hanged for the brutal Murder
of Mr. Damien Gracen of Thorne Hill, Connecticut. May
God have mercy on her soul.*

I'm surprisingly calm as I read. It's only when I look out
the tiny barred window that I suddenly can't breathe. It's a
beautiful June day outside. The birds are singing. The trees in
the distance are green, and a light breeze rustles through them.
My window is open, and I can feel that gentle wind, can tell
that it's a cooler day out there than the one on which I came to
Thorne Hill three years ago, but it's not the weather that stops
the breath in my throat. It's that a man is outside, sweeping
dust from the gallows.

I am going to die.

It's a simple fact of everyone's life, right? Everyone dies, young and old, sick and healthy, friend and foe.

I'm not ready to die.

And that's the crux of it. Everyone dies, but why do I have to die today? I'm not ready. I'm not guilty. I don't deserve this. I want to be with James again, feel his arms around me and look deep into his fascinating eyes. I want to hold Jonathan again, kiss his sweet face, and calm all of his fears. I want to see Alex again, marvel at how tall he's gotten in the last few years, tease him about his new driving skills or his video game habit. I want to hug my dad again, assure him that mom's ancestress was not a killer, and just remind him how much I love him—how much I love them all.

I wonder what will happen after I die. I am not a religious person. I have no celestial assurance that heaven is waiting for me after I stop breathing at the end of that rope. But if I have to die, what I wouldn't give to join my mother and my best friend in whatever afterlife there may be. That, at least, will be some consolation for what is happening here.

I am jolted from my reverie by the sound of a key in my door. *Is it really time already?* I look up, trembling, as a guard enters for me. It seems the sun is high in the sky; it's almost noon. *How did that happen?* The tears begin to run soundlessly down my cheeks.

Then another noise coming from the open window catches my attention. Not the sound of the small crowd that has gathered outside. Something different. Hooves. But not a gentle trot up the cobbled street… It's galloping, by the sound of it. The noise stops, and is quickly replaced by the sound of running feet and a pounding at the door.

"Stop!" A breathless shout rings out as soon as the door opens. It's a voice I recognize now, fancy accent and all. *What is he doing here?* I told him yesterday when we said our goodbyes—I begged him, pleaded with him—to stay home today. He can't really think that he can stop it. He doesn't need to see this.

The guard fusses around my hands, ties them together behind my back.

"No, stop!" James shouts again from outside. "You can't do this! She is innocent!" There is the sound of a scuffle, even a blow, but the guard who is in with me doesn't stop what he is doing.

I'm led out of my cell, through the office, and finally outside into the clear summer's day, a day so incongruous with what is about to happen. James, in his black suit, is being held back by three men. He is straining against them, his face red and swollen from where he has clearly been hit. A trickle of blood drips from his nose, now more crooked than ever. I look at him desperately and shake my head back and forth just once, slowly. He stops fighting then, a look of absolute anguish on his face.

There are some, but not too many people gathered here to see "justice" done this day. My friends have all stayed away, knowing that I don't want them to see this. I wish James had stayed away as well.

Libby, on the other hand, is here with her husband, a smug smile on her face as I'm walked out to the gallows. So are Glory and Emily, and more people that I don't recognize, here for the entertainment value, I'm sure. Some people were bound to see it in the paper. I notice that Angelica is not here today. Perhaps she feels bad for what she has done to me. She should. And I loathe her all the more now, for not having the guts to come watch what she helped to put in motion.

I hold my head up high as I walk through them all. I make eye contact with everyone I pass, unwilling to be cowed, forcing those who lied to face me. Libby doesn't even bother to flinch. She just smiles even wider and stares right back at me. I falter for a moment though, when I see Damien's mother and father in the front, closest to the scaffold.

Mrs. Gracen spits in my face. Mr. Gracen is holding her back, and the look on their faces almost breaks me. It's so hard to hold up my brave facade after that, but I don't have far to go now.

Up the steps. I stumble once, and the guard holding me yanks me back up harshly. I hear James make a choking sob behind me, even over the noise of the other onlookers. When they turn me around to face the crowd, I seek out his face. He's closer to the front now. I don't want him to see this, but since he is here, I will take advantage of this last moment. My eyes lock on his and I am able to keep the tears from spilling over.

His pale green eyes are clouded with despair, but they are still as beautiful as ever. He is not fighting now, but he is still being held by two officers. He looks tense enough to try something, but he is already out of time. There is nothing more he can do here.

My breathing speeds up as two men move in on either side of me: one holding a canvas hood and the other a rope. I concentrate on James's eyes, desperate to avoid thinking of Jonathan, Alex, Dad, and everyone else I'm really, truly leaving behind. The green of his eyes stays with me even after the hood is lowered onto my head.

The man with the rope slowly tightens the noose around my neck. But still, James's eyes stay with me. And I realize that I will see those eyes again someday. I may be about to die, but in the year 2000, more than a century from now, I will be born to Jonathan and Rachel Franklyn in this very town. That is a fact.

As I grow, I'll see his eyes, first in my dreams, and then I'll follow them back here. Back to the farm to bask in James's indescribable love, back into town to dance in my best friend Damien's warm arms, back to my home to revel in Jonathan's sweet hugs. I will do it over and over again. And so, I smile, even as my feet drop out from under me.

Epilogue

Isn't it strange how we sometimes remember the smallest details of a dream, but not the entire thing? Some pieces slip away easily, like stray feathers on a windy day, while others remain embedded in our minds forever.

This is what I remember: bits and pieces of a face that I've never seen in my waking life. Short, straight hair that's parted on the right; sometimes dull russet, but sometimes lit with sunlight, creating fiery red highlights. An ever-so-slightly crooked nose, striking in its imperfection. Strong, neat brows firmly set on an unlined forehead, and straight white teeth behind plump pink lips.

And finally, most of all, I remember dazzlingly beautiful eyes—eyes the color of the lightest jade, that look directly into my soul and seem to glow from within.

That is all.

Acknowledgements

To my family and friends: Even if you didn't know I was writing it, you helped me just by being there for me. Thank you.

To my copy editor, Julie Blattburg: I can't believe you deleted every double space between each of my sentences in addition to everything else. That is some dedication to your craft. Thank you for your hard work.

To my cover/book designer, Caroline Teagle Johnson: Thank you for helping me find the perfect cover. Your vision for it really was better than my own. I truly appreciate everything you've put into this.

To my proofreader, Mark Shultz of wordrefiner.com, thank you for your hyper-spelling expertise. I never would have found those last few stubborn typos without you.

And finally, you may have noticed that I took some liberties with Victorian social niceties, among other things. That was necessary for the continuation of the story. However, I never would have managed any of the true Victorian details you saw in these pages without these four sites:

http://www.beautifulwithbrains.com
https://mimimatthews.com
http://www.tudorlinks.com
http://www.wikipedia.org